A Mail&Guardian book

The White Life of Felix Greenspan

Lionel Abrahams

M&G

ISBN 0-9584402-8-X

First published in South Africa by
M&G Books
a division of M&G Media
7 Quince Rd
Milpark
2092
www.mg.co.za

Cover design by **Disturbance**
2nd floor Innesdale
101 Innes Rd
Morningside
Durban
4001
e-mail: disturb@mweb.co.za

Page design by **Lynda Harvey**

Printed by **Formeset Printers**
22/23 Kinghall Ave
Eppindust
Cape Town
7945

To my Jane
who daily proves
what seemed impossible

The completion of this book was supported by The Foundation for the Creative Arts.

Author's Note

This narrative is an overlapping sequel to *The Celibacy of Felix Greenspan*, 'a novel in 18 stories', and is intended to be read as fiction containing no report or judgement on actual persons and their circumstances.

L.A.
Rivonia, near Johannesburg
1999

PART I

The Life of the House

PART II

Wars and Rages

PART I

The Life of the House

1

Africa, Russia, Shadows

Felix looked down through a veil of low cloud. Pastel dabs of light patterned the black velvet floor of the highveld with a drifting collage of rivers, lattices, grids and loops. As he sank lower he identified, here and there, fish-like glimmers and red pinpoints of traffic tentatively threading the darkness. Ordinarily, he was one node of identity moving amid all the others down there, tracing its minute particular pattern within the huge pattern of that city. But now, balanced in the sky before re-entering his stories, he peered into the field of his absence, and for the moment every association was obliterated. All history and expectation were cancelled, forgiven, and this view of Johannesburg was neutral, innocent and beautiful. In a whim of proprietorial pride and protectiveness, he saluted it. Home ground, his city.

However, from what he plunged down into he had been absent for only a few days, and this return was no new beginning. It was back to his white life in the golden city. Only, the life he led there was no more white than his skin. And the city was no longer even mythically golden. If it did still possess an identity by which it impressed itself on all the white, black, brown and yellow lives it located, its distinction was to be in Africa an anti-Africa, not the only one but the hugest. All to whom this dangerous, potent anomaly was ordinary were its true purblind citizens.

There was a painting that had come with Moh's family from Vilna: a mansion by a green-banked river where filmy figures rowed in a wisp of a boat under a silvery sky with a strange sweet darkness in the woods, the clouds, the water and the house. "That's Russia," she told Felix.

That was one of her dreams of "Russia". Her real memory was of being locked in a house day after day alone with her sister Ella and their dolls and some food, waiting for evening to bring their mother home from her business of selling drapery door to door. Their father had left for Africa when she was still a baby, and when she was five the family left "Russia" for the East End of London, there to continue waiting.

"Ella and I used to leave for school in the dark and it always seemed dark again by the time we got home. I never saw the sun... Our class once sang in front of King Edward..."

She was ten by the time they went to Africa.

"Father was a stranger when he met us...someone I'd never seen, and to me he always remained a stranger. He was always disappearing with a book to read under a tree in the veld. No wonder he lost Harry. Mother was the hard-working one who held the family together, the responsible, honest one. And she was wise. You would have liked her so much."

There were three sons and three daughters, the girls all younger than the boys. For Vera, the youngest, her family—those lives—formed the core of her culture and traditions. Less curious and attentive than he should have been, Felix picked up fragments of those stories over the years as Moh let them fall during rare reminiscent moods—glittering splinters of narrative under a shadow of lost time and foreignness and secrecy, but to him, after all, only crumbs of his mother's ordinariness. Sometimes particles of that history would spark out in conversations he overheard between her and siblings or cousins, especially their arguments hot with the aches of the past. At such moments curiosity allowed him glimpses of a river of connections, repeatedly interrupted, sunk away into its sandy terrain long before it could reach him.

Her elder brothers, Meyer and Boris, had filled their father's place as providers, alongside their mother, and as guides and protectors, during the years of separation and even afterwards. Meyer was aloof and remote, but Boris, a dreamer and raconteur and joker, who designed jewels and penned little verses, was Vera's mentor. So it was she who felt his absence most achingly when, though still a newcomer to South Africa at the outbreak of the Great War, he volunteered for the army. He had felt it his duty to disprove a common calumny that Jews were cowards. Starvation and disease in East Africa left their marks on him. "He was never the same after the war," Moh grieved. "You should have known what he was like before."

Felix could not see the damage. The only visible hurt had nothing to do with war: it was the diamond-setter's thumb, swollen to twice the normal thickness by innumerable small injuries, which Uncle Boris would whimsically flaunt, as though it had some kind of comical or magical significance. A rare charm survived in him and numbers of women felt the enchantment too. "They all fell in love with him," Moh would say, while leaving a mist of secrecy over many things. Had some embarrassing entanglement led to his long sojourn in South America? Were modest earnings all that kept him unmarried until past forty—long after all his sisters and brothers had started families of their own—while his willing bride had lost some of her bloom waiting for him?

Jessica, the elder of Moh's sisters, also had glamour, but hers began not in closeness, like Boris's, but in remoteness. As a child she had contracted lockjaw and undergone surgery and spells in hospitals. Her scarred left cheek was only a blemish that emphasised the fragile cast of her ripe Pre-Raphaelite looks, and her illnesses were not enough to subdue a certain quiet vivacity or dull the sharp mind she exercised in family matters and business. She was courted by a handsome accountant, Howard Massingham, whose looks, gallant considerate manners and talents dazzled the women in the family, Vera not the least. He painted, he sang, he acted (Felix was even occasionally to hear him in radio plays). After a time, Jessica and Howard went, like Boris and with motives equally swathed, to live for a time in South America, where the first of their children were born. "How I missed them," Moh told Felix. "I used to dream about them." When they returned they often left their babies in her charge, and to them also she gave her heart.

At some stage she had saved a little money, which Jessica borrowed to help finance a business plan. It failed, and the money was never repaid. Thus much, in a late year, Moh told Felix, but said no word as to whether the debt had simply gone forgotten, or she had asked for the money and been fobbed off, whether any kind of quarrel had taken place. But he guessed at some humiliation for her, some disappointment—a blotch of shadow in the brilliant aura surrounding Jessica.

The youngest boy, Harry, as an uncontrollable seven-year-old had been taken along to Africa by his father, and there lost for several years. Only after the family had settled in Johannesburg and placed advertisements for him in newspapers was he found, or rather, did he find them. Vera was the first to see him—an unknown young man with a bloodstained bandage round his head (soon to be made the pretext for a yarn)—prowling cat-like from window to window of the house and spying in, crouched as though in caution, intending mischief or a prankster's surprise (so Felix filled out the picture from his knowledge of Uncle Harry). He brought to the family a store of anecdotes out of his years of adventurous wandering in a strange country and an irrepressible playfulness. The mischief he brought was an unforgiving resentment of the father whose carelessness had let him go astray. But he attached himself closely to the rest of the family, and closest of all to his brothers, whose ideas and dreams he drank in thirstily. During conversations with them the entertainer in him, his ironical mischievousness, became invisible. Here, for once, he was fully serious, as otherwise only in respect of his bitterness against his father. Yet he proved more in command of the world's ways than they ever were to. He went into business and prospered, then married and produced an anarchic empire of eight children, ever ready to hear his stories and relish his tricks.

Moh's other dream of Russia was the Soviet Utopia that Lenin had forged, and like the painting, it was something she brought from her family. Russia's communism became the most commanding and rousing of the ideas Harry received from Meyer and Boris. Embracing the revolution that overthrew the anti-Semitic Tsar they had given up the old religion and turned instead to Karl Marx. "Russia" became more than just the place they had come from. It became the new destination, the model for a world cleansed of religion and class and race and money, freed from poverty and snobbery and hypocrisy and war.

While she was growing up—learning millinery and the piano, minding baby nieces, nursing first her mother then her father through their long months of dying—the dreams of "Russia" had been redreamed in the sweet intervals when the scattering family came together. "My happiest times..." The conversation was rain and honey to her, the calls for her accompaniment to songs of love and sorrow and comedy.

At death, her mother's face had grown marvellously peaceful. "She had a kind of smile, such a look of peace—I'll never forget it." This was a recurring recollection, but only once did she tell how her father, the stranger, had declared on his death-bed, "Vera is the good one." Her pride in telling it wrestled with her bitterness that this was his first and only sign of appreciation.

It was Harry who introduced her to Reuben Greenspan. He also had come from Lithuania when he was ten. Like Moh's brothers, he had had to go out and make his living while still a boy. He had worked at many jobs and then gone into business after business. During the Great War he had been conscripted for a cavalry raid into German South-West Africa. He loved to regale any audience he could buttonhole with rambling stories of his exploits. His father had been pious and learned enough to have headed a Yeshiva college, and his older brother, Nechemiah, was a fragile, clever autodidact who always entertained ambitions of great wealth and intellectual influence. Reuben looked up to him humbly, submitting to his irritation and mockery with a shrug, and ever ready to put his hands or his car at his languid brother's service. He, more dutifully than Nechemiah, kept up the family habits of religious observance, and believed in salvation through Zionism. Impatient with daydreams about "Russia", he took on some of his brother's habit of indignant ridicule, and did not get on with Meyer and Boris.

But Vera married Reuben and left her piano in the family nest. In their new home Reuben kept closing windows against drafts, and Vera kept flinging them open for fresh air.

From the first, Felix remembered shadows. The street in that first suburb was full of the shade cast by the oaks that lined it, and nearby loomed a ridge covered in pines. A few times he was taken in his push-chair to where the rising street ended against the foot of the ridge, and he looked up into the strong waiting darkness under the near-black fur of the pine branches. In the shadowy street in front of their house, everything was partly hidden as he looked out through the lattice that fenced the high verandah where he played. He stared out at broken images of passers-by and traffic and the houses opposite and the little shop on the corner.

One day out there a crowd gathered round the shop and a bald man with blood on his head stepped about waving his arms, shouting. A native pushed people, struggled, ran, was absorbed by the crowd, struggling again. Someone waved a long stick. An ambulance came, then some policemen, two of them terrible in hats with wide brims turned up on one side and chin-straps in front of their ears. They took someone away. The crowd stood and stood.

On another day a uniformed man on a bicycle stopped and handed in an orange paper at one of those houses across the road, small and squeezed together and built of dark red brick. Soon a low screaming came out of the house he had been to. People began to go in and out. Mommy told Felix the lady was crying because her sister far away had died. How did she know? Because of the telegram, that orange paper. But when Felix asked, "What is died?" he could not find out. Only the howling went on and on. After the first day it would start up again at any time for a while, and then it seemed to be the house itself, with its squashed-up dried-blood face under low eaves and dark leaves, that tore the street with its howling.

But the shadows fell from somewhere beyond the reach of his earliest memories—from something they had survived, a threat they had to be protected from. Like the darkness he had woken to one night, piled thick and heavy on his face. When he could find his voice he screamed, and Mommy had come running to his room, screaming too: "What now? What? What? O my God, that damn cat, sitting on his *face*...!" She and Daddy had had to soothe him a long time before he stopped crying and could let himself go back to sleep.

Daddy seemed sure they were out of it, safe, or he had forgotten or never known. He wore white flannels on Sundays, teased Mommy, joked with everybody—"Felix, my boy, take my advice: *Don't Get Married*!"—and made a sort of jolly light around himself. But Mommy had not forgotten. The shock and anger of those shadows, the vague sad darkness around the edge of things, belonged to her. And the explanation, Felix eventually guessed, must be himself.

No one knew at first, no one knew why the baby was unwell, why he cried all the time. He cried his way into Vera's nerves and she became as brittle as all the feeding bottles that slipped from her tense hands and smashed. After the many months spent nursing her dying mother and father, she had hoped for things only to be "normal" when she married. But her first baby fell into convulsions, cried relentlessly, wouldn't sit when he was due to sit. He was brain-damaged, the doctors decided. He would be a sick, helpless child. And there was no help for her. Her sisters were concerned but had their own babies. It wasn't in her nature to allow responsibility to a servant. Reuben was awkward in handling the baby and a bit playfully sceptical about her predicament. There was only her anger to carry her through. She drained her life to the economy of survival, like an animal.

Things were worst when her mother-in-law came to live with them. She was (as Felix would come to know Bobba) a pious little lady, proper and genteel, who spoke no English, murmured and rocked over a prayer-book in the lounge for half an hour daily, baked a batch of little jam tarts every week, and always wore a hat when she went out. Vera had no patience for frills and gestures, and spent days in her dressing-gown when she felt too worn out and distracted to dress. The old lady's disapproval finally turned to spitefulness.

"One day when I was nearly crazy because of your crying, she mocked me and laughed at me. I waited for her to go out, then I went to her wardrobe and took three hats I had made her as a present when we became engaged, and cut them up with a scissors and left the pieces on her bed."

2

The House, The Motor Car

Felix is five-and-a-half and is sitting with his five-and-a-quarter year old cousin Vivvy on the steps leading down to the yard from the kitchen door of Auntie Jessica's house. In the yard, because no room in the house is big enough, is the tail-end of a birthday party—a long cluttered table and a clutter of chairs and cousins and aunts. Vivvy whispers in his ear: "Let's go and play rude."

Felix feels a tingle at his wee-wee. "Where?"

"Behind that door...watch where I'm going." She goes, and he makes his way after her, down the steps and along the yard toward the back gate, not walking, not even yet crawling on his knees, but bumping himself along on his hands and bottom. Someone asks, "Felix, where are you going?" and he happily explains, "I"m going to play rude with Vivvy". Everyone laughs.

In the alcove where the dustbin stands between the wooden door from the yard and the wooden door to the street, a dim, secret place when both doors are closed, he finds Vivvy waiting. She pulls down her broeks and squats and shows him the little sticks and beads she wants him to push into her wee-wee. Felix does his best. But suddenly one of the big cousins bursts in through the street door, stops, stares, gasps, "Ooh-woo! I'm going to tell," and rushes through the yard door. The game stops. Vivvy runs out frightened. When Auntie Jessica hears what they were doing she is angry and says Vivvy will be punished. Felix is not punished, but he knows why they hid in the little space between the doors.

Back-yard beginnings. Only once did Felix get close to the Native Maternity Hospital where the piccanins lived. They were showing him to their mother, who wore a nursing sister's uniform and talked to them in stern cheerful Zulu, interrupting a brisk volley of instructions to a nurse. The low red-brick building sat on the sandy earth in a banked hollow amid tall grey grass, and where they stood was a yard with washing lines and over-heaped dustbins buzzing with big flies and smelling sour in the hot sun. There was the sound of crying babies.

Dinah, Daisy, Dora and Timothy were the piccanins who came across the veld from the hospital behind the row of bluegums, to play. They were of different heights, from Dinah the tallest to Timothy the smallest, but they all had the same long face and mysterious big eyes under eyebrows that met in a fine arrowhead pointing down to the nose, and the same impala legs under floral skirts or khaki shorts. Except when they squeaked with excitement in a chasing game, they were very quiet and shy and as clean as if they were going to church. They spoke English almost in whispers and to each other Zulu in strong pressed-down voices full of zeds and clicks.

They would come day after day for a while, then not appear for weeks. What attracted them? What made them withdraw? After a time Dinah vanished for months because she was at school in Zululand. Later, Daisy also went, and still later the other two as well. But now and again one or another of them would appear for a few minutes to report and show how they were growing up. It was over years, but the piccanins remained like wild buck. What made them keep returning, yet kept them impersonal and remote? They arrived for play on the veld or on the pavement, or came up onto the front verandah. In the end Timothy had become the tallest of them, and perhaps the shyest, full of the secrets of his obedience and education, which remained secrets because, like creatures in a nature reserve that must not be fed, he and his sisters had never stepped through the door of Felix's house.

Back-yards had dustbins and lavatories and girl's rooms and coal heaps and washing lines. People came to the back door to see the girl or to bring the meat or the groceries or to ask for a job. A few times a native named Hendrik stood on the back verandah talking to Daddy, saying often, "That's right, my baas... Oh, yes, my baas... Thanks, thanks very much, my baas..." eating thick bread and drinking tea from a huge enamel mug. Once he was given two shirts, trousers and a pair of shoes to take with him. The next time he came he showed a shaved head and explained that the police had arrested him for stealing those clothes. The jacket and trousers he wore were torn and dirty.

"They keep them so poor," Daddy said. "It's very wrong." They—the natives—walked torn and dirty in the streets expecting the police to catch them, and they lived in rusty dusty locations with streets busy as ant-paths, or in back-yards. In the girls' rooms they used boxes for tables and newspaper for tablecloths and jam-tins for cups and their fingers to pinch off and knead the lumps of doughy porridge they dipped into their gravy. A punctured paraffin-tin brazier was the fireplace and a candle was the light. The bed, raised high on bricks stacked under its feet, was a real bed and the blankets were real. The natives did all the hard work. And some of them were the burglars. When night came the darkness was full of them, bogeymen in dirty torn clothes or Malaitas wrapped to their noses in blankets, waving knob-kerries as they jogged along whistling the promise of murder.

Like the Malaitas, with the same fierce rushing of muscly bodies on strong stamping feet, were those who brought the coal. The lorry with its mountain of knobbly bags stopped outside the yard gate. One of the workers (Were these "boys" like the rest? They were more like big dangerous goblins.) stood on the mountain. The others took turns to stand below, alongside the lorry, back on, arms lifted in a huge V, each with a grunt to receive and bend double beneath a load as massive as himself. Then each stagger-ran, "hoo-hooing" for a clear path and scattering a rain of black nuggets, through the gate and down the yard to the coalheap, there to tip out the clattering load over his head as though he were emptying himself. But this gigantic vomit of black hardness did not leave the man whole and clean: when each huge hump had dissolved and its containing sack been flung aside, something remained stuck on, obscuring, misshaping his head and back. Years later Felix realised it was only one of those same heavy sacks slit open and worn as a hooded cloak for protection. But those men had looked as though they had been damaged by carrying that weight, reshaped to do nothing except carry coal for ever.

Daddy stopped the car outside one of the small new houses, asked the man working in the little space behind the diamond mesh fence if Mrs van Wyk was home, and went to the front door. The man came to lean on the fence for a minute and talk to the children in the car with friendly smiles on his leathery face. Then they watched him digging grass and weeds and stones out of the patch of dusty soil that was going to be a garden. He was shovelling hard and dust was rising around him in the hot air as he pounded the soil to get it loose and clean and threw aside stony clods and weeds.

Suddenly a big dusty stone leapt over his shoulder and hit a closed window of the car with a loud crack. The gardener turned to see, but before he could come closer, before a child could cry with fright, a lady burst shouting from the front door trailing Daddy behind her. She raged at the gardener as she ran to the car. Then, still shouting at him, she fiercely soothed the children and hugged the one who had been nearest to the cracked window. The gardener explained and apologised, but she scolded him more and more angrily and after a while said, "I'm phoning the police," and went toward the house.

Daddy said, "I don't think it's necessary to have him arrested. It was an accident."

"Oh, no! I know these people," the lady said. "He nearly killed your child. Poor little things! Look how frightened they are. I know what he wanted to do. Don't lie to me, you skelm, it's tronk for you!"

Felix was surprised at how angry the lady was and wanted her to stop, but the more she showed what a shocking thing had happened the more he kept seeing the stone come flying over the gardener's shoulder growing more dangerous every time. When she had telephoned she stood talking to Daddy near the gate while the gardener stood against the fence, his head down, not trying to speak any more. At last a pick-up van came with two policemen. The lady showed them the car window, the stone, the gardener and the children. They handcuffed the man and took him away.

Mommy is the house. Daddy is the motor car. Mommy is always there. The car takes Daddy and brings him home again—he is like a visitor bringing presents, like a present himself. The car is business and shopping and going out to uncles and aunts and bioscope and picnics. Any drive, even when Daddy is only going to see the factory or collect rent or inspect a demolition or buy some delicatessen, may be better than staying at home. The car shows Felix town, streets, shops, buildings, traffic, crowds, houses, gardens, locations, veld, farms, everything that is not home.

One day when Daddy leaves him in the parked car it begins to roll downhill. It is disobeying. It is carrying him off. It is plunging toward a steeper slope, towards a wall. It is gathering speed. Not yet indoors,

Daddy hears something, turns, shouts, runs to catch up, wrestles the door open, lunges in, wrestles the steering-wheel, wrenches the hand brake, halts the car. But now there is treachery and viciousness in a parked car. For a long time Felix will not be left alone in a car, will not trust the slightest slope. Another cowardice.

Shadows pour into Felix's mouth and nose and chest and head from a rubber half-ball of darkness that a gang of soft-spoken white-coated strangers wearing blank masks clap over his face to kill him.

The clinic is a place of long bare passages between big white halls where clusters of people wait. Mommy brought him here because medicines have made his teeth bad. A fat woman in a passage chatted with Mommy and told her the way to the place where she gave him over to the gang. They pretend gentleness until he struggles, then they grow merciless, throwing their weight onto his kicking legs and onto the instrument of murder by suffocation. She has left him to them. She is on their side. He goes down into the blackness.

When he revives, his mouth is sore and full of blood and Mommy is with him again. She shares the terribleness of what has happened to him. They go on being lost in the clinic. They go into lifts. Outside the lift door the world changes, but it is still the clinic. Centuries after the first time they meet the fat woman again, now in a dressing-gown and with her mouth bleeding. The walls look white yet are splashed with blood from bleeding people. He knows that all the terribleness is also happening to Mommy, even though she chats quite comfortably with the bleeding lady.

Yet later again, two or three times, she will hand him over to gently-murmuring gangs who will suffocate him with cups or cones of rubber darkness. And she is on the side of any hypocrite-enemy who can make her believe they intend his good and know what is necessary—first, doctors armed with suffocation, enemas and needles, later, teachers armed with schedules of homework, and institution staff with the power to hold him prisoner away from home for years and years.

3

Little Empires

A small sunlit lawn, enwombed by tall, soft, dark hedges. Angel children playing timelessly with beautiful toys, clay, paper and colours, while an angel lady watches them, guarding their safety and happiness. Felix had given Mommy and Daddy many reminders about his needs and his likes and dislikes to pass on as instructions to the people who were going to be looking after him. But still, his picture of the place was that little garden-heaven, that womb.

Instead, a tarred path flanked by hydrangeas, cannas and stretches of lawn, sucked him and his suitcase of new clothes toward the beetling portal of a rambling stone-and-shingle mansion. And that door thereafter, when Mommy and Daddy had left him, sucked him into a world of routines, hierarchies, disciplines and codes—codes above all, and lacunae, a vast weight of broken history. In the grand staircase-embraced vestibule behind that well-porched door-behind-a-door stood a pedestal bearing the black, gleaming head of a rhinoceros, never to be explained. Nor would the beads be explained—the thousands of tiny red and white beads that lay embedded in the grass of one of the lawns, perpetually to be scraped up in little hoards by children at play. Nor would so many other mysteries of the place ever be explained. But the force of his curiosity faded as his months there made things uncomfortably familiar—certain rooms, corridors and portions of the gardens, the rhythms of the days and the weeks, certain kinds of dismay and lack, and alienness itself.

One of the familiar rooms was called Small Dorm. Between its door and its two big uncurtained sliding windows, its moulded ceiling and bare polished wooden floor, it contained a fireplace with a mantelpiece, eight metal beds and a ghost. This was the quarantine room Felix had to stay in when he caught German measles. Among the boys with him there was his friend Percy. Together they made up stories about being home.

Another was Ronnie Spavic, bigger, hampered only by a limp. He loped about on ropey, tense legs, often muttering through his skew tight lips and teeth, in growls, whines and hisses rather than words. His habit was to sidle close and pounce on a smaller boy, seize on him with a trap of hard fingers and wring his head as if he wanted to test its firmness, but would be gleeful if it caved in. Sometimes a cage of fingers would be clamped over the victim's face, or bottom, or arm. And sometimes the small boy was wrapped in an embrace while Ronnie pumped at his backside for a few seconds. He seemed to want to do something terrible, violate, damage, kill, if only he dared. But something stopped him. When staff talked to him, making him nervous or angry, his lower jaw would pull back in a sort of yawn then jerk down again and again, like a choking dog's. Meanwhile he would walk or stand as though nothing unusual was happening. Sometimes when he was quiet he would moisten his smallest finger with saliva, push it deep into his nostril, let it rest there for long minutes, then pull it out well coated, and return it to his mouth. He seemed not to care whether smaller boys saw him at it, as though confident that they found him too dangerous to denounce. This habit must have caused the sourish smell that hung about him.

Felix was not always able to get to the lavatory in time, and one day was trying with Percy's help to clean away the evidence of a small accident, when Ronnie came on them. "Hey! You shit yourself, little Jewboy? And on the floor? Hey, lemme call the nurse..."

"No!" Felix begged. "We cleaning it up. It's cleaned up already."

"Hiding it, hey?" Ronnie clamped his fingers on Felix's head. "Thought you could get away with it, hmm? But I copped you, didn't I, little Jewboy, little crook?" He squeezed hard, and Felix's pleading turned to a moan of pain. "I'll tell if I want to, you hear me, you dirty little nit?" A last fierce dig of his fingers seemed to satisfy him for the moment. He dropped Felix and turned away.

But from now on the secret was there all the time. He used it to make Felix squirm and plead or give in to his demands. Any reluctance to come and be mauled or queerly caressed or to hand over a toy or a piece of tuck, any complaint, would be met with a clench-toothed mutter: "You want me to tell? Hey, little shitpants! Little Jewboy! Hey? Hey?"

Though Ronnie never really hurt him, Felix never dared to resist or defy him. Their miserable cowards' partnership went on for long months after the quarantine was over.

Ronnie-the-wolf, and the ghost in Small Dorm, and snakes that came in from the koppie at night, and the beam from the night watchman's torch swirling shadows through dormitory windows, and the wind in the pines, and the roaring of lions and sad peacocks' wails from the zoo, and a bleeding nose streaming into the dust where he sat on the floor of the summerhouse rondavel, and boils on his legs, and sharp, impatient nurses...

Two of them, herding a clutch of small children, converse in a code of spelled-out words, and show they are tired and annoyed. The children are "it". "Oh-oh! Now it's going to blub, would you believe!" Another, feeding him at lunch, claps her hands in relief when he says he does not want a second helping of the burnt, chloroform-tasting roast pumpkin. When he lies in bed before lights out, proudly reading aloud as he always does, one of them snaps, "Read to yourself". From then on, he reads silently, for himself alone.

He lies in bed tickling his bottom, thinking of a place, a rondavel like the summerhouse but smaller and all closed up, and hidden deep in a forest. And he is in it with a lady. And they are both naked. And he is doing something to her, he doesn't know what, but something rude. And it seems cruel, cruel.

Time with Percy was hours of quietly making up some game with stones, sand and grass, string and sticks, pencil and paper, or whatever toy or annual had come their way. Sometimes they wrestled for a while, but even when they hissed, "Now I'm vicious!" they did not hurt each other much. Most often they talked and talked about what it was like at home. Percy's father was not at home but in an asylum in Pretoria. It was, he told Felix at first, because he was deaf. He had gone deaf on a ship because everyone was shouting and there was an enormous noise. Only much later did he tell Felix that really his father was in the asylum because he was "off his head". His mother couldn't walk and nor could his youngest sister and his elder sister was very wild. He never tired of telling about the wild angry things she had done.

But they liked best talking about Gerald. They had discovered that Felix's cousins' cousin Gerald lived next door to Percy's mother's house. Felix had seen Gerald only about twice, but he was a link. Not like the link of Percy being, as he sometimes said, half Jewish—so that once when a Jewish holiday came he sat outside with Felix instead of going into the

Playroom for school. Gerald was a link because he was someone in that other world who was known to someone here. He proved that the other world was real.

Even though he did not make his own bed, Felix took so long to dress and wash in the morning that he was often late for breakfast. Sometimes the nurses in charge made everyone line up and wait in the Big Playroom until the last latecomer had arrived, before opening the big door into the dining-room. Felix's "Sorry! Sorry!" would meet with scowls and grumbles.

One morning he woke before the up-time bell. It was dark still, but he decided to give himself an early start. He managed to get his shirt, pants and socks on, then, feeling gleeful, he crawled through two dim dormitories of sleeping boys out to the big corridor where, beside the door to the bathroom, the shoes and boots were left for polishing. There was light enough from the duty-room at the end for him to find his boots in the big pool of leather, and he was doing the bow in the second lace when the night nurse came up the corridor.

"Felix? What are you doing?"

"I'm getting up early, Nurse Duncan," he explained.

"I'll say you are! It's only half past one..."

"Is it?" Felix sat gaping. "But I..."

"Off with those boots and back to bed with you." She pulled off the first one. "Getting up early!" she exclaimed. "You noodle!" And then they began to laugh.

The castle on the ridge had been a Witwatersrand pioneer's mansion. In the hall of the grand staircase hung photograph portraits of the pioneer-donor and his wife in modest black-and-white with their names beneath. No one but Daddy—studying the portraits on visiting Sundays—seemed to remember who they were. This piece of Africa belonged to Christendom and the Empire. Above the first landing of the staircase hung a large photograph of the cold, lofty nave of a cathedral. Elsewhere, three or four Bible pictures. In the Small Playroom, which served as the Grades' classroom, a picture of Saint Francis surrounded by creatures great and small, and one of a pretty family at a prettily laden table saying the grace that was printed across the top and bottom: "We thank Thee for the food we eat. We thank Thee for the world so sweet...". On Sunday mornings when the Big Playroom, the old ballroom, became the chapel for Service, the sunlight that streamed in at the huge north-facing windows and open door seemed gentle and very clean, the child-welcoming light of a Gospel meek and mild. The same light at other times wove into other things of the Big Playroom: school when he understood something new, Saturday or public holiday free time, time with 'Swiss Family Robinson', 'Gulliver's Travels', Pip, Squeak and Wilfred or Robin Hood, the aching days when one of the pretty girls—he thought perhaps—liked him.

And for the Empire, there were two pictures in grandly sober colours, of the king, encrusted in medals and braid, and the queen, doubly encrusted in jewels, her towering neck made all out of pearls. They ruled from above the dining-room mantelpiece on which swam a four foot long model of HMS Queen Mary, the greatest ship in the world. Their mystical Golden Jubilee produced golden confusions and golden-looking medals for the children. And when the king died all the things nurses, children and teachers said about it were as awesome as the endless gossip about the end of the world. A pane of the skylight in the duty-room fell in on the night the king died, which was a sign. His doctors had sewed a green thread through some part of his body: if it had come out stained red by blood they would have known he was still alive, but it had come out green, so they were sure he really was dead. Was that because he was a king? The cruelty of that needle!

There was a war in Africa. Eyetalians in aeroplanes were dropping bombs on Natives who only had assegais and shields. It wasn't fair, so everybody sang:

"Will you come to Abyssinia, will you come?
Bring your own ammunition and your gun.
Mossaleeni will be there,
shooting peanuts in the air.
Will you come to Abyssinia, will you come?"

Then the greatest empire in the world sent exhibits from all its colonies and dominions to show their colours and their pride, and crowds of people from all over the world came to the Golden City to see the Empire

Exhibition. A convoy of cars collected the children one day for their visit. Their route to the showground lay through the university, vacation-hushed, its palaces of learning with their clean new Classical shapes establishing symmetrical order within the light and space of the young country, this obedient arm of empire. In the showground colourful and obedient throngs streamed along a network of roads to pay homage at a score of shrines.

The children were herded onto little open trams whose two long back-to-back benches faced outwards so that passengers could see at least half of what was to be seen. Special nurses, belonging to the Exhibition, rode with them and saw that no one fell off the seats. At one of the shrines black waiters in white nighties and red flower-pot hats served them cakes and drinks at little wickerwork tables on a terrace. In another, a low oval wall enclosed a model of the world, lumpy continents surrounded by real water on which little ships (the biggest, the recognisable Queen Mary, nearly half the size of Madagascar) plied their fascinating courses while their tiny lights and and those that showed where the cities were came on and went off as an electric calendar counted off miniature days and nights. This was better than the Giant and Midgets, the Fat Boy, the Wild Man from Borneo, even the Performing Fleas. Felix could have gazed for hours, gorging his imperialist eyes on this little, visible, orderly earth.

4

Shadow Adventure

Over school holidays Felix went home to the new, half-built suburb spreading onto empty veld. Even after municipality workers came and made the streets and lined them with baby trees in little round cages, it was still a naked airy place. The nearest big trees were the bluegums along the fence of the Native Maternity Hospital (where the piccanins' mother worked) beyond a stretch of tall veld grass. The high black pines and cypresses of the cemetery were further away and houses between hid all but their pointed tops. Yet on windy winter days when yellow-grey sand from the mine dumps coated the verandahs and long drawn out hootings filled the air, the soft howls and sobs on the wind seemed to come not from the nearer bluegums but from the piled up darkness of the cemetery trees.

On the veld near the hospital fence was the opening to a tunnel which ran all the way underground to a sort of ditch with cemented sides and a fence around it deep inside the cemetery. So some children said. The tunnel was a huge pipe that spilled rainwater and sand and little stones out onto the veld. The opening was in the angle of a V made by two tapering walls that met where they were highest, like wings or thighs. It was a favourite place with the children of the suburb because a little way in it began to be dark and was good for adventures and hiding and secret games.

The only time Felix went into the tunnel Moh was walking him, holding him up from behind by his arms as they went. "No," she said at first when he asked her to take him in. "It's stuffy and dark and dangerous, and goodness knows what dirt there is inside." But he pleaded and nagged until she gave in.

They plodded along the bed of washed-down sand that made a level floor into the echoing pipe. There were rude words and drawings in chalk on the curving wall which held a feeling of all the secret things that had been done in here. The thickening shadow ahead was full of it. He strained forward, wishing he had a torch, wishing he could know it all. But soon the dim air began to smell more chokingly and Moh said, "No, I don't like it, it's stuffy. Pooh! And it's too dark. Come on, out now, back to the fresh air!"

Felix stared for a moment into the blob of pitch blackness that swallowed up the depth of the pipe as it tunnelled on underneath the veld, underneath houses, and underneath the main road, perhaps to the cemetery. Then he let Moh turn him round toward the dazzling whiteness of the opening, glad that as she walked him out, she was between his back and that greedy shadow.

5

Something Left Over

They had moved into the small Mayfair house when business was not going well, and it took a long time for them to get a wireless, a refrigerator, a telephone. Moh claimed the minimum for herself, tried to spend the minimum, and used things carefully. She wanted thorough work from the servant, yet only reluctantly, uneasily, called on her services. "You can't rely..." she said. Or, "I haven't got the patience to train her. I'd rather do it myself."

The black maid, the girl, chopped the firewood, brought in the coal, set the fire in the stove and took out the ash, did the house-cleaning and most of the washing and ironing, and made the beds. But cooking and serving the meals was Moh's work, also nearly everything to be done for the children, the mending and sewing and all the rest, as well as some of the heavy tasks when the girl was off or otherwise occupied. Though doing the minimum that was necessary, Moh filled her days with work, often to exhaustion, as though that were the way to get full value out of herself. Work was economy and economy was survival.

Mavis and Becky, schoolgirls now, grew more and more to hate the scrimping, the makeshift repairs, the bundles stored in corners of rooms, the making do, the holding back on things other people could have and do, when Moh couldn't see the "necessity". "What have we got to do with the Prince of Wales?" she said when they begged her to buy them little Union Jacks and take them to town where their friends and the neighbours were going to see the royal visitor. They protested, especially Mavis. And sometimes Dad complained, "Why can't you lay a proper table like everybody else?" There was a proper way to do things, there were things that everybody did, and because the same things didn't happen in their house it was not a proper place, and Moh was not a proper person.

Who else would spend minutes coaxing the last knife-smear of jam from the tin and then rinse it with a spot of hot water to add to a cup of Russian tea? Who else would press the sliver of old soap onto the new cake so that it stuck, mend broken china with smears of egg white from used shells, save string, newspapers, paper bags, pencil stubs, broken ornaments, toys, used envelopes for scrap paper (or for the sake of the gummed flaps, if they'd been only tucked in)—anything that could conceivably be used or rescued for service some day? Who else would treat the old half-witted egg-hawker, when he complained of being hungry, to a *pfankuchen* made from two of the dubious eggs from his own basket? Who else would react with annoyance when given a present? "What for?" she would snap. "It's unnecessary."—so the giver felt punished instead of thanked. She regarded careless givers with suspicion, as though they might turn out to be grabbers or as though, like grabbers, they didn't have enough respect for the line between Yours and Mine.

She put up with the nuisance of having a cat only to keep down the mice, and never hesitated to kill flies and ants and mosquitoes in the house. Yet one day she ran screaming out into the street to rescue a bird from the mouth of a dog. Felix was surprised, and glad. Here she was suddenly wildly dashing to save a hurt creature that didn't belong to her. This was something she did not have to do out of duty or for economy's sake.

She had got back her piano, and with Felix away at the Home she had the leisure to practise her old pieces and the new ones given to Mavis and Becky by their music teacher—the one they called "Firralees", and Choppin's "Polonaise" and the Strauss waltzes. In the dining-room, where the furniture had been squeezed up to make a corner for the piano, "Tales from the Vienna Woods", "An Artist's Life", "Wine, Women and Song" and "The Blue Danube" coming from her careful hands, so obedient to the sheet music and the metronome, seemed to rescue them from the gritty meanness of the suburb. During endless homesick terms in the mansion on the ridge above the zoo Felix yearned, more even than for being made comfortable and given good things to eat, for these half hours of music that she snatched from her cooking and cleaning and mending. Warmth and cleanliness and tasty food had to do with health, with survival. But when she read to them and when she made her music (even though she explained it away: "The piano is instead of a rest, it does my nerves good.") it had to do with something left over from survival. She could sometimes do something more than her day's work, something more than need or duty required.

It was grim duty when she accommodated her mother-in-law as a house-guest for a few weeks or months at a time. And it was duty when she put up Auntie Ella's son Joe during the first part of his apprenticeship at a garage in their suburb. Felix, Mavis and Becky grew drunk and rowdy on the laughter as Joe bantered with them or sang, whistled, raspberryed and snorted through ridiculous songs about Old MacDonald's farm or Popeye or Susannah "a funnical man", or made a circus out of preparing his sandwiches and squashing them flat enough for his lunch-tin. The noise and wildness grated Moh's nerves and made her grim with strain.

But when she let Uncle Boris come and stay with them for nearly a year there was something in it for her that went beyond duty. Any house-guest would be a burden, and Dad and Boris often wrangled about politics, and Boris sometimes fell into moods of bitterness and pessimism, drawing Moh with him, and even Uncle Harry if he were visiting.

"All I want is to rest forever", one of the uncles would say, or "Oh, well, fifty years from now we'll all be under the ground".

These gloomy slogans seemed like some kind of joke, frightening but not really meant, since Boris and Harry were so often playful and could do even extravagant things simply for fun. But it wasn't like Moh to pretend gloom or to disguise it. When she was shadowed by Boris's darkness, in which even survival became a luxurious vanity, Felix became threatened. Whenever she said anything like "All I want is to rest forever", the words did not dramatise a weary pessimism but reflected anger and exhaustion, and made everything seem bleak.

Yet there were times when she sat and listened to Boris, in a thirsty way which she seemed to have reserved for him—the foster-father of her childhood—absorbing his anecdotes and reflections and visions of "Russia", words with no useful purpose, but tuned especially for her listening, and yielding her something she could take for herself alone.

Again, it was more than duty, that something left over from survival, when she invited Auntie Jessica and her family for a Seder dinner one Pesach. The Passover cutlery and crockery and candles and matzo and wine and horse-radish and charred egg and other symbols set out on the best tablecloth, always made a Seder night seem rich and different in an ancient Jewish way that belonged to Daddy. But for once, with these handsome guests who knew how things should be done, Felix felt that the kind of special night that proper modern people went in for was happening at their house.

The daughter who was famous because she had won a beauty contest came with her fiancé, and they squeezed together in one armchair, and chased each other around the table and through the house, and spilt their jollity over everyone, even before dinner was over and some of Daddy's Seder rituals were still to be gone through. And afterwards Uncle Howard struck a fork against a plate and made it zing, then plucked the sound from the prongs with his finger and thumb and carried it across (Felix thought he saw a singing spot of pale blue flame) and placed it on the rim of a wineglass, which then magically continued the tiny music of the fork. His magic was different, it seemed somehow more magical, than the other uncles' tricks.

These days Auntie Jessica was ailing, but she could still make everyone join in a jolly game of hunt the thimble. Then Uncle Howard persuaded Moh, though she was flushed and dizzy with the effort of serving the big meal, to sit at the piano and play so that he could sing "Who were you with last night?" and "D'ye ken John Peel".

He came back a few days later and Moh let him take down the big monochrome print of people at a fair that hung above the sideboard, remove it from its frame and spend the whole day tinting it with his water-colours at the dining-room table. Felix sat by and watched until Moh shooed him out to the fresh air. Uncle Howard did not go in for the teasing fun that Uncle Harry and Uncle Boris did. The miracle of the singing glass was his only magic. But his quiet manners, and expressions read in stories but never before heard spoken (his greeting for children was "Hello, chicks!"), excited Felix in a different, grander way. And with his warm courtliness toward Moh, he brought her none of the gloom that her brothers sometimes imposed.

The picture he tinted fell from the wall a few years later onto a vase filled with flowers, and the paper was so damaged by broken glass and water that Moh did not try to patch it up. But by that time both Auntie Jessica and Uncle Howard had died.

6

Big Boys

New patients or staff were always so interesting at first, but afterwards mostly disappointing, especially big boys, who did not usually waste their time talking to small boys. But Petrus was different. He was a big blond boy from a farm, and he had had a fall from a foofie-slide between a tree-top and a dam and broken his leg and concussed his head. He was a bed-patient during his first days at the Home, and one day Felix was sick in bed in the same dormitory. The new big boy surprised him by talking to him straight away. Petrus liked to explain everything—his accident, how he had nearly died, what his home was like, what he believed in, his longings, his sorrows—and Felix listened with all his heart.

For the next few days he got permission to spend his free hours in the dormitory, keeping Petrus company. Once Petrus was up and about, taking his place as one of the biggest boys, being his friend was a special privilege, and Felix clung to it. He did everything to show that he was loyal, that he understood and cared. Especially about Petrus's bitter sadness in life, his knowledge that he would never fully recover from what his accident had done to his brain, his loneliness at home, his certainty that God wanted him to die young, his longing to die, to kill himself one day soon. Felix tirelessly pleaded with him not to be sad, not to feel lonely (he, Felix, would always want to be his friend, would never desert him, always do what he wanted) and above all not to kill himself. But Petrus would lie on his bed, his face hidden, buried in his sadness for hours on end. More than once he lifted his head and mumbled to Felix, "I'm going to kill myself today," or "Tonight". And Felix was shocked not only by the words but by the sight of tears on Petrus's cheeks. He had to find the right thing to say, the right thing to promise. It was up to him to save Petrus from killing himself.

One winter's night, long after lights out he heard Petrus leave his bed. "Petrus, where you going?" he whispered.

"I hate myself. I can't take any more. I'm going to die."

"No, no! What are you going to do?"

"I'm going to that stoep and I'm going to lie down on the stone floor and let myself get cold until I die."

"No, Petrus! Please!"

"I must. If you try to interfere I'll know you are not true to me."

Even Felix's two blankets weren't enough against the cold of the night. He lay in his bed clenched against the air, every minute murmuring a plea to Petrus who lay dying on the marble tiles a few yards away, but did not dare to anger his friend by shouting for the night-nurse to come and prevent this tragedy. Luckily she came by after a while and her torch-beam fell on Petrus. "What are you doing? Don't be silly! Get back to your bed." Petrus seemed to be sobbing softly as he climbed back under his blankets, but Felix thanked God he had been saved, though perhaps he would still get pneumonia.

More than anything, he wanted to be able to do things for Petrus. He wanted Petrus to need him and allow him a place as his special friend. But Petrus often found other boys more useful and interesting, especially Henk Malherbe. Henk was very good at carving things out of the chalky stones that were to be picked up in the grounds and on the koppie—not only the hearts that everyone else tried to make, but medals and badges as well, and even faces. He was also champion at drawing and bows-and-arrows and other things, and he could go with Petrus up or down the koppie or wherever he wanted to go.

"Henk is true to me," Petrus said.

"But I'm also true," said Felix.

"You have to prove it before I can trust you."

Everything Felix did was meant to be proof that he was true to Petrus, that Petrus could trust him more than anyone else, even Henk. And sometimes Petrus did things on purpose to try him out and make him show proof. He swore him to secrecy about certain things: the name of the girl Petrus liked, and things about other girls and their ous. And he told him things he had to believe: how if you shook hands with a girl and you did a little ticklish circle with a finger-tip on her palm it meant you wanted to jig and if she did it back it meant yes, and things God had told him. He made him agree to back Buck Jones for best cowboy, even though Felix's favourite was Ken Maynard.

And there was Stingball. Henk began it. "Sit still so I can sting you," he said, and threw a tennis ball hard at Felix. It caught him on the arm.

"Don't..." Felix protested.

"See if he can take it," Henk said, throwing again and missing.

Then Petrus picked up the ball. "Can you take it?"

"Yes," Felix declared, knowing that if he let Petrus stingball him, it would be proof. Petrus and Henk threw the ball again and again. Back. Shoulder. Knee. Back. It became a game they often played. And the harder they made the ball sting, the more it proved that Felix was true to Petrus.

One day a nurse saw them at it. "Petrus, what in heaven's name do you think you're doing?"

Petrus stayed silent and it was Felix who answered: "He's only testing me, Nurse. It's all right!"

"Well, don't do that," the nurse obstinately said. "Give me that ball."

"No, Nurse," Felix said. "I said it's all right. I like it!"

"Yes, you *would*," she snapped, and then as Felix went on protesting, "Oh, shut up, Felix!" She took the ball Petrus handed her and said, "Listen, Petrus, and you, Henk, if I ever see you doing anything like that again I'll have Matron on to you."

"Oh, Nurse," Felix screamed, as she walked away, "you don't understand. You're just spoiling everything..."

Morning school ended just before lunch. Coming out onto the driveway that led to the outside door of the boys' daytime lavatory, Felix whispered to himself: "Subject, object, predicate—extension of predicate qualifying time, place or manner." As he walked he soaked in the midday sun. Wednesday. Good. Nice lunch. Steak-and-kidney pie (no tripe or leeks or pumpkin) and then fruit salad for pudding (no sago or tapioca). He felt hungry. And grown-up and important. Grown-up because of being able to at last walk by his own balance. And important because of the after-school feeling that came when he had done well or learnt something special, something new and hard. "Subject. Predicate. Object. Extension of predicate qualifying time. Extension of predicate qualifying place. Extension of predicate qualifying manner."

One morning soon after Petrus had left the Home, Felix was putting on his boots in the corridor when he heard singing:

"When there's a rainbow on the river
You get that feeling
Romance is stealing
Right out of the blue and into your heart..."

It was a voice as good as Bobby Breen's, or better, and it rang out loud enough to be heard all the way to the Small Playroom.

Felix asked, "Who's singing?" and someone answered, "That new guy, Roy." There was no time then to find out anything more, but later in the day Felix went into Big Dorm and saw the new boy in bed with a cage on his bed to hold the blankets off the foot that had been operated on. He had a handsome thin face and black curly hair smartly greased and combed, and lay reading a comic.

Felix said, "Hullo," and the new boy responded, "lo," and went on reading, so Felix walked through. But he wondered what that closed face looked like when a song was coming out of it. A couple of days later he saw Roy singing: sitting up in bed, swelling his chest and letting the rich music come easily out of his wide mouth, while he looked toward the ceiling or downward with half-closed lids, as though he didn't care who was listening—he was singing because he could and because he felt like it.

Felix was now one of the oldest boys in the Home, so Roy had to notice him sooner or later. In any case they were in the same class at school, and when Roy heard Felix reading and giving right answers in mental arithmetic he decided that Felix was educated and worth talking to. So they spent a lot of their time talking about who was educated and the advantages the two of them had over most of the others because they were educated. It was interesting because they found encyclopaedias to read and talked about lots of different subjects: astronomy, watches, George Formby, Robin Hood, bioscope, Roy's gang at home, their favourite foods. Even though no one else shared their educated conversation, except a friendly nurse now and again, Roy was popular, strong and even more talented than Henk Malherbe, so Felix felt lucky that Roy was interested in him. And when Roy sang he not only enjoyed the music but felt proud of being the singer's friend. He felt sure that Roy's wonderful singing would make him famous.

When Roy's voice broke after a few months Felix was sad, but Roy wasn't because he said it meant his balls were getting ripe. Now he would be able to dig without getting blue-balls. He knew a lot about girls, called them "cows", "bitches" or "wimmen"—instead of "dames" as the other boys did—and told Felix which ones had nice legs and how to tell which ones were game. Felix was puzzled about legs and Roy had to explain to him what was a good shape, but he still didn't understand why it was important."You must get educated," Roy said to him.

Roy sang no more, but he was still the king. He was the handsomest boy and lots of the big girls liked to flirt with him. He could hit just about any target with a catty and was very good at Meccano. Once he made a machine with a clockwork engine inside and a propeller that spun so fiercely that the whole thing almost lifted into the air like a helicopter. And he knew how to get all kinds of privileges from the staff. When he had his second operation and had to be a bed-patient for a month he got permission for Felix to keep him company every day and was allowed to have books, games and a Meccano set from the toy room. There was also a gramophone and a pile of records, including a lot of George Formby songs.

Only with Percy had Felix shared so many things, but Roy was the king and he made the rules. "Let's bet," he said when they played draughts or fox-and-geese. "Penny a game." He nearly always won, and when Felix owed him a shilling he said, "When are you going to pay me? You better pay up."

Felix had no money and didn't look forward to asking Daddy for a whole shilling to pay for betting. Later on Roy said, "I'll give you a chance. Let's play again, double-or-quits. Any time you win you owe me nothing."

A day or two later the debt was over three pounds and Felix said, "I never win. I'd better not play any more."

"You better pay up," Roy said. "Don't say you can't. A bet's a bet... Or d'you want another game? There's always a chance." So they went on playing and Roy went on winning until they both knew that Felix would never be able to pay. But that was never said and he went on worrying about it.

Sloping down to bottom lawn on a ramp shaped like a wedge of cake on its side was a brick paved path, safely wide enough for a wheel-chair. Going very carefully because keeping his balance on a slope was difficult, Felix could walk down the ramp, but for a long time the climb up was too much for him. Then at last, one day when he was in a daring mood, he took it on, climbing in little spurts, almost sideways, right foot pulling, left foot braking and pushing, as he puffed, "I can, I can, I know I can...", doing it for himself but also making a show of it—a circus feat to impress Percy and Roy and the watching nurse and anyone else who could see him—and reached the top. It was too much of an effort to make every time he had to go up from bottom lawn, but he had done it at least this once.

Another day he was sitting about half-way up the ramp with his legs dangling over the edge, above a flower border with nothing in it but three cut back rose bushes, when Roy came up the ramp and said, "I dare you to jump."

"Never!"

Roy was armed with a whip made from a stick and some knotted string. He flicked Felix. "I mean it. C'mon, jump!"

"I can't. It's too high." It was a four foot drop from where he sat to the ground.

"You can," Roy said. "You gonna. Let's see it." He flicked again, more sharply. "Jump! I said jump!" Flick. Flick.

If he sat and squealed loudly enough, Roy would give it up in disgust, or a nurse might come to see what was happening. But perhaps if he slid forward and stretched his legs, his feet would be so near the ground that he would fall softly, perhaps even land on his feet so that he could lean against the side of the ramp while he found his balance.

The lash stung him again and he yelled "Ow!", and launched. He came down hard, grass and grit jarring his heels, his back, elbows and hands, and a hard, splintery rose stump ramming his bottom. "Eina! Oow! Ow! I hit the stump!"

Roy laughed a bit, then jumped down to see. "It's bloody sore," Felix said, rubbing himself and beginning to get up. Then he flopped down again. "But I jumped."

"Yeah," said Roy. "I said you could."

Tuck was precious. Sweetness. As one sucked or chewed, what was happening in one's mouth made up for everything. Not only hunger or the disgust of slimy boiled leeks or rubber-gluey tapioca, but also being cold, and soreness, and being afraid or anxious, and all the things one yearned for and couldn't have, and even homesickness. Now was the syrupy saliva. Pause with it. Make it last. Now was sweet.

They got three sweets each that tuck-time. Felix kept his best one for last, a toffee, he hoped a hard one that would bulge in his cheek and go on melting out its buttery sweetness for a long time. Roy had finished his. "You still got?" he said. "Hey, orps! C'mon! Orps!"

Saying "Orps!" was more than just asking for a share. The word had a power in it. If it was said before the owner said "Nix-orps!" the asker had a right to a share.

"It's not fair," Felix said. "You've had your tuck."

"So, if you're slow? C'mon, I've got orps..."

"It's a hard toffee," Felix said. "We can't break it."

"I've got a knife. I'll chop it." Roy reached for it.

"No, man, Roy! It's my tuck." Felix pushed Roy's hand away and tightened his fist around the sweet.

"Well, stick it, Shylock!" Roy said.

Felix pushed the sweet into his mouth.

Roy had in his hand a small toy gun that could shoot matchsticks a few inches. He was trying Meccano axles for ammunition but they were too heavy and just fell out of the mouth of the barrel. "Hell, hey! I didn't know you were such a spoily. I had orps, didn't I? Sis!" He put the gun against Felix's head and pulled the trigger.

In spite of the toffee deliciously pressing his tongue, Felix began to cry.

"Hell! You're a cry-baby as well as stingy. What a pip-squeak! What a drip!"

But Felix, his hand over the place on his head where the gunpoint had been pressed, could not control his sobs. After a minute Roy came and lifted his hand away.

"Oh, crikey!" he said. "There's a hole in your scalp. That bladdy axle went right in. Shit, it looks nearly a quarter inch deep. Shit, that must be sore."

Felix saw a spot of blood on his hand. "Yes..." he tried to say. "Yes... You see..."

"Hell, I didn' know it would do that. Hell, I'm sorry."

"You see... You see..." Felix, his toffee hugged in his cheek, was laughing and sobbing at the same time.

On the tarmac of the driveway a leaking hosepipe was creating a creeping rivulet. Felix watched how the shiny, rounded edge of the water, as high as a flat penny, pushed its way over the dusty dryness, stopping at bumps, spreading, feeling its way round to the lower places, making different shapes, sometimes splitting into two branches, sometimes joining up again to make an island.

After a while he touched with the tip of his boot a place where the stream-tip seemed to be holding back behind its elastic edge, stuck. The curve broke and the water trickled forward into the next patch of dryness. Then at a place where the water was spreading, swelling into a pool, he dipped his boot and scraped sideways to start a new branch, and helped it whenever it seemed about to be stuck. Drawn along by his boot the new streamlet split and rejoined and he saw that on this island an ant was caught. It ran from side to side, testing the little water-wall for a way out. But there was none, and as the streamlet trickled, the water-edges crawled toward each other, shrinking the island.

Felix wanted to throw himself down and try to save the trapped ant—give it a bit of grass or twig to climb onto, or even a finger, then lift it over onto dry tarmac and see it continue its journey—but things were happening too quickly. The lip of water closed on the spiralling ant and swallowed the island. Tiny kicks rippled the surface. The ant was drowning and it was his fault.

Nurse Manchester was young and kind and pretty. One Saturday midday little Nurse Manchester, off duty, her head free of the meringue of starched linen that was her cap, but still in her royal-blue tunic and black stockings, stood on the landing of the fire-escape outside the nurses' quarters and chatted with a handful of boys on the driveway below. Felix, on his way from the lavatory back to top lawn, paused to say hullo. Then he found that he could not go on. Nurse Manchester, bending forward to lean her arms on the rail, easy and timeless, was everything friendly and lady-proper in the grown-up world. But looking up at her he saw how the blue of her dress contained the stockinged knees and thighs, and he saw that she was something else as well in the grown-up world.

He had to stare and stare, he had to see as much as he could of what her skirt was meant to hide. He leaned on the Virginia Creeper ivied wall as near the fire-escape as he dared, as nearly underneath her as possible, slightly behind her. He could stare up for only a few seconds at a time, then look down, away, anywhere. His greedy staring must not be noticed. He had no right.

But his body set about to betray him. Now he had something of his own to hide. He slid down against the wall and sat, with his knees up, on the tarmac, and looked at her again and again. He wished she would look down and discover the state of his flesh, wished she knew what was happening to him, what he was feeling and doing, wished she would look down and, seeing all that, would smile and call. He whispered a call to her: "Nurse Manchester..."

But she must never know. He had no right. He was a boy of twelve, one of the children, but a criminal wanting wild, impossible, grown-up things. Nurse Manchester on her iron Juliet-balcony—he wanted her life, he wanted her to invite him inside her rich, mysterious grown-up life, he wanted her to quench his flesh, his childhood, his darkness. Nurse Manchester, up there, far, far away, a neverness away.

She looked down at him. "Why are you sitting there, Felix?" It was an odd place to sit, on the driveway. "Are you all right?"

"Yes, Nurse, I'm all right... Just sitting in the sun," he mumbled. Soon she went inside, but he remained sitting, whispering, "Nurse Manchester... Nurse Manchester..."—sitting until he could walk away without shame.

7

Enemy

A strange elation overtook Felix a few minutes after he had bumped into Willem Prinsloo one day in town. Over the years, chance meetings with other former fellow-inmates of the Home had usually rather depressed him, reminding him too keenly of how disliked he had felt there ("unpopular" was the word used then), how often displaced and endangered. Yet Willem Prinsloo was the bully he had particularly hated and feared, while most of the other boys in the senior section for children over fourteen had shared his feelings, had been his allies against the tyrant.

His throat contracted when he recognised the robust man limping toward him across Harrison Street with a young woman on his arm. He had often toyed with fantasies of facing Willem in the grown-up world, but now that it was really about to happen he did not know what to expect. He was trembling a little as he spoke the first words of greeting.

"Willem... Hullo. How goes it?"

"No, it's okay with me, thanks. And you?"

The perfectly civil answer amounted to a reprieve, and not now needing to escape, Felix dared, "And what are you doing nowadays?"

"Oh, diamond cutting, you know..." There was no sarcasm, though Felix ought to have remembered, that being the trade many of the boys became apprenticed to. Then, unprompted, Willem added, "This is my wife."

And so, with a minute of cool politeness while they waited for a robot's permission to move on, the encounter passed and they walked away from each other. Perhaps it was simply relief that accounted for the elation that now swept Felix up. There had been, on Willem's part, none of the old harshness or rudeness or menace, and no sign of recrimination—and this softening might have had to do with his wife's presence, the public place, or some ten years of forgetting. But on his own part, Felix was surprised to discover a complete freedom from bitterness. So there was more to his little euphoria than just relief. That decade-old toxic element in his memories of Willem seemed suddenly to have been neutralised. He allowed himself a fanciful regret that he had not invited the pair to join him for coffee in a nearby tea-room, so that once more after so long he and Willem might partake at the same table. How different it would have seemed, how delicious the contrast with those many meals at the long tables when all he wished from Willem was not to be noticed by him.

Why had he been so daunted? It must have been some particular degree of unripeness in his adolescent outlook that had induced him to hug his fear and caricature Willem into a monster. Reflecting now on the face he had just re-encountered, Felix found no quality there, after all, that necessarily bespoke brutality and arrogance. Those quick-moving eyes under the brow that so readily rumpled in heavy frowns, need not seem fierce or suspicious. He recalled noticing just such features on someone he knew only as mild and tractable.

And Willem's gestures and habits also appeared in a new light. Even the way, with his grin or laugh, his tongue-tip would protrude, pressed against his lower lip as though to restrain his eagerness, keeping the curve wet and hungry-looking, had lost its malign aspect. Felix had recognised that old habit, when it had reappeared while they chatted, with something like a secret greeting for itself.

But he could remember how in the old days when Willem Prinsloo laughed, when his tongue-tip showed and his bull voice leaped up the scale into a shrieking giggle, smaller boys would melt with terror. It made Felix smile. What queer exaggerations had stifled their reason and moused their courage. How grossly their lack of perspective had distorted reality.

In the hierarchy of physical strength that framed the society of thirty or forty boys at the Home, Willem Prinsloo's place was at the summit. Felix's was usually near the bottom. The only boys on whom he could impose his will were bed-patients—like Nemus Marais who was paralysed from his chest down and who died during his second winter there. He was a thoughtful, older boy with gentle manners whom Felix liked to chat with and play at chess, drafts or Chinese checkers. Yet from time to time he could not resist teasing Nemus for a little, pretending to try to push a cake of soap into his mouth, amused by his helpless giggles and breathless protests as they came by turns.

But Willem Prinsloo, with his cabinet of strong henchmen, ruled the whole community. And regarding him from his station in the system Felix was bound to perceive him wrongly. He figured as a simple, all-powerful instrument of motiveless cruelty, at once despicable and fearful. Felix would freeze in a stupor of dismay as Willem appeared and strode toward him, bawling one of the contemptuous nicknames he favoured—"Joodjie... Pigmeat... Proffesssorr...!"

What followed was often a treacherous game. Taking his subject gently into the strong circle of his thick arm Willem would adopt an almost fatherly tone, murmuring, "Come on, come on, Joodjie, it's about time I got you a bit tough. Let's teach you how to take it, eh..." Then he would begin, flicking Felix's ears with his fingernails, perhaps, grappling knee muscles with timber-hard hands, punching biceps, blowing illicit cigarette smoke into his face. There was always the chance that his mood would push him across a certain boundary, and he would bring the burning end of his cigarette close and closer to blistering point, until enough terror showed. Once he rubbed with a moistened thumb at a spot on Felix's hand until the skin broke and was left to leak and fester...

"I'm only playing with him," he invariably explained if any of the staff happened on the scene of his game.

With his new perspective, Felix judged that he would feel quite differently about such things if he had to undergo them again, far less negatively. After all, the bully only rarely inflicted a real injury. The way things appeared now, if Willem puffed smoke at him, the knowledge that cigarettes were strictly forbidden to the boys would add, to his sense of grazing up against Life as he choked and struggled to turn his face away, a touch of admiration, a tickle of mirth at Willem's bravado. And he played with the thought that the other ex-inmates of the Home, similarly broadened by experiences of life away from that protected hilltop, ought also to see the remembered Willem cloaked in this benign nimbus of revised appreciation. When, with the benefit of maturity and detachment, they recalled the things he had done to them, they ought to chuckle nostalgically, or even feel grateful.

There was, for instance, the tall, big-boned fellow whom Willem once dealt a black eye. Granted some perspective, that boy might find the memory more than a little amusing—especially recalling that the bruises round his eye were outlasted by the days that Willem's sprained fist had had to be wrapped in sticking plaster—and laugh out loud while rocking on his callipered legs and crutches.

And the feelings of the dwarfish boy whom Willem had swung round in the air while holding him by the ankles should be, whenever he looked back on the incident, a surge of gratitude for a unique experience. Counting up the number of times his head touched the floor as he whirled round and round through that switchback circle, his gratitude should grow in proportion to Willem's ingenuity and determination and strength. And so through the ranks of all who had lived in fear of the top dog's whims. All would be able to recall his "punishments" and "lessons" in a light-hearted, positive spirit, instead of with the bitterness of victims. Ripeness had surely endowed them with the same genial balance that Felix now felt he enjoyed.

In those days, however, his outlook had been as distorted and narrow as any. It was as though, somehow, he had remained fixed for months and years in the after-effects of his first fright from Willem. As still a new boy, he'd been jerked awake one night by the suffocating pressure of a heavy hand clapped over his nose and mouth while the dark simmered with giggling. While he kicked and squirmed, Willem muttered in his ear, as though giving some kindly advice, "Suffocation... You shouldn't of told anybody this is what you scared of."

He had led a gang of pyjamaed raiders from upstairs to give the smaller boys' dormitory a little skrik, just for fun, just to remind everyone who was boss. But the shock had left Felix unnerved and bitter. In the shallow soil of his inexperience he had, after that, rooted an unrealistic tree of heroic righteousness. He conscientiously hated Willem with the abhorrence of a Round Table knight for villainy. He cherished dreams of revenge; and meanwhile, whenever it seemed possible to do so, he regarded it as an honour to foil the bully.

That was why, when he had seen him swinging that pigeon-chested boy by his ankles and heard the thump that came each time his skull bounced on the floor, he had burst noisily into tears and created so much surprise—perhaps it had never before happened that one boy cried because of something that was being done to another—that Willem had stopped what he was doing and turned to growl, "What the blerry hell's the matter with you...? Shut your bek or I'll donner you," before stomping out of the common-room.

And then there was Basil, the Catholic boy with the good singing voice who slept in the next bed to Felix's in the downstairs dormitory. When Willem had wanted to push Basil in his wheel-chair around the building to the quiet, hidden part of the lawn, and then to undo the hank of rope he always had hanging from his Scout belt and fold it into a thick lash, and then to have one of his henchmen take Basil out of the wheelchair and place him on all fours on the grass, and then to... When Willem announced that intention to his justice committee, Felix found that he had to intervene. He came out with, "No, Willem, don't give him lashes. He's weak and you might damage him seriously."

"What the hell you talking about? You shut up. He's got to be punished."

"Yes, sure. But, Willem, listen, I know what... Just let us *tell* him that on Wednesday after supper you are going to take him and there and do that..."

"What you mean?" Willem demanded. "He's got to have his punishment. There's got to be no stealing from lockers."

"Yes, I know. But he will be punished." And then Felix explained how they would let Basil wait three days in suspense, and how at the end of that time, on Wednesday after supper, they would have him wheeled out to that hidden part of the lawn as though that were the time for it, and how only then Willem would tell him that he had been punished enough.

"That won't teach him not to steal."

"Oh yes, it will," Felix pointed out. "It will be even worse than the other."

Willem looked at him suspiciously. "But listen here," he growled, "I'll break your blerry neck if you tell him we not really going to punish him. Hoor jy?" Then he told someone to go and fetch Basil into his presence.

The reason for Felix's sudden promotion to Willem's counsels was that it was his locker that had been robbed. It was his purse with his one-and-tenpence in it that had disappeared. He had hunted for it and told the boys of his dormitory. The word had got to Willem, their policeman, judge and executioner, and he had summoned all the boys into the common-room and commanded them to own up, and in the usual way had been met with a sheepish silence. Then he had ordered a search of all downstairs lockers. It was fruitless, but afterwards the purse had been found under Basil's mattress.

The recovery of the purse satisfied Felix, but of course it also meant the finding of a culprit, and that demanded Willem's judicial attention. "There's got to be no stealing from lockers," he proclaimed. "Anyone who steals from lockers has got to be severely punished."

Basil, the dormitory's songbird, omitted his usual ritual of singing softly to his room-mates after lights-out that night. In fact he remained very quiet during the whole of those three days leading to Wednesday evening. He sat drooping in his wheelchair, bothering to drive himself only when and where he was compelled to. His eyes avoided every face, and his answers to anyone who addressed him were short and absent.

When Felix saw that no one else was nearby he came close and said, "Listen, Basil, don't be anxious about what is going to happen on Wednesday. Believe me, you don't have to worry about it. I..." Basil gave a start, thrust out his trembling lower lip, glared for moment, then turned his head aside without answering a word, and began to propel himself away. It was the same the other two or three times that Felix tried to pass him a hint about the real state of affairs. "Look, about old Willem and Wednesday after supper, you don't have to..." But each time a surge of blind fear and anger made it impossible for Basil to take in the comforting news.

On Wednesday at sunset, when he was wheeled round the building to the hidden part of the lawn his face was very pale. And it became even paler when Willem said to him, "Nou ja, boykie, you in for your punishment now," and lifted him out of his wheelchair and set him down on all fours on the grass, then ordered a hanger-on to hold Basil steady while he got ready. He undid the hank of cord on his belt, folded it to the right length for the lash, and tested it noisily two or three times on his hand. But Basil's features retained that greenish shade even after he had been lifted back into his wheelchair and Willem had announced to him that he had been punished enough, and explained, "But, hoor jy, Basiltjie, next time you won't get off like this if I ever hear you been stealing again. I know you always praying, but that's not gonna help you. There's got to be no stealing from lockers."

While he was giving each of the little justice committee a smile of gratitude and relief Basil's cheeks remained pale, and immediately he was done he hung his head. As soon as he could suppose that no one was watching him, Felix saw him cross himself and mutter something with shaking lips. That night again there were no songs in the dormitory after lights out. Basil had climbed into bed and gone to sleep very early.

Looking back on it all from the vantage of his new perspective on Willem Prinsloo, Felix saw how a similarly broader vision might have opened Basil to happier possibilities. Instead of being so shocked and angry, so damaged because he had let himself be terrified, Basil might at least have relished the relief of his reprieve. And he might have taken a little comfort from the realisation that after all Willem was not absolutely and uncontrollably dangerous. He might even have appreciated a kind of joke in the charade he had been through. The lesson Willem had intended might have been the least of what he had learnt about life that evening in the hidden corner of the lawn. And he would have given that half-hour after lights out to singing, to more exuberant singing than usual. And might, out of something between mockery and gratitude, have sent someone upstairs with a note to Willem, inviting him to come down in his pyjamas and listen to the recital.

At that time nothing would have been stranger to Felix than the idea of Basil reacting in any such way. The victim's restricted vision was equally his own. Indeed, his perspective on Willem was even narrower and gloomier than Basil's and everyone else's. He was on their side and against Willem. He even felt, as perhaps the favourite subject of his attentions, that he was secretly their leader against the tyrant. In some way it was left to him to exact retribution for all his crimes. He dreamed of a distant day when they would be men and Willem would somehow be in his power, and he would darkly and mercilessly torture him until he had exacted from him as much agony as he had squeezed from their hearts.

That was why, on that Sunday some weeks after Willem had left the Home to take up his diamond cutting apprenticeship, when according to the custom of old boys he paid the place a visit, his reception was so unceremonious that this first visit was also his last. When Felix glanced around himself that Sunday afternoon, he found that all the boys on the lawn were gathering and forming themselves into a crescent behind him, like a Zulu impi.

"You, Willem Prinsloo," he shouted, "listen, I'm going to tell you a few things... And you're an outsider now, don't think you can bully any of us any more..."

As his taunts and insults poured forth, his limbs trembled uncontrollably, but his voice remained so strong that he felt it could flood the whole huge plane beneath them with Willem's humiliation. "You thought you were the king because you could boss us around, but nobody respected you. They were only frightened because you were such a cruel bully." And though he saw that face darken and twist in anger, those huge legendary fists fold up into terrible hammers, he knew that now the bully was impotent against them, so nothing could stop his tirade, which went on until Willem turned and began to limp away, shouting over his shoulder, "You going to hear from me. I'll see you with the police! Just wait..."

Since that day Felix had not seen him again and lately rarely thought of him until this casual crossing of paths with Willem as an ordinary pedestrian walking arm-in-arm with his wife. So he was surprised at how a bare minute of contact in Harrison Street alongside the City Hall could change his feelings from that last rancorous triumph to this broadminded and worldly forgivingness. No, to an emotion even more positive than that. For the truth was that Felix found himself suffused—as he threaded his way among streams of strangers who were excluded from the experiences Willem Prinsloo and he had lived through together—with a feeling of brotherliness towards him.

8

Economy

At the Home Felix was often uncomfortable, cold, hungry. The habit of hunger between meals gave the smaller children an appetite for anything that looked edible—orange peelings, grass tubers, even toothpaste. Once he picked up a clod of pure salt he noticed on the servers' table as he was leaving the dining hall. Swallowed whole, its fierce strength left him gulping and gasping for breath. Moh and Dad's Sunday visits were always feasts of carefully chosen tidbits which Moh fed to him. So, knowing what she provided, knowing that she never held back on what she thought was necessary and good for her children, he respected her economies. But he resented them when they deprived him of pleasures. And they frightened him when they shrivelled the imagined possibilities of life.

Once, when he was fifteen, she displayed this strangling parsimony in connection with an unusual extravagance. The supervisor of the boys at the Home then, the one nicknamed Pluto who practised astrology, persuaded Dad and Moh to let him cast a horoscope for Felix. The cost was half a guinea, but they were curious and fancied that they might learn something to Felix's benefit. And besides, Dad was always eager to please anyone in an official position.

On their next visit Pluto handed them an envelope closed with sealing wax. "Felix's present incarnation was premature," the document inside declared. "His soul rushed into a bodily life that was not ready for it by many years. Therefore there is malfunction. All the channels are incomplete and defective, and energy tends to short circuit and explode. Felix will be wise not to expect normal social and bodily fulfillments in this life. He must try to learn to postpone his aspirations and desires until his next, more mature, embodiment."

The more Felix understood the message the less he liked it, but it made a certain sad sense to Moh, this economising on hopes. "If you don't long for what's impossible you can't be disappointed", she said, drying her eyes. Her agreement froze him, because she was the one who identified and named the necessities of their life. She was the one who drove her children to do their homework, their exercises, their practising on the piano, who faced and outfaced their terrors over doctors and dentists, the one who could have kept him at home in his school-years but accepted the necessity for him to be away if he was to have an education.

Moh screamed into the telephone, "What? What? Seriously? Do they say seriously? Oh, Ella, Ella... Poor Joe..." Then she wept loudly. Auntie Ella's son had lied about his age and joined up and been away Up North for over a year. Now he had been injured by a landmine. Moh's weeping shocked Felix as much as the news. He hadn't known she could weep like that. It was because Joe was so young; it was because it was war and waste; it was because Auntie Ella on the phone was full of the shock of the news she had freshly received. But he hadn't expected that Moh could be broken through Ella's breaking.

Felix came home for good at last and enrolled in a matriculation college. Mavis had been trekking across town by bus and tram to and from school for two years, and when Becky passed Standard Five, the last class in primary school, they moved into a bigger house with lawns and fruit trees, in a suburb near the girls' high school. There was more money and they were buying this house, but still Moh and Dad were reluctant to spend, especially on their own needs and pleasures.

"Money is nothing if you never spend it," Felix protested, "and that's a real waste. It's as if you saved food that you never ate."

"Did you ever hear such nonsense!" Moh spat the words. "Food goes bad if you don't eat it but you've always got the money if you save it. We've got to eat, but I don't believe in unnecessary spending."

"But this isn't unnecessary. It's letting the money do things to make your life better."

"Oh, how you talk! What do *you* know about life? You don't know how the world works."

It was her way of quelling him when they argued, using contempt to defend herself against his outbursts of criticism. She was too untrusting, he felt. Why so suspicious of strangers, so automatically critical toward all who came close to her—Dad, the girls, the servant, traders, workmen?

With guests who were self-indulgent or vain or tried to flatter her, she became embarrassingly sharp.

"Did you ever see!' she exclaimed when a niece asked her for a drink of water. "I don't have to *make* it for you. You know where the tap is. Help yourself."

This made sense and only awkwardness made Felix groan, "Oh, Moh!"

"Don't you interfere," she responded. "She isn't helpless."

Mavis matriculated and found a job. Out of her first month's salary she bought Moh a pretty jug and matching set of drinking glasses. She presented the parcel and unwrapped it proudly.

But Moh was having none of it: "What for? This kind of fancy goods—a waste of money. It's unnecessary."

Mavis stiffened under the punishing sharpness, and spat back, "It doesn't have to be necessary. It's a present. Don't you know how to accept a present?"

Like Moh, Felix often quarrelled with Mavis, but now for once he was on his sister's side, stabbed by her pain, perhaps sharing some of her soft longings. The ritual was important to her, symbolising her adulthood, her independence, her freedom from Moh's bleak economy. At the same time she was paying formal respect to her mother, according to the gracious conventions she yearned to follow, and making a peace offering after a thousand battles. "Oh, Moh, I don't understand you," he railed. "Your daughter gives her mother a present out of her first wages, and you... Can't you show a bit of grace, a bit of ordinary manners?"

Moh might have softened after a few minutes and yielded Mavis some sign of appreciation, but now, with irritation added to her embarrassed annoyance, she turned on him—"Don't you interfere!"—and their anger flared and left its fumes to sour the air.

He tried to hold back when she was in the right, but when she overrode someone's dignity, someone's tender feelings, he could not help rising to the victim's defence. "Moh, don't insult people..." The victim this time was the servant.

"Where 'insult'? She doesn't do her job properly. She can't see dirt right under her nose."

"Yes, but you don't have to call her a stupid idiot. That's attacking her dignity."

"I like that! Who's got time for dignity? What does dignity matter if she can't clean the house properly?"

"It matters, it does matter, to everyone..."

He was shouting, and now she flamed at him: "Oh my God! there you go again. Don't shout at me! I can't stand it when you get excited. If you knew what you look like, what the sound of your voice does to me... I'd give anything if you could learn to control yourself. And if you'd mind your own business..." She flung from the room as though she needed to be at a distance or her anger would go on fuelling itself and never die down. And he was left stung, reduced, confused in the face of her certainty that what she did was what necessity and survival required to be done, and suspecting that he might be a dupe of sentimental theory, or of some childish vanity.

Yet sometimes when they quarrelled she stayed calmer than he did, and when his face showed that one of her barbs had pierced him she exclaimed, half in mockery, half in surprised recognition, "Ah, you're so touchy, so sensitive!"

Over the years it was as though she were trying to tame him, and he her—tame or arm, for life in the world of other people.

9

An Orderly House

Mrs Katz from next door brought the scandal that the mother and three daughters who had lately moved into number 27 were running a brothel. Moh's face stiffened with shock. "Did you ever hear! How dare they, in a decent neighbourhood! It's a disgrace. How low can people get? Why haven't the police done something about it?"

Felix was twenty-two, blocked in the ice of his virginity, fixed on the seven-year-stale message of his own undesirability that had flared from the shocked face of that pretty friend of Mavis's when he had asked her to lie with him. Mrs Katz's gossip seemed to promise him the possibility of a crack, a living thaw, if it could be true that the thrilling kindness of attainable bodies was being offered three doors down the street. If he could find the money, if he could summon the courage to risk being seen going there. Moh's indignation immediately destroyed the possibility and placed her with the cold powers that were refusing him the chance of joy and release. He could say nothing, but he let himself hate her with a hatred he nursed for days.

Perhaps she could not afford to know what his needs were because she still had Mavis and Becky in the house. Those women at number 27 who did not care by whom they were used as long as they were paid, threatened the wholeness and wholesomeness she was guardian of. So that she could fight this danger off, another had to remain unseen, or at least unspoken of: the danger in Felix's yearning—the danger that would go on unfolding another seven years and far beyond, in intervals of frenzy, fantasy, disappointment and shame.

To Dad some sort of disorderliness was at least thinkable. Helping Felix dress because they were late for some family party, he noticed a scratch on his thigh. "You must be careful of bad women," he remarked. Felix could not picture the lurid connection his father was supposing. But the worst of it was the inaccuracy with which he was being guessed at, the mocking irony of the timing—in the hopeless middle of one of those long dry spells when he was cut off from any but the loneliest sexual resource. It was worse somehow than having his urgencies ignored, or quite unknown.

But after all, this side of him had to be and remain unknown to his parents. He had to guard his adult separateness against the humiliation of their sympathy, or their shame, or their judgements on the wild shapelessness of his desires, the squalor of his resorts, his successive follies of hope and disappointment over every visible girl. When he fell in love with girls he met at university, first Bathea, then Janine, then Bathea again, it was enough for him to discover, as each drifted untouched and untouchable out of his reach, how he could be deluded, how he could delude himself over and over again.

After Mavis and Becky married and left home Felix lived on in the house with Moh and Dad, his years refusing to take on a serviceable shape despite his intentions and ambitions. He had defected from university in the middle of his second year, and was unable to find a job. He typed letters and filed invoices for a few hours a day at Dad's timber yard, and tried to dream his way into stories and poems. Time was loosely spiralling, like the flock of pigeons he became fond of watching from his bedroom window as it described circles over the rooftops in the dip that fell away behind the house.

"Mavis says you live like a prince," Moh told him one day.

"What does she know about how I live?" he objected. All the same it was a shock to find he could be thought of as parasitically idle. He decided to finish his degree.

His second spell at university brought him at first more sterile months of tantalising closeness to unattainable young women, but then the mercy of his first sexual requital. Evelyn's bodily kindness was a grace he thought he had done nothing to earn beyond needing some such rescue. But even if she bestowed her love in a spirit of charity, it surely saved him from the poisons of his frustration. All the same, gratitude was not a passion strong or sure enough to hold a lover for long, and Evelyn was soon drawn away from him in favour of the man she eventually married.

By the time he had attained his degree he was being asked to contribute articles to magazines and had edited a volume of Johan de Waal's essays, but the sense of his successes was eroded by yearning. Whatever he accomplished was surrounded by dissatisfaction and his energy was dissipated. At the best of times his work was slow and he earned meagrely and irregularly, and remained dependent—less shamingly so after, at last, one of Dad's eternal sweepstake tickets moderately fulfilled the promise of fortune he had daydreamed on for as long as Felix could remember.

One day when Felix forestalled Moh's quickness and cut a slice of cake for himself, she exclaimed, "How well you can manage!" He was half embarrassed by her applause.

"But why are you surprised? You know what I can do."

"Yes, I know, I know! You can do anything if you have enough time. I know how independent you are. But I haven't got the patience to watch you struggle. I only want to save you the trouble." She did that so promptly, so thoroughly, that she was unused to the sight of him doing things for himself. In fact he relied on her help, only sometimes resisting, feeling that perhaps she went too far, perhaps she shielded him from some part of his own reality. And reality was something he more and more did not want to lose, either by giving too much or too little meaning to any part of it.

With scarcely less sense of danger, he accepted the awkward tribute of the tears she shed while reading an article of his: "But why? What's there to cry about?"

"You express yourself so well," she explained with a sort of shyness. It was as though, for her, after the way things had begun this were no less a mercy than his being able to walk, feed himself, dress himself, take a tram; whereas, if his adulthood meant anything, *he* had to take all this for granted. But her acknowledgement of his ability moved him, as, conversely, her jeers had a power to hurt, like the "Oh, what do you know about the world? You've never been out in the world. You're a baby" she would fling at him when they were tangled in one of their political arguments.

She too did not go out in the world. She left the household shopping to Dad, joined no societies, had no close friends who were not relatives. Her own house was increasingly her retreat.

When Dad and Moh took a trip to England to visit Becky, Felix insisted on his independence. He would not stay with Mavis or any other relative. He would remain at home. With the servant to help him he knew he could manage. The two and a half months became a strange subversive interlude. Master of the house, for the first time at large in Johannesburg with no one to account to, he found himself strangely spilled out. At a friend's request he allowed the lounge to be used for a clandestine political meeting, and later let a man in danger of "detention without charge" lie low in the house for several days. He found and repeatedly visited a brothel in the city. He encountered an amenable black girl at a party, invited her to the house and, against the law, risked an afternoon of love-making with her. Afterwards he looked incredulously back on the dangerous games he had been playing, relieved to have escaped exposure and repercussions.

Moh returned from her visit to Becky to learn that her best-loved brother, Boris, had suffered a stroke. His wife was a working woman and could not stay home to nurse him, so Moh offered to have him with her. His walking and speech were impaired and most of his memory had gone. Moh and Felix tried, by talking to him, questioning, reminding, explaining, reading him simple and familiar things, to recall him to himself. But after a few weeks their hopes for him faded. Moh knew him as a a mindless burden and expressed no regret when she let him go to the Aged Home. He died a few months later. Meyer and Harry too were dead by now, and of Moh's siblings only Ella remained, a nervous widow so wrapped up in vulnerable pride that conversation with her always had to be a childish game of diplomatic humouring.

Gail had treated Felix with sisterly concern since they had become friends at university, and he had supported her through the stress of examinations and the stormy early days of her marriage. "I feel as if I'm drying up," he confided to her one day. It was years since he had become discouraged about seeking out prostitutes when ones he knew of became inaccessible.

"Let me see what I can do," Gail said. "Let me ask someone I know. I think I can find something out for you."

After a week or two she brought him an address in the southern suburbs with a telephone number and the cover name he was to use in making his first appointment. He took a bus to the place one afternoon. The woman in her meticulously kept cottage was kind but elderly, and the mystery of her situation did nothing to romanticise her ministrations. Felix accepted the relief with a kind of dismay. This was a sort of paramedical service. It implied that there was no hope for him in the world of passion between persons. And when, at the end, she refused to accept his payment, he felt it signified not affection but pity. If this was how he was to be saved, then he was lost indeed. He kept the appointment made for the following week, bringing a bottle of whiskey for her, but did not go to her again.

Moh needed her "outings", her weekly bioscope, the occasional drive when Dad had a business errand in a convenient direction, but more and more her life was in the house. She was the life of the house. She alone knew where to find everything. Dad had as his own the secrets of the sideboard drawers where he kept his papers. Felix had his desk and files and bookshelves. But all the secrets that were of the house itself were Moh's. They were her special knowledge.

For Felix the house meant home, food, bed, desk, telephone, his choice of books and pictures in his room. But he was the recipient and things were never perfectly according to his design. Returning from a trip to town one afternoon he found that Moh had rearranged his furniture "Why did you have to do that?" he remonstrated. "You know how I hate to change things."

"I'm only trying to make things more practical, more convenient." She was no more than half apologetic. She seemed also amused, both at her own compulsion and at his irritation. But it was her role to protect and preserve the house and seek out ways to improve its running; and it was he who endangered its safety, subverted its decency, admitted alien intruders: the security police preposterously sniffing some red herring in one of his publications, a sexual adventuress who wanted him as her pornographic scribe, wayward white writers and indigent black ones.

Moh gave its value to the view from the back of the house—suburban roofs and a jacaranda avenue and spurs of hills and a spread of highveld plain that outreached the suburbs and stretched pale and naked to the horizon—enjoying it as though to exact the full worth of something she owned. She scrubbed walls and killed ants and flies and drove the servant after dust and cobwebs, and salvaged the detritus of their lives — the string and bits of flex, the broken plugs, the used screws and washers and nails, the cardboard and paper bags, the jars and rags and keys, the newspapers and magazines—on shelves, in drawers and cupboards and boxes.

It was salvage, not hoarding: everything was stored in the hope of realising some value or use. Best would be if each bit of rubbish could be used up, consumed in the fire of its usefulness. But in a drawer of her dressing table she saved even the long grey and white strands of her own hair, rescued from the brush and wound into a ball that grew to the size of a baby's head. If she had a purpose in mind, it remained her secret. Felix could not ask her about that.

On sloping ground, the house stood higher at the back where his room was, with a cellar beneath and steps down from the kitchen door to the backyard. Often, at his window, Felix looked out, not across to the horizon and Moh's favourite view—the backdrop to the swirling flock of pigeons that fascinated him—but downward, into the yard. This was when his torpid curiosity, baulked usually by the glaze of long familiarity, was prodded awake by sounds of the entire alien life that was lived down there.

"*Ko-ko!*" he would hear from the back gate in a restrainedly raised voice, "*Ko-ko! Ko-ko!*" And for years he supposed it to be the servant's African name or nickname (how strange that several should answer to the same), before discovering that the call meant, "Knock knock! I am here, let me in." The same sound announced clients when the servant's room in the yard became a shebeen, and congregants when, under another occupant, it did service as a "Zionist" church. And then might come hymns and sermons rising to the frenzy of a visitation of tongues, or sometimes the thumps and shouts of a police raid for pass or liquor law offenders. The room was burgled more than once, and more than once its occupant, screaming, fled the terror of nightmare or ghosts or attempted murder. A man with an unknown name, whose face became familiar as he came evening by evening and left morning by morning, slept there for years. The room housed illness repeatedly and once the birth of a baby. Moh and Dad were drawn into that backyard life now and again to mitigate its threats and distresses.

It was his Africa, Felix sometimes ironically reflected, and he failed it, he wasted it. For his interest to be aroused he needed human identity to be spelled out and issues dramatised, as they were in the case of Timothy Mabeko, a novelist, semi-literate in English, whose manuscript he was editing, and Wilson Nthuli, a young poet he was guiding. Their testimony and their needs made him wish he were affluent enough to afford more than some surreptitious help to Mabeko in paying his daughter's school fees—surreptitious because Felix wouldn't risk his parents' indignation at his presuming, in his financial situation, to give lumps of money away, however deserving the recipient.

Mabeko's poverty made Felix find, after all, a decent appropriateness in Moh's and Dad's reluctance to spend on inessentials even when some affluence had come their way. Moreover, the large remnant of Dad's windfall had gone to finance some persuasive schemer's gamble. Had it succeeded, his problem concerning Felix's security would have been solved. But, alas, the schemer miscalculated and Dad's thousands vanished. So even when he was well past seventy he could not think of retiring from business.

If Moh had been allowed to know, she would have identified Felix's folly over Susan from the start. Her ingenue's face with its intense expressions, her tormented dependency, which would have aroused Moh's distrust, were precisely what overwhelmed him. When Susan, as always armoured in a heavy pullover down to mid-thigh over her slacks, lay in his arms urgent for his reassurances, for the safety of his embrace, she would give way to a prolonged shuddering that came, she told him, of an old anguish. She explained that she was in retreat from sex after years of compulsive promiscuity. Holding her so taught him feelings of tenderness and protectiveness he had not had the chance to exercise before. He thought he could wait for her to resolve her conflicts, or could even sustain permanently the kind of loving they had achieved. But soon she was eluding even this degree of intimacy. By the time she flew to England at the call of a former lover who wanted to marry her, her departure meant to Felix mainly relief from a tension and confusion that had become unbearable.

When he returned from the airport after seeing her off, the pigeons were circling. He couldn't remember now how long ago his pleasure in watching them had first begun—eight, ten, twelve years? One of the tiled or iron roofs below his window was the pivot of their wheeling, their "home"—he had never cared which, being simply glad that his valley was their haunt. But he wondered why they favoured some hours and some seasons more than others, and how and why those dozens of birds held together like a single creature with tendons of air.

He had also wondered about the cause of his own fascination. The pigeons were replete with mystery as they flew, in their easy muster, again and again past his window, now on the near now on the far side of their orbit, now clockwise, now against the clock, usually driving themselves with brisk or slower strokes of their wings, but sometimes stretched and rigid as kites, gliding as though only the wish to move moved them. There was the flowing position of each pigeon within the flowing flock, there were the switching facets of their wings as they dipped or sharply faced about, the sudden driving flutter after a long swoop of still-winged gliding, the strum of broken shadow sometimes thrown into his room as they came past the face of the light. And there was the always surprising sound that reached him when they widened their loop and flew within feet of his window, perhaps just above his roof, a living whirr that made him intimate with the feathers, wind and flesh of their strong wings. On certain winter days, against the khaki of the opposite hill and the drained gray of the sky, their mere shadow-black and gray and white flashed out like flames and flowers, simply because they moved, moved with that rhythm, grace and mysterious accord, and so bespoke life.

More than once when an irrational reluctance to be away from home had made him hesitate over an invitation to holiday or travel with friends, he had jokingly explained his feelings as coming from the influence of the pigeons.

"They hypnotise me. Gyrating like that, they lay a spell on me."

Today they yielded him another meaning. His by favour as they circled an invisible cote somewhere down there in the dip, they symbolised the girls, the women who had stirred him, entranced, roused, teased, enriched and eluded him, kept nearly all their real secrets, but sometimes enclosed him in their widening gyre and passingly whispered to him that there was flesh beyond the glass of his window, flesh beyond the limits of his own flesh—all the different, mysteriously similar women of his young manhood, Marjory, Bathea, Janine, Melissa, Evelyn (even Evelyn, the one who had brought substantial proof) and now Susan. When the pigeons had been circling an hour or more, their way was, one by one, each choosing an individual moment, to drop away out of the flock and out of sight.

And yet another meaning. Enclosed in their pool of suburban air, and contrasted with the arterial road in front of the house that linked the city centre with the airport and the wide world, circling and circling and making no journey, they pictured something of his own years, of himself. Of course something of himself was also in the road, the scene and channel of so much that had come to him—but to see that he had to be facing a different way.

After Susan, came the visitation of Lucilla, dazzled visions, breathless aspirations, a year that tempered him, converted him to an intention of devotional celibacy, but in the end left him bereaved and confused. He revenged himself on that restraint in the letters he exchanged with Veronica Steen. But her complicity in the game of lewdness was ambivalent, guilty. They went through a cycle of hints and invitations, decreasing tentativeness on his part, rising to frenzy, and then revulsion and bitter reproach from her—and repeated the pattern twice more before he recognised its persistence and tore up his cache of her letters.

Lucilla and others had declared Moh's face exceptional, fine in some rare way. "I can't really see it," Felix confessed. What he could see was that it was increasing in pallor, until it almost matched the hair that had grayed so early and then steadily intensified in whiteness. She became translucent. That face she so rarely touched with a bit of lipstick, naked, spare of flesh, tactlessly hiding nothing—neither tiredness, illness, anger nor pleasure—was candle-white, with its eyes hollow above the high cheekbones, its lips bladed, spare, drawn and serious.

She did her work vigorously and took her food or rest fiercely, at a point of sharp need. It was a healthy pattern and there was always a shock when she admitted to being ill. Now that she was past her mid-sixties, winter colds repeatedly went to her chest and she was racked and drained by coughs for weeks on end. There were days when arthritis in her hip flared up and laid her low. An attack of angina pectoris sent her to hospital. The house then failed. The servant gave Felix his breakfast and lunch, unless he ate out, and when Dad was home he did the cooking—but he did it with a stricken fussy awkwardness. The house was without its rhythm, without its authenticity.

Back home, Moh dealt with pain and illness like an animal, drawing aside, hiding, folding the sickness away inside herself, alone with it because she was the only sure source of help and caring in that house. Whenever her illness became visible, Felix could do hardly more than worry. Dad fussed, nagged with useless solicitous questions, did his confused and clumsy best, but only wildly irritated her. After a while she would scream her instructions, badger him, insult him. The air became electric with desperation. At ordinary times Dad would retreat from her castigation with a wry appeal to Felix: "Your mother is an impossible woman." But now his worry seemed to swallow it all.

As soon as she could, Moh threw herself back into her work—making the meals, giving Felix the extra help he needed since his right hand had begun to weaken, looking after grandchildren who were brought to her for a few hours or a few days, nursing when either of them was ill, darning and sewing, harvesting the fruit from the trees in the garden which she could not bear to let go to waste, the figs, the apricots, the mulberries, the persimmons.

On routine days Felix did not take the bus to town (trams had been replaced) but was enclosed in the house with his desk and his books, with the telephone and the radio, with the view of the pigeons, with Moh. In the ordinary hours of the ordinary days of those years he was cloistered with her. When not on his own business, he often watched the industry of her hands, so brisk and sure with spoon and knife and needle, so carefully tentative on the piano keys until a piece was mastered, so fumblingly nervous with pencil or pen (yet every month or so building a letter in response to Becky's regular missives). He saw the way the skin of her fingers dried and wrinkled and that of her face grew papery over the broad Slavic bones. He told her the things about himself that he could, sometimes even needing the injustice of her criticism against someone with whom he had had a difference. Yet, taking a meal at her hands, he often brought a book or a portable radio to the table and voiced nothing beyond functional grunts. There were no routine greetings or thanks between them and any ceremoniousness would have been as embarrassing as to have been caught talking to oneself. She carried his life (even in a way the invisible weight of the chaotic things he could not tell her about) but she was simply what he had, there, daily, ordinary, like the floor, air, bread. And so she was nothing. She could not change him. She could not rescue him.

The persimmons came from one small tree that bore larger fruit than anyone had seen in the specialist fruit shops. Though rare, they were not much favoured. But rather than leave them to the ants and birds Moh brought them in, the occasional one or two that burgeoned, having swelled from green marbles into moons, full and shiny as giant tomatoes, orange-gold, with the promise of a new rare taste. It was chiefly Felix who ate them. If he broke into one while there remained any firmness in the flesh its bitterness would coat his mouth with a floury astringent layer, to be cleared by the tongue and spat and spat in sticky yellow crumbs. The beautiful saffron fruit had to darken to reddish-brown and attain the yieldingness of a breast before its sweet slime and slippery cell walls (the gummy richness, tasting faintly like mango and faintly like plum but with no acidity) could be scooped and scraped from the thin burst skin, the lumpy core, and safely eaten.

10
Politics

"Jews will never be safe unless we have the whole of Palestine," Felix yelled joyfully at the voters making their way between tables and posters to the polling booths in the Shul hall. He loved slogans, especially ones he worked out for himself.

"Vote for real Zionism, not for half Zionism, fake Zionism or disguised anti-Zionism... This is the only party you can rely on to get us a state that can protect us... Vote Revisionist!"

It was election day for the Zionist Federation. Felix was not old enough to vote, but was doing his best to spread the truth.

Dad was in charge of the Party office in a house across the road. He was a lifelong supporter of Jabotinsky, who stood for "A Jewish state with a Jewish majority both sides of the Jordan", and during the years between Hitler's war and the birth of Israel, the time of illegal immigration and the guerrilla struggle against the British Mandate, Dad became chairman of the local branch of the South African Zionist Revisionist Party. He arranged for Felix and Becky to join Betar, the Revisionist youth movement—Mavis had slipped away to one of the rival movements—and took Moh and Felix to several mass meetings. The news from Palestine and UNO kept the excitement simmering, and now there were these elections.

The Revisionist Party was competing against three other parties for representation in the Zionist Federation. Felix fell under the spell of the leader's booming speeches. How could anybody not see the case—the homeless people Hitler had nearly wiped out, desperate for a national haven in the native land of its religion, against a cruelly obstructive Mandate, callously selfish Arabs and treacherous, weak-kneed Zionist rivals?

He kept attending Betar meetings and camps until after Israel was achieved. But then, when the leader and the Party newspaper and the Betar speakers went on insisting that those partitioned slivers of land could never be a viable state, he became bored. He remembered during the election, on the basis of his own logic, insisting, "As soon as we get our state the Revisionist Party will go out of existence." In any case, by now he was under Johan de Waal's spell: politics was full of "obvious" thinking, all moral pretentiousness and low cunning. And from earlier, some of Skipper Ross's truths resurfaced: "reality" was shaped, not by the facts that newspapers could report, but by thought and faith; political argument, with all its negativity, was destructive of the spirit's potencies.

So when, at twenty-one, he arrived at university, he was disinclined for the campus politics. Lunch-hour protest meetings in the Great Hall did not attract him. Still, three or four times, when friends pressed him, he filed with them into the crowded, hectic auditorium to listen to the student leaders' speeches. One of the meetings was about the new government's Christian National Education policy. He couldn't understand how it came about that all these hundreds of his fellow-students, most of them younger than he was, knew enough about the threat to care so intensely. Another protest was about the expulsion of foreign black students. One of these had been a classmate of his, so he understood for himself how ugly and unfair that government order was. But he couldn't imagine the dutiful, self-important mood of the Great Hall somehow producing the message that would bring back to the classes the princely young Alfredo who had suddenly been deported home to Mozambique.

What did shake him were the obstructive cat-calls and heckling from a phalanx of white-coated engineering students. What did they know that made them, all as one, so contemptuous of the protest, so determined not to listen to the speeches or let them be properly heard? They were having fun in their mockery. But there was something anxious and brutal about it as well. In any case, this clash of wills and certainties had nothing to do with his business as a student.

But his business as a student, he found out soon, also involved things he was less than happy about. He had groped his way to the secret that literature's combinations of symbols, syllables and cadences were inscrutably magical keys to wisdom and delight. But none of that accorded with the English Department's analytical processes. Still, only vaguely protesting, he played their game until a few weeks into his second year. Then the course came to *Humphrey Clinker*, to whose aliveness and humour Mr de Waal had introduced him. Hearing it begin to be interpreted, at the first tutorial, as a responsible satire on some aspects of eighteenth century English social life, he felt that things had gone far enough.

After all, too many heresies seemed to be expected of him, acts of defection he would not lend himself to. He dropped out.

Five years later, feeling stagnant in his job at Dad's timber yard—typing the letters, filing the correspondence and invoices, answering the telephone—he decided to go back to university. He was hungry to enlarge his understanding and ready now to bend to the academic discipline and learn whatever he could. What he owed Johan de Waal (who had died by now) was not, after all, a pious faithfulness, but an openness to life, a readiness to discover and enjoy. And as for campus politics, they were also part of the pageant: he would take or leave them as the spirit moved him, and otherwise simply observe their show for interest or amusement.

In fact he found very soon that an unusual flurry of politics was disturbing the calm of the Department of Texts & Times in which he was now a second year major student. Its new head, Professor Carfew, was not one to inspire confidence. He was an awkward man whose ingratiating smile punctuated his sentences like a nervous reflex. What mattered, though, was that he was a desperately boring teacher: his lectures, confined to the technicalities of archival evidence, consisted of strings of mostly uninteresting facts, with no visible argument or structure. It was no wonder that his appointment was unpopular, but it also stirred up a lot of political suspicion. Between classes, in corridors and foyers, on the steps of Central Block and in the canteen, Felix caught snatches of the students' grumbling.

"I don't think he's simply incompetent. Why would they appoint an incompetent? You can see, he's deliberately lowering the level."

"Well, it's pure politics."

"I've heard that he used to be a member of the OB"

"But he's English-speaking."

"So...?"

"And the people he's brought into the Department—my God! That van Jaarsveld can hardly speak the language...and that argument of his about the trekkers being at a disadvantage because their firearms had to keep being reloaded while their attackers had spears!"

"Well, he *was* in the Ossewa Brandwag."

"No, he's in the Broederbond, I've heard."

"That's more likely."

Another time it was, "Look, Carfew's been been brought in under government pressure for political reasons."

"What political reason?" Felix wanted to know.

"His job is to lower standards."

"But why?"

Frank Potts, a sharply clever fellow in second year explained: "The idea is to undermine techniques of objective textual assessment, to make it easier for the Nats to instil their indoctrination."

"How do you know this?"

Potts shrugged, but someone less discreet said, "It's what Dr Vesey told James de Villiers."

Dr Vesey was a senior lecturer held in awe for the rigour of her scholarship. She had a following that included most of the brightest students.

One day Felix arrived for a tutorial by Professor Carfew to find that none of the other nine students in the group had come. Carfew appeared at the set time, exchanged enquiring looks with Felix and fiddled with his books and notes for five minutes. The room remained horribly empty, and at last he pushed his things together, gave Felix his pleading grin, muttered, "Ah, well, I suppose we'd better have this another time," and returned to his office. Felix could hardly blame his classmates for preferring to avoid forty minutes of tedium. But soon things were taken further. Notices in the canteen and in the Central Block foyer announced a general meeting of students in all the Departments of the Arts Faculty to discuss "the crisis" in the Department of Texts & Times.

Felix went along out of curiosity. Apart from the chairman and secretary, as far as he could see it was students of Texts & Times only who crowded into the lecture theatre, and the meeting seemed to have been thoroughly planned. A spokesman for each year of study presented an aspect of the case against Professor Carfew.

James de Villiers, for the Honours class, spoke first. He was troubled by the level of discussion in seminars, the triviality of assignments and the inadequacy of responses to submitted work. "Professor Carfew and the people he has appointed tend to treat us as though we were in first year, if not matriculation. What should make this a matter of urgent concern to society at large is the indisputable connection between the soundness of textual studies and political vigilance."

Felix supposed he had somehow missed the formal meeting at which Frank Potts had been chosen to speak on behalf of his and Felix's class. But clearly he was fit and eager for the task. He had armed himself with some information about Carfew's doctoral thesis, and smiled when he came to, "It analyses the punctuation in 18th century correspondence, and reveals—wait for it!—that inconsistency is pervasive. That dazzling illumination suggests to me a first rate mind!"

The fresher spokesman delivered his complaint about the lowering of standards with no less assurance than the others. Felix recalled the confused, lost condition of his own first months at the university. These freshers had enrolled a bare three months before. How had they come to know enough to be able to compare present and past standards and take such a definite position on the issue?

"In the light of what we've heard," a third year student in the front row declared when the formal statements were completed, "I move that we petition the University Council to rescind Professor Carfew's appointment to the Chair of Texts & Times." She read her draft petition out, then the debate was thrown open and the wording and details of the motivation were discussed. Nothing was said, after all, about membership of the Ossewa Brandwag or the Broederbond, and little about corruptive pressures from the government. But as comment followed comment it became clear that the motion was going to enjoy huge support.

The proposer was pretty and it would have been tempting to please her. But suddenly Felix, seated near the back, found himself speaking, shouting to make himself heard and relieve his feelings: "I think there's something wrong with this. I don't like it. This ganging up on a man to get him thrown out of his job. I agree that Carfew is an uninspiring, a damned boring lecturer and doesn't seem to be doing the Department much good. But a petition to his employers seems to me out of proportion, and ugly. Why can't those of us who feel strongly about his teaching criticise him directly, to his face? Interact with him in class...has anyone tried?...or send a delegation to him in his office. But don't gang up like this behind his back to get him discredited and sacked... and ruin his career. It's unfair and even cowardly."

There was a blaze of surprised stares from all round the room, but no one replied to his point. The discussion rolled on about the exact form of the petition and other details, then came the vote and the motion was carried almost unanimously. He felt faintly embarrassed. He did not quite wish that he had remained silent, but realised that he had spoken without much control.

However, during the next few days people took to greeting him who hadn't before, and James de Villiers and even the girl who had proposed the petition came and chatted with him for the first time—though not about Carfew or the meeting. In fact, except for the friendship that began between himself and James almost nothing seemed to come out of the whole affair. Unless Dr Vesey's emigration a couple of years later had anything to with departmental politics. Felix picked up nothing about the University Council's reception of the petition, no sign or rumour of a humiliation for Professor Carfew, who continued in his Chair for the next several years.

It was as though, after all, once the petition had been drafted and circulated some kind of catharsis was achieved, so that there was no motive actually to submit it to Council—for the whole agitation seemed to die away a week or two after the meeting. The result, if so, was not the best that could have been wished for for the Department, but for Felix it contained the relief that he did not have to imagine the cruelty of the moment when the uneasy little man learnt of his denunciation. Yet he was sometimes to wonder whether his own odd little performance had ever come to Carfew's knowledge.

The final scene, as far as it concerned Felix, was played out a few days after the meeting. He was walking from the last lecture of the day with two friends, when Frank Potts fell in beside them. He bore a copy of the petition, on which he was collecting signatures. He asked the two friends for theirs, but they had already signed. Then he turned to Felix: "And how about you?"

"Good god!" Felix exploded. "You were at that meeting. You know what I feel about this petition. How can you ask me?"

"Oh, well, just trying..." Potts gave an apologetic smile and shrug, and held the paper behind his back. Then, "By the way," he remarked, "some of us were chatting with Dr Vesey yesterday and she was telling us how impressed she was by your middle era essay."

"Oh! I'm surprised. That's very nice to know." He had seen little of Dr Vesey and hadn't imagined her noticing him much. "Thanks for letting me know."

"Yes, she said it's a long time since she's come across student work where there was such a fine sense of how to assess the sources and balance the argument. She thought it was at Honours level at least."

Conscious of his listening friends, Felix blushed with pleasure and stammered monosyllables of gratification while Potts developed the theme for another minute. Then, choosing his moment, he once more produced the petition and a biro pen: "Look,"—his voice urged decency, gratitude, friendship—"won't you sign?"

And Felix fluttered, huffed, shrugged and, finally, took the pen, and signed.

11

The Child

While he fought for breath Moh stooped over him, her face wrung as though the injury were her own. He had tripped over a border brick in the garden as they were going out to the car, fallen and bruised his ribs. And indeed, at least the burden of nursing him was to be hers through the next two weeks while he kept to his bed helpless because, once the contusion had set in, his chest would seize up in a breath-blocking spasm each time he tried to move.

His first sick-bed visitors were Vernon and Tanya, new friends from a group he had been meeting weekly for readings and discussions. They brought him a huge wedge of Toblerone chocolate, and came several times more. Despite the difference between his age and theirs, they had seemed eager to befriend him, had visited him more than once, taken him with them to visit other friends. Though Vernon was the more articulate and humorous, the easier in reaching out—his scientific appetite to understand new things, his incisive questions, making conversations run easily—they were both enthusiastic and full of ideas. Tanya at first seemed rather like the shadow to her husband's light, then later like a shadowed opening out of which unpredictable things might come.

In the few months after Felix's fall the friendship grew. Their life seemed very full, and it surprised him that they went on having the time and appetite for his company. He was being wanted in a new way, by a new kind of people—people who were free in a new way, and hungry for knowledge and excitement. Then Vernon was awarded a research scholarship at an American university. Although he was to be away for at least six months, Tanya was not to go with him, having embarked on a dissertation for an honours degree at Wits.

He had been gone a short while when the members of the reading group were invited to a wedding, and Tanya asked Felix to partner her. The evening together revealed that Vernon's absence left a space between them which they filled with a certain shyness, as though they were still almost strangers. Leaving the hall after the reception, they passed a tipsy guest near the doorway who teased, "Ah, you lucky dog! I wish I was going home tonight with such a lovely lady." The banter was received with an awkward laugh and then silence from both of them. For Felix there could be no intimate advantage in escorting his friend, however lovely, whose husband was also his friend.

A few days later Tanya telephoned to ask if she might come and show Felix some poems of her own that she had not yet read to the group. They sat in mild autumn sunshine on the lawn and she read to him from her file. There was something in the writing that went with the small girl curve of her brow and cheek as well as something that went with the experienced set of her mouth and the amused, enquiring look in her eyes. Despite all the conversations they had shared in before, as they talked now—the poems having licensed Felix to criticise, praise, advise and interrogate—it was as though they were making their first full communication.

"This is the newest one," she said when he had heard the rest. Part of it ran:

"Voice of the Shadow whispers to me -
suffer the dance in that darkness
the midnight gate
to frenzy and wisdom,
peril and light..."

It surprised him. "I thought you had your life all under control, but you're not at peace."

"No, I'm not... I've been going through a strange time, a stormy time with my feelings."

"What about, Tanya?"

"Don't you know? I wish you did..."

"Why?"

Her voice was breathy, tense, as she said, "It's about you, Felix... I haven't been able to stop thinking about you for days."

"What are you telling me?"

"I need you. It's as though some part of me has always been waiting for you. You help me to feel sure about some things in myself that I couldn't ever before... And I want you, I just want you."

Felix looked wildly around him, checking the reality of the surroundings. "But what about Vernon?"

"That's why it's been so disturbing... I love him. We love each other. We have our marriage. But things get very tense and confusing sometimes... That's why we need to be apart for a while. So...he's away, and... this is how I feel about you. It hasn't been easy, but... I've decided not to be guilty."

"Oh, God! What are you offering me?"

"Until he comes back I want to be with you, if you—I need you."

"Until he comes back... He asked me to look after you." Felix felt hot and dazed. But only one answer was possible. "Yes... Damn! I'm not going to ask any questions. Yes. Oh, God... But it's so hard to believe..."

"I know, I know..." Tanya's face was half turned away. "But if you'll let it happen, it's what I want... Does it sound crazy?"

"No... I don't care. I want it, even if only until Vernon comes back, even if... How could I help wanting someone like you... loving, if you would let me? Please, help me also not to feel guilty. Surely it doesn't have to be a matter for guilt. There needn't be any hurt, and... anyway, I need this so much."

Urgent as they were, they needed to proceed tentatively. The proving of their possible new joy was a thing his house would not contain in its dangerous entirety. When she visited him the next evening they lay together in the quarter-light of his darkened but uncurtained room, ensured of privacy by the height of his windows above the yard and garden, caressing each other in the restraint of amazement, to test the reality of what they had, talking in murmurs so as not to disturb his parents who were asleep nearby.

They, over the years, had known only three times where his passions were taking him. They knew about Marjory, about Evelyn and about Lucilla, each of whom had represented a crisis—the first of adolescent confusion, the second of release and cure, the third of romantic delirium. Otherwise all was shrouded in the protective shadows of his privacy. And they could not be allowed to know of what was beginning now with Tanya. Their wish for his happiness would not spare them the shock of judging this liaison a scandalous betrayal of her husband, an invitation to trouble. This time, however, it was not only from his parents that things had to be hidden. Just because Tanya did love Vernon, and because Felix held both of them dear, she and her marriage had to be protected with secrecy.

The day after that first night of incredulous, tentative caressing, she telephoned him: "Won't you come and have dinner with me? On Wednesday? I wish it could be tomorrow, but I've got to see my parents."

"Yes."

"It seems a long time..."

She and Vernon had a small flat high in a tower block near the university where Felix had been as their guest several times and the reading club sometimes met. He knew their Scotch terrier, Petrouchka, their furniture, their posters, records and books. But he still felt like only a transient stranger when, having fetched him from home, Tanya ushered him in there. He was her only guest but she had set a ceremonious table with candles and wine glasses. All the same he found a shyness that he could only get through by talking and making her talk, about the jobs she had had before coming to university and meeting Vernon, about her family and her childhood in war-wrecked Europe.

As she talked the thought came to him that perhaps this was all the closeness she could permit. Perhaps Vernon's presence in the flat was too palpable for her, for them, to push aside. But when she stood near him gathering up the dishes at the end of the meal, he put his hand tentatively on her waist. She covered it with her own and drew his head to her breast. "Let's sit on the bed," she said, hoisting him from his chair by an arm. "I'll clear the table later."

And then it was that she admitted him to the sweet river of her flesh. There, where it was broad and deep, he drowned, and emerged shining and gasping with joy. They left the bed when night was waning, and she drove him home through the chill dark empty streets, because his parents knew with whom he had gone out and it would be too eloquent if his bed were found unslept-in the next morning.

"When will you come again?" she asked when she stopped her little car at his house.

"As soon as I can. As soon as you'll have me."

"Come on Monday."

"I can't... Tuesday?"

"Yes. But this time stay with me."

"All night?"

"Yes. But I want you to stay longer. Be with me..."

This time he made his own way, by bus with a walk between termini in town, having told Moh only that he would be away for two days. In the past, he had usually taken care to tell her where he was going, or at least give her a telephone number, especially if he was to sleep out. He knew gratefully that, unlike Dad, she would not press him for information he did not offer, even though she might be anxious about how to reach him in case of need.

When he arrived at the flat Tanya was preparing supper. He went to the kitchenette with her and fondled her as she worked, touched and touched her body in the wonder of possession, as though her flesh were something new on earth that he had discovered. At first there was something raw and thrusting about the way he took, but she absorbed his caresses with laughs and endearments and he was filled with more tender feelings.

While researching her dissertation, with no obligatory classes to attend, she was at her own disposal and treated the ordinary working weekdays of his visit as a holiday. They lay next morning making love until they were starving for breakfast. When they had eaten she said, "Would you like a bath?"

"I would," he told her, "but I wouldn't be able to manage it. There's nothing for me to take a grip on climbing into the bath. At home I hold the taps for support, but yours are in the wrong position for me."

"I'll help you in."

Permitting that would mean letting go a fragment of his independence, perhaps of his dignity, but at the same time filling in their intimacy more than he had imagined she would want. "But getting out will be even harder. I don't think I... we'd manage."

"I'll manage, even if I have to lift you out... Wait, I'm going to get the bath ready for you. I want to give you something special." When she fetched him into the bathroom the air was dense with perfumed steam and the water was covered with a deep layer of yellow foam.

"What is it?"

"Badedas. You need no soap."

"God, such luxury!" he said as she lowered him into the foam. "Hey, you're not going to wash me..."

"Why not?"

"It's too much. Tanya..."

"Come on, give me your leg."

Afterwards she lifted him out and wrapped him in soft towels.

"You do things in such a delicious civilised way."

"Let's see your toes," she said, then clipped his nails and powdered his feet. "You must dry your feet properly. Otherwise the skin between goes funny."

"I"ll be so spoilt after this."

"Let me spoil you. Do you mind?"

He had come to her on Tuesday afternoon and his return home was promised by Thursday evening, but he slept with her for most of the third night. As long as he got home before daylight things would be in order. When the alarm clock woke them he pulled reluctantly away from her and dressed. He had to use all his powers of insistence to prevent her from dressing as well to drive him home. Instead he telephoned for a taxi, then summoned up a self that managed to separate itself from her and everything of his that the flat now contained, to sink with the lift through floors and floors of unreality and meet the car down in the street. He rode through the echoing half-pink twilight and silhouettes of the new day, wrapped against the cold of his aloneness by her kisses, her protests over his safety, her reluctance to let him leave her.

This visit set the pattern for them. They refined their stratagems for safeguarding their privacy and increasing the time that he could spend with her. She disliked the idea of his having to cross the city in two slow bus trips, and taxis were expensive. Twice she was able to persuade a friend who was not known to Moh and Dad to fetch him from home. When on a doctor's recommendation he began attending twice weekly at the General Hospital for physiotherapy to strengthen his weakening arm, it became usual for her to meet him there after the treatment. She would take his hand, caressing and helping at once, lead him to where her car was parked, almost lift him into the passenger seat, then enclose herself with him, give her welcoming kiss and look, and take him, via whatever errands she had to do, to the flat. Alongside her in the car as they moved through familiar Johannesburg streets he felt as if he were holidaying in some remote place of marvellous beauty and poetry.

"I'm in your life," he said one day as they drove. "I'm right inside your life."

"Isn't it yours?' she asked, half amused.

"Oh, yes, it's mine too now, because you've given it to me."

"I want to. I want to give it to you."

When an article of his was published in a newspaper, with a photograph of him alongside, she snipped it out and taped it up on a wall, giving the flat a mark of his occupancy. Whoever came would know that he had a place there, without the secret being betrayed. They visited, together, friends who knew only that they were friends, and they made forays to exhibitions, films and parties. But mainly he remained in the flat, enclosed and hidden with her, especially when deep night had made visitors and telephone calls unlikely, sharing her hours, her food, her bed, making the substance of his new life.

One Sunday morning while they were still in bed the telephone rang. She went to it naked, and crouched where the instrument rested on the floor. The caller was Peter, one of the reading group, who was fond of long telephonic gossips. Felix lay still, watching her, savouring the secrecy that had to be protected by his silence, the irony of the two separate intimacies she was containing (as though beneath the arm that covered the chill of her breasts), the sweetness of memory and anticipation, the sureness she had granted him—and, as the minutes passed, sharing the little ordeal that her patience exposed her to. Had he been confident of moving quietly enough not to be heard by the inquisitive Peter, he would have risen and spread her dressing gown over her shoulders.

Sometimes he was alone in the flat while she was out doing an academic interview or some shopping or walking Petrouchka. He was left to dress if it was early, or to read or write. If the telephone rang he would leave it unanswered, and hoped no one would come to the door. There was an evening when she had to dine with old friends of Vernon's in a town some thirty miles away. She locked the flat from the outside, and Felix settled down with a book and Petrouchka for company. Late in the evening he heard thunder and lifted a curtain to watch lightning and a veil of clattering rain that blurred the lights in the streets below. The downpour continued past midnight. He imagined Tanya's drive back and the possibility of an accident. A small panic overtook him. He would be lost if he lost her. How was he to know? How long should he wait? Whom could he telephone? How was he to get out? What if people came? Her parents? What if Vernon suddenly returned?

At last she was there. "Thank God you're safe," he said. "And now I'm safe."

Vernon wrote lonely yearning letters. Sometimes he sent affectionate messages for Felix, but even if Tanya had not had a reason to mention those letters to him he might have detected that her feelings were torn. She was tense and abstracted, though she shed tears only once, when telling him about a telephone call from Vernon. Momentarily, each time, his ease with her was baffled. Could he try to comfort her without heightening her distress, or intruding where her thoughts and feelings were centred on Vernon? But when he touched her hand or shoulder she responded with warmth. "Hold me..." she said after the telephone call. "He misses me so much, and it's hard sometimes."

"And you miss him."

"Yes, of course. But we had to break for a while. And I've got you. I'm so glad I've got you. Only, what's it going to be like for us afterwards? I'll be absorbed in finding Vernon. But you? I want you nearby always. But how are you going to feel? Aren't you going to wish the whole thing hadn't happened?"

"Tanya, my darling, don't take it away from me, even in words. I can't stand your being sore. I don't want to cause that, and if you had to, perhaps I could let you go now. But whenever it ends, it will have been the richest happiness in my life and afterwards is just what has to happen after that."

She looked at him solemnly and stroked his face. "Please don't worry about me. I'm so glad I've got you."

It was more often than not he who set the limit to his sojourns, pulling away against her tender resistance when he felt the need to go home to his desk, to take up the work he had in hand, to be at Dad's disposal for the occasional business letter he needed Felix to frame and type, and perhaps above all, to relieve Moh. Home contained the habitat which his parents' support had allowed him to create for his writing—Dad's permissive providence, Moh's particular way of supplying a presence in the house for his needs yet at the same time, during his working spells, a necessary absence, a receptive withdrawal that left him as free as possible from distraction.

Unable to reach him at will by telephone, she would be worried about messages and post unattended to and about his safety, and sometimes she would be finding the house bleakly empty. In the evenings Dad was there with her. They had got into mellow ways, often passing an hour or two over Scrabble on the kitchen table after supper. But during the day, even when conversation with Felix descended into abrasive quarrelling, even when they did not talk and his presence promised her only additional drudgery, he knew it represented company that Moh missed when he was away for more than a day or two. It was a thing she had told him more than once in the past. She did not say it now, respecting his reserve over his disappearances.

On days when she was not required at Mavis's house to help while the maid was off, or when a grandchild was not left for her to look after, she would enjoy the peace and restfulness, the chance to work out a dressmaking problem without interruption or compose a letter to Becky in England or read a chapter or two of a novel at her painstaking pace or give an hour or two to the piano, which, these years, she never played except when alone. He sometimes caught her last notes and the sound of the closing keyboard lid as he entered the gate or turned the door key after an outing, and guessed that there was something more to this reticence than her wish not to disturb him when he was reading or writing.

But when there was a child in the house, she would miss Felix's share in entertaining the little visitor, which relieved her for the occasional spell of other work or a rest. And when she was alone there would be time enough for anxieties, some about him, even if she guessed that an uncommon happiness was keeping him away, and some, certainly, now that she had been visited with angina pectoris, about herself. He knew this because, musing as she watched him eat one day, she had asked in a half-joking tone, "How will you manage without me?"

He had not known the answer, even for himself, and yet was not frightened. He remembered how in his childhood the thought of either parent's death as even the remotest possibility had contained pure terror for him. Now he found himself feeling almost nothing, merely reflecting that he often needed kinds of help that she could not give, things that were beyond her skill or that he would not tax her strength or patience with. And he wondered whether this safe nullity were some special dullness of his own, a cowardly self-numbing, or some ordinary part of what it meant to be adult.

Dad had always had a delicate digestion and been prone to dramatic bouts of illness, and from early years had made a point of occasionally confiding to the children that one day he must die, as though this were one of the facts of life he ought to teach them. When Moh now broached the subject of her own absence it was with an unfamiliar tongue. She asked her strange question with a glimmer of teasing humour, but reflecting on it afterwards Felix received an intimation of dark hours. It was full of the awful aloneness he had been allowed to witness enacted once when they had been walking to their car after a family wedding reception. In the parking lot Moh stopped, immobilised by some cruel access of her angina, gray-faced and grim with resentment at Dad's useless questions. Words, even words of the deepest perceptiveness, could not have reached her where she was at that moment.

Her wry allusion to mortality when she asked how he would manage rose from a serious recognition she was inviting him to share. When he was with Tanya it became a remote abstract shadow behind his bliss, but it was a thing that repeatedly urged him back home from his lover.

By the energy of her encouragement, Tanya was enabling him to work a little in her vicinity too, but there were many things he could only do in the place where he customarily worked. "You know," he told her, not meaning to explain what pulled him home, but simply to describe his relationship with Moh, "although she can make me feel small and sore and unreal when we're quarrelling, as if she had no confidence in my opinions, in me altogether—when things are calm I usually feel that she really does trust me, my thinking. And that she understands...not abstruse references, complicated discussions, but what I'm trying to be about. Or at any rate she cares about what I actually want to do, not where it will get me or what it will get me. Most people can't see that difference — my dad certainly can't. There's not much she can do about it, beyond leaving me in peace to get on with it, or shedding a few tears when she reads something of mine that impresses her. I hardly ever think about it, but perhaps it is the most important of the things she still does for me."

Another abstract shadow was his knowledge that the love affair was an interlude that must end when Vernon returned. The marriage was in recession, leaving Tanya with this time and this freedom for him whom by some miracle she needed and wanted. The thought of Vernon, weighted with love, was in each of them, but they were carried by the occasion and its propitious circumstances, by their interlocking needs, by their mutual love that grew as they embodied it. They had broken the rules, yes, and yet it seemed there was also something given—rather than taken, taken advantage of—by them, in the situation.

"Why didn't you come to me fifteen years ago?" he asked her one day as they lay down together, caressing each other into rest, after hours spent deciphering one of the authors she was working with.

"I was only nine."

He joined her laugh. "No, I mean.... When I was about twenty-five... Why didn't you, as you are now, come into my life then?"

"Why then?"

"I've needed you so much all these years. It was this way of being with somebody that I was looking for, expecting then, and all the time of disappointment has...done something to me...dried me up at least."

She kissed him. "Silly. You're not dried up."

"No, I suppose I'm not. Or if I was, it doesn't matter any more. You've made me juicy again."

But restoration was the least of her gifts. She was bringing him more than any of his other loves—more than Lucilla who had inflamed his imagination for so many months, more even than Evelyn who had actually given herself at a time when he had started to believe it impossible that anyone could and when his aliveness and balance had been imperilled. Tanya was bringing him the honey and brandy, the bread and meat, the cleansing and education of a complete love, allowing him the first full season of his manhood.

They couldn't celebrate with a party of their own, but when they went to others' parties their feelings appropriated them. There was one in particular that suited their mood. It was an afternoon house-warming at a cottage that had been remodelled for an artist. There had been a shower of rain but now the sun was negotiating luminous clouds and the light was both soft and brilliantly silvered as it drenched a view of washed hills set back across a broad suburban valley and pedestalling the city centre's poignant clustered skyscrapers. Felix chose to sit in a courtyard where Tanya brought their wine and savouries. Talking with friends, he was ebullient in response to something more than friendliness in those conversations: he and Tanya were receiving a kind of congratulatory affection for being with each other. They couldn't caress or speak intimately, yet, without losing their secret, they were making it visible, as though the embracing tender light came from them, their happiness. Felix had so often been the outside witness to the attachments of men and women, or the perplexed petitioner for an attachment of his own, but now at last he was inside the sweetness of the mystery, he knew what it felt like not to yearn and strain and dread the withdrawal that any overture of his must produce, but to stand in confident belonging beside a lover as desirable as his wishes.

At another, more intimate party the mood was so light that after Tanya's unhesitating draw on a dagga cigarette doing a round, Felix set aside his uneasiness over the fashion for experimenting with drugs and took a compliant puff or two. For the moment, sitting beside her, whatever he had been afraid of seemed not to matter. All that mattered was to make love and celebrate. But the mouthful of fumes he had sucked in left him unaffected.

"I wonder why that should be."

"Who knows? Perhaps you didn't take in enough. Try another puff." But the cigarette did not come round again.

Days later she said, "Do you want to try smoking pot properly? I can get some."

"I don't know. You know how upset I got about the way Piet and Fanny were affected after that trip of theirs."

"They tripped on LSD. Pot isn't a hard drug."

"Yes, I realise it's not the same thing. D'you think...?"

"No, you must choose. Whatever you want..."

He hesitated a little. "Will you be with me?"

"Of course."

"What the hell! Let me at least find out what it's about."

The next time he came to the flat she rolled and lit the smoke for him. He drew deeply several times and after a few seconds felt a lift of excitement and lust. He wanted to dive whole into Tanya's sex, and immediately stretched his hand under her skirt. But before his fingers touched cloth or skin the emotion fell away, cancelled by the hallucination of a tribunal. Gabbling judges accused him for a few seconds, then were gone. He tried again to concentrate his desire, but the idea of Tolstoy's *War and Peace* came into his mind. He wanted to tell Tanya, but before he could start speaking, there was an image of airports. Then it was a daisy, then his cousin Alf, then the daisy again... He tried to hold one of the thoughts, return to one of the images...

"Oh my God, Tanya, help me!"

"What's the matter?"

"I can't control my mind. It's jumping around like..."

"Well, let it. Don't try to control it."

"Yes. Yes... Oh, no. I can't stand it. It's like..."

"Listen, just relax. Just let go. You're having a trip. It can't harm you."

"But it's like being mad. I can't stand it. My mind's drowning, exploding. It will drive me mad."

"No. No, darling, it's just a trip. Try to relax and just let it happen. I'll hold you."

But his terror mounted minute by minute. "How long is this going to last? I can't stand it! My mind's like a neon sign, flick, flick, flick, flick... I'm out of control. It's still hours, isn't it? Out of control. I could do anything. Smash... Oh, I'm mad..."

"I'll give you some vitamins to try and bring you down. But try to relax. You'll be all right."

"No... This is madness. I could smash. I could hurt you. Myself. I could push myself through the window. Through the window... I'm out of control. There's nothing..."

"No, you won't do any of that. I won't let you."

"Oh please... Don't let me. I'm mad. I've gone mad. I can't see why this flick, flick, flick, flick should ever end. It's been waiting for its chance. This is its chance. I've lost my control. Flick... Oh...it will never end..."

"Believe me, my darling, it will end, it will end soon. You'll be all right. It's only a bad trip. I'm here with you. I'll hold you safe. I'm strong."

Through the hours his panic receded and then surged again and again as new terrors and despairs occurred to him, and she sat on the bed beside him, holding him, stroking him, talking his hysteria away. It was well after midnight when one of his silences deepened into a doze that he woke from to find that his thoughts were easier to hold and control. Eventually she drove him home and helped him get to bed.

"You saved me," he said. "You were so strong...and so brave."

"I didn't have to be strong. You could hardly move."

They laughed together ruefully over that. Then he said, "I meant strong in another way."

She said, "You're also strong in another way."

He awoke one morning at home, his head full of a dream. Later he told her, "I was in your flat. Near me Petrouchka was hunting a mouse among the long tufts of a carpet, like grass. Through the doorway I could see into a different place. There was a hospital bed with attendants changing the bedclothes. The patient was out of the bed waiting to get back, shuffling back and forth across the room. It was an old man, or maybe a woman, and his head was shrunk to the size of an orange and blank, and I knew that had to do with agony. He was dressed in a vest and long-johns. Then I saw it was a clown or acrobat's white costume, and it was decorated with diamond shapes and flowers. Someone with a wide broom was sweeping round his feet, obstructing him. The longer the bed was delayed the worse the suffering grew, but at the same time the footsteps became stronger and stronger, till they reminded me of a tiger striding, and I could see the muscles bulging under the cloth of the costume, and the design became stronger and the colours brighter."

Joe was Aunt Ella's son. He was a veteran of three wars, wounded, malarial, alcoholic. He had been married and had fathered children, but now was divorced. The family rarely saw him, but Felix had bumped into him in town, and one day he came to visit, bringing a copy of the regimental magazine he had edited in one of his wars. While he was there a friend named Manfred dropped in to invite Felix to a party. Expansively, he included Joe in the invitation, and it was arranged that he would pick them up here at seven on the evening of the party. Joe was to come by bus in good time for the lift.

By the Saturday, however, Felix was again with Tanya. She was also invited, so they went together from her flat, confident that Manfred would fetch Joe as arranged. They arrived at about eight o' clock when the party seemed fairly under way, but neither Joe nor Manfred was there. His wife explained that he had left much earlier to ferry in those of his guests who had no transport, including some from the far side of town. She expected him at any moment. There was no telephone, but Felix said, "Joe's probably joy-riding with Manfred. I see no point in driving across to my house to rescue him."

There was food and wine and dagga. In the mood of these days Felix was drunk on Tanya when they arrived and scarcely needed the glass or two he drank to prompt him into stroking her arm and thigh only half surreptitiously as she sat beside him. Some of the other smoke-abstracted guests knew Vernon, but the atmosphere was so easy that Felix felt no restraint, none certainly from Tanya, on his desire to express his excitement.

When a harassed Manfred finally arrived it was after ten and he brought with him a car-load of guests, but not Joe. He had gone for the others first, he explained, had had a puncture and other delays on his journey and then had found that the car was full. He had tried at some stage to phone Felix at home but hadn't been able to get through, and had hoped that when he was late Felix might get his father to run him and Joe across. He insisted now on going immediately to rescue Joe, but fifteen minutes later was back with the news that there were no lights on at the house.

Felix was stricken, but there was nothing to be done at this stage. He returned with Tanya to her flat that night and next morning telephoned Moh.

"It was terrible," she told him. "Joe arrived about six o' clock with a ready-roast chicken and a bottle of brandy. I gave him your message, but he was disappointed not to find you here, and even more disappointed when no lift came. Later on we had some tea and were sitting and talking in the kitchen when he started shivering and turned yellow. And then, while Dad and I were trying to do something for him, he vomited right in my face. Oh!"

"Oh my God, Moh!"

"Yes. A black stream of it that just gushed out... And onto the table and over the floor. We had to clean all that up, and Joe lay shivering under blankets. Dad drove him home when he felt a bit better."

"Oh God, oh my God!"

"And he left his chicken and his brandy behind."

"Valium," the neurologist announced "It could be a miracle drug for someone in your spastic condition."

"But it's my arm I'm worried about," Physiotherapy had produced no visible improvement and Felix was seeking help at a higher level.

"Your arm should benefit when your whole body is relaxed."

The drug affected a loss of appetite, listlessness and lowered spirits. The doctor urged persistence with the treatment: "It needs time. You'll adjust to the side effects."

Perhaps it was as well that he was so dulled when the time came for Vernon to return. Tanya did not let Felix doubt that she loved him and was determined still to have him in her life, but lovemaking would now be out of the question. The Valium miseries numbed his desires, removed him from the reality of all the joy she had given him and made even his loss remote.

The first of February was a Sunday. Aunt Ella came during the morning and stayed to lunch. She had a way of muttering on, voicing her stream of consciousness without pause, liable at any moment to become offended and sink her voice to an ominous, petulant growl. Moh could find her a strain to deal with while cooking and serving. But on this day Ella somehow merely amused her and she laughed her way through all the crossness and muddle.

Becky had come back from England some months before, and during the afternoon she and her husband Wally arrived. Moh served tea with her home-made ginger biscuits. Afterwards she and Becky went into the spare room to look among the hoarded bits and pieces for something to serve as temporary curtains. Soon Wally went to see what was afoot, and then Dad, Aunt Ella and Felix also drifted into the spare room. Moh was energetically unpacking, sorting and measuring pieces of cloth. Finding a use for something she had saved was the sort of task she enjoyed.

Suddenly she stopped still, moaned, and brought her hand up to her face: "...feel sick..." She sat down on a bed.

"Put your head low down," Becky suggested.

Moh started to bend, then doubled and slid off the bed onto the floor with her legs bent under her and her skirt pulled high, the impetus of the fall rolling her to lie face up. She was still, but the deepening colour of her face showed that she was suffocating, she was drowning.

"Oh my God!"

"What's happening?"

"Call the doctor."

"...ambulance."

"Oy! Oy vei!"

Is she feeling sick? Is she all right?" Aunt Ella fluttered, and in a fright left the room. Wally followed to the telephone.

"Mouth-to-mouth...artificial respiration..." Becky got down and placed her mouth over Moh's. Felix was on the floor next to them, breathing with the deep chestsful of air Becky was blowing through Moh's lips.

"Straighten her legs." Dad went to do that and drew her skirt down.

Felix was shouting. "Her false teeth... Take them out! She'll swallow them and choke." It was a rule from the First Aid he had learnt as a Scout. Becky went on a while, breathing and blowing, but his hysteria was too strong to withstand. She forced her fingers into Moh's mouth and struggled to find and, at last, dislodge the bridge, put it down on the floor, then started the rhythmic inhaling and blowing again.

Wally returned with some outrageous message from the doctor: he wouldn't come—they must wait for the ambulance. Could Becky keep it up? There was no result anyway.

At last the ambulance. Two men in white coats and berets. An oxygen cylinder. The transparent plastic mask over the blue lips and white nose. Surely this. She always wanted air, fresh air. Breath. The young man thumped his brute knuckles on the sternum over the seized up heart.

Nothing. He shook his head. "No. I think she's finished." She wouldn't be there with her indignation to resent the bruise.

Sitting and covering his face, Dad said, "Oy vei, Vera... What will we do? She was a good woman." Why had he never said that to her?

The only thing was to get her to hospital. The family would follow the ambulance in Wally's car. But Felix had already surrendered to the fact. There was no hope for him to chase after to the hospital. He would not go, he insisted, he would stay here. He watched her being carried out through the gate, and felt the house collapse on its emptiness, into rubble and dust, as she was taken from it. As soon as the ambulance doors thumped closed he went to telephone Tanya. "My mother just died...please come."

Back in the spare room he stared at the emptiness of the floor. Her denture had been pushed almost under the bed. He picked it up, touching something nobody was supposed to touch except herself. There was emptiness everywhere. He looked through the window at the oaks of the avenue. Between their leaves, emptiness. On the street, emptiness. In the houses opposite, in the sky, empty room only for death. He had seen it, the way children would see adults copulating. It was real. Nothing else was. The knowledge, a vast settling weight, ripped away the ground of things inside him, like paper, and let through from the abyss a darkness of black dust that drowned him and everything.

At last Tanya and Vernon were with him. They led him to a settee and sat either side of him, Tanya holding him. And then, from below his stomach, in total unthinking grief, for Moh, for his sins against her, for the advent of death's reality in the world, he howled like a damaged animal.

PART II

Wars and Rages

12

Valium of the Shadow

It was only after emerging from the state of mind he had been lost in for four years, that Felix would identify its ambiguity. Grief and its processes had been complicated, prolonged and masked by side-effects of Valium, while the drug's psychological effects had been reinforced, distorted and disguised by grief. Near the beginning he had run out of tablets, missed his doses for a day, and been racked into a state of intolerable tension, relieved only after he had swallowed the next pill. This episode had left him believing he was trapped in a chemical dependency, but it did not make him aware that his other entrapment, in an emotional pit, had anything to do with Valium. The Valium of the shadow of Motherdeath.

His bereavement was long past, yet the rolling months failed to bring the promised healing, failed to erode away the stony heaviness dumped low in his chest by the shock of that day. He went on being oppressed by faceless dread, by anger, distaste, weariness. The sight of Moh suddenly subsiding into her death seemed to have dislocated and diminished all other knowledge. Mortality alone was real, the thought of it now displacing even the sense of his loss, filling the abyss of Moh's absence with the darkness of horror. And this obsession was a mortal sickness. Waking in the mornings he wanted oblivion. There seemed no reason not to choose oblivion.

What could he do? He kept a sporadic journal in which he wrestled with his by now causeless depression, as though it were a moral or psychological problem, an intellectual mistake that could be reasoned or "talked" away.

> *A black amoeboid mass, no more than a fistful in quantity, destructively infested a single head of a multi-branched succulent shrub. Thing or substance, it glittered in the sun and squirmed without rhythm but without rest, chewing and devouring, vomiting and excreting itself, but not visibly changing. "Newly hatched locusts," someone explained—and*

then I made out the miniature locust shapes, the brown and gold stripes around slender, almost elegant abdomens, and half understood what was happening in the blindly wriggling mass impelled by three imperatives—move, eat, cohere. So the creatures crawled and crawled over and around each other, emerging, climbing up humps of bodies, burrowing back into the mass—passing through an hour or more of total vulnerability, while some only guessable process was completed: the last of the pupae were bursting in the heart of the mass..... the winglets were drying...... something...... To bloom so hideously, so precariously, into being, and yet with a challenging insistence, like the bark of a dog, the roar or pounce of a lion, the inescapable confrontingness of a nightmare. Life affirming itself.

He was in the garden of Tanya and Vernon's house outside Port Elizabeth where they had moved so that Vernon could take up a post at a large laboratory. No sooner had they settled in than they had begun urging Felix to come to them for a recuperative spell. Tanya, back in Johannesburg on some family and academic errands, had overridden his inertia, winkled him out of the stale den he lurked in, and taken him with her when she'd driven the six hundred miles home again.

Affirmation. A word from a different era. Did it come into Practical Criticism? I can't remember. It might have been dubbed "emotive" if it occurred in a "woolly" context. Or into Leavis's morality? Era of non-violence and rationality, of (despite and because of Hitler) an innocence that wanted to be on guard against itself. All my doubting and quarrelling with the wisdom of the English Department in 1949 and '50. But I liked affirmation, affirmative. Works of art had to be affirmative—life-enhancing. I understood and embraced that. Nothing else seemed quite sane.

But now, twenty-three years later, I renege. The law has ended for me. In these permissive, anarchic times, I've been holding out for art and its kinds of order, for reason, for self-in-communion, for traditions of humanity. I fancied all had a bearing on what I sometimes dared to call the making of God. But now I have nothing to offer, just formless self-indulgence, confusion of presentness, fragmentation of memories, desper-

ation, revulsion, anger. Once I wanted a story or series of stories out of my life—I thought a pattern would do—now all I want is a meaning, a clue about the way back in. That is what differentiates me from a suicide. I have still to make sure whether or not that clue exists to be found.

Another morning in the same garden, trying to warm himself under the wintry sun, he noticed fat yellow ants, some with black heads, some with red.

They formed no single line like the ants I'm familiar with, but spread wide on the lawn a tangle of trails, all westward of the nest's entrance. Yet each individualistic journey contributed one more needful shred of grass or wood for the purpose hidden under that little hole. Two or three feet away a twig much larger than the other fragments being collected—the weight of forty or fifty ants together—was tackled by one of the foragers whose tug barely made it stir. To other ants it was still just an obstacle in their path and they barged or squeezed under it or dragged their own loads over it. After a while one of them stopped and joined the first in the task. Soon, a third and a fourth reinforced them, and their trophy began to lift and tremble. The task itself seemed capable of generating the intelligence and co-operation necessary to its own accomplishment. There was a process of life going on. Then the puppy arrived and in a moment noticed the yellow creatures moving. She snapped up five or six, then took to catching and crushing them with a forepaw before lapping them up in ones and twos. Of course, the busy paws and snout had completely disrupted the enterprise around the twig. Suddenly, a change in the way she was moving. Uncomfortable shakes of the head and the paws. A retreat from the area. One forepaw repeatedly shaken, a yellow body, black or red head hidden in the fur, high on the leg. A moment's scratching rid her of this attacker which was crushed and eaten. But the ants were still there. They had won. They could continue. Whatever it was. The task. The purpose. The end. They could not choose not to. They must just go on. Probably never knowing or meaning. But, in their near silence, affirming.In a sense, I'm suddenly stripped of everything except an abstract imperative to affirm. But it isn't good enough. How, in what acts, does one affirm? The locusts, the ants and the puppy are fixed in affirmation, but I'm imprisoned by my freedom to choose—unless that's an illusion with an attractive name, an emotive trick, one by which human biology generates the intelligence and co-operation necessary for the attainment of its particular ends. Do I have choice? My sigh at the morning's first gulp of hot coffee is affirmation. My gasp at the cold gush in the shower implies affirmation. They're involuntary. But so is this unbudging boulder of depression. Affirmation has lost one of the qualities I used to believe it had: it is not selective, it does not necessarily favour the beautiful, the good, the true—the life-enhancing. What affirms itself is simply being. Being and becoming. That's why that clump of baby locusts was somehow terrific, terrifying. I could, for my individual, conscious self, choose a moment for ceasing to be. I could negate all this involuntary negation that dominates my feelings month after month. But is that what I want? That silence? I'm losing myself in words. You step under the cold shower protesting or assenting. I want to give assent. I know my case is far from the limits. Disaster, atrocity, tyranny. Apart from those populations of victims we all know of, I have known individuals who were inconsolably bereaved, deprived, tortured and oppressed—some whose psyches must have been atrophied, rubbed down and diminished by the impingements of illness alone—who, nevertheless, held and manifested faith in the life-long objects of their faith, in even such a sumptuary god as artistic form. I think of Cynthia Green in her last days—to deal with person-to-person, exhausting, wasteful, bleak, in a sense mad with her agonies and despairs (and her hidden knowledge of the imminence of her death), to me a shard scraping my mind and spirit—yet, in her vision, her heart, her faithfulness to the values—even most minutely manifested—that made so many of her poems marvellous, in all those respects steadfast, concrete, vigorous to the point of belligerence. In the sense of faith to things beyond her suffering self, she remained herself to the end. In this sense she presented the opposite of self-indulgence, self-surrender.In this sense I do yield. I break faith, break free to rant and howl, expose where I am broken, where I am naked, where I am perfidious.

He pieced out in hundreds of free verse lines what was as much an existential quarrel as a bellow of lamentation:

There is ending
as there is beginning.
Were there no beginning there would be no end.
Logic betrays us.
In the beginning was the word,
the whorl, the whore, the hole.
Sh'mai Israel! Hear, o nations, hear!
Thy god, the word without image, is one,
and his name begins with D.
His first commandment was "Ignore!"
And he commanded us again
against the taking of his name.
Yet, nations, hear!
The lord, this one word which is all,
moved at the first and made the world,
in his imagelessness made heaven and earth
one squared-off hole........

He talked about his inner malady, to friends, even to mere acquaintances. During his second long visit to Tanya and Vernon at Port Elizabeth, Dan, who had been the closest of his friends for more than twenty years, happened to be in the area on some cultural business and was invited to dinner, along with the writers he was visiting, Pierre and Sandra. As wine and conversation ripened the evening these two grew to seem as much Felix's intimates as the others, and finally he gave way to the temptation to pour out his distress.

"...it stays there, month after month," he finished, "this stone of deadness.... Like a heavy boulder sitting in my chest...."

"Felix, you must go *into* the stone," Dan tendered.

Pierre nodded approval. "Yes, yes. `Go into the stone.' That's good."

"Into the stone — what does that mean?" Felix demanded.

"Don't keep struggling to get rid of it. Look at it and find the way into it."

"Dan, I don't understand your words."

He did not scorn words or aspire to transcend them—he lived by words, breathed by words. But often the way others spoke or wrote defeated his understanding or quenched his sympathy. Dan was one who increasingly over time (whether by right of inspiration or by some lesser form of license) had seemed to be claiming a habit of freeing language from the possibly pedestrian orderliness Felix observed and needed to observe. Until now, he had wryly, even fondly, tolerated his friend's wild-winged style of discourse, even at times welcomed its healthy challenge to his own stiff literalness, his timidity.

"Look," Dan explained, "you said that all the levers you could have used for budging the stone—"

"My image for the values I used to believe in."

"—were broken. So you're telling yourself the only thing is to move into the stone. Explore the stone. Let yourself move with the molecules of the stone. Even become the stone."

"But there *isn't* a stone. The stone was only a damned metaphor I made up, borrowed out of the air, just to try and make my feelings describable. There aren't any molecules."

"Why are you trying to deny your stone? Don't you see the dignity of claiming it, entering it?"

"Dignity! Oh, God..." Felix groaned, but Dan was in spate.

"And those broken levers—those certainties of yours..."

"As I said—things I thought I believed in..."

"Throw them away." Something in the manner of Dan's argument, like a misplaced game, verged on affront.

"Are you telling me," Felix acidly burlesqued, "that I must unselve myself in order to go on being?"

"Exactly—that's exactly it. It's always a thing of growth to let go of certainties. And a thing of courage. The kind of courage that's somehow missing from your poem about your mother."

"What do you mean? Why are you looking for courage when all I was trying to express was my terror and despair and confusion and this ache. I couldn't *find* any courage. All I could do was try to think my way out of this to something liveable."

"*Think your way out.*" That's exactly what I mean. All that intellectual metaphysical theorising." Felix recognised Dan's loyalty to the anti-intellectualist ethic they had shared in the early years of their friendship. "You use your thinking-out like a sweet on a stick that you're trying to suck some comfort out of. If only you'd stayed with your mother, her death, what it is to you. Instead you write two poems in one. You bring in all that public, rhetorical head-stuff about death in the abstract and history and civilization. It might have been interesting on its own, but you use it to avoid the personal thing that's really hard to stay with. That's why I say the poem lacks courage."

"I had to look everywhere," Felix protested, "for some kind of answer to death. You seem to be saying I should be thinking-*in* instead of thinking *out*... But Pierre and Sandra haven't read my poem, so this must be boring them."

"No, no," Pierre protested. "I'm thinking about this enormous illumination you've been offered. If you could take hold of it, this grief would be a hell of an opportunity. It's a Zen koan. And, man, I like what you said earlier—'unselve myself'. I think that's exactly what you have to do. It's pure Zen. 'Moving into the stone' is also classic Zen. These are your koans, man: 'Enter the stone', your mother's death, 'Unselve myself'. Claim them. Use them. Get rid of the effort to understand. Hey, look, that stone of yours—it's the Sisyphus stone. Do you know what Camus says about your stone? I wish I had *The Myth of Sisyphus* here."

"We've got a copy," Vernon said, and fetched it.

Mellowed by wine and attention, Felix felt tempted to quip that the rationalist in Camus might not have had much to say to Dr Suzuki. But his radical mood demanded more ruinous subversions than the mere queering of a debate. He listened restlessly to the reading of a longish passage, its point in Pierre's argument elusive, its rational sonorities too demanding, in any case, for this recital.

"Thank you," he commented at the end. "I heard one sentence that helps me...to the effect that life goes on and individual deaths are swallowed up in it." In fact, Camus's insight amounted to a reassertion of one of those broken beliefs of his own that they had been urging him to jettison, but he kept this thought to himself, while his having conceded a point seemed to permit both Pierre and Dan to let the argument lapse for now.

He slept on their enigmatic counsels, but could find no meaning in them, unless as an urging to some version of Christian-Buddhist resignation. Recalled next morning, all that had been said to him smacked less of understanding than of mystical rigmarole. He suspected there had been an element of vain display in his own part in that conversation. But that did not soften his resentment at being offered the bafflement of Zen koans without the resulting illumination. Only much later, too much later, did it occur to him that his inability to hear wisdom in his friends' counsel might have been the deafness of his own inner noise. When he next met Dan they quarrelled bitterly. From now, perhaps coincidentally, began a distancing between them, a gradual attenuation of their friendship.

They had been used to seeing each other frequently under all sorts of circumstances, and Felix's dependence on Dan for transport supplied a pretext rather than a reason for them to spend time together. For several years the most regular lifts were to Sunday evening meetings of a film society. Among audiences that had drifted to the cinema from the suburbs and buzzed with eagerness to give the wilted rest-day some shape and point, amid a spattering of acquaintances and friends, Felix partook of a modern richness he might otherwise have missed, and Dan's eclectic enthusiasm helped to open his own receptiveness to masterpieces like *Bicycle Thieves, La Strada, Closely Observed Trains, Hiroshima Mon Amour, Woman of the Dunes, Pather Panchali....*

Now that custom fell away, but not that only, and nor was it only because they now lived further apart. Dan's career became more demanding, taking him more frequently out of the country. And when they met, Felix found in himself a less controllable impatience with Dan's paradoxical habit of cryptic inarticulacy, his dark river of visionary words whose sense was often elusive. So if the old friend showed a new evasiveness—habits of rarity and distractedness, a nun's or detective's trick of never visiting alone, never unchaperoned—this may have been his defence against Felix's irritability. They might have lost contact more or less completely despite the magnetism of shared history and habits of laughter, but they were knitted into an enduring network of friendships, especially with Gail and others who went on year after year creating occasions to meet, to celebrate and remember, and kept congeniality alive.

Apathy was no less destructive than anger. It endorsed the destruction of the home that might have been Moh's only material legacy.

"The place looks terrible. Can't you get someone to cut the lawn?"

The brother-in-law's remark was justified. The screen of ragged grass was up to two feet high, and there was a part-time gardener available. But the fastidious irritation in the friendly advice affronted Felix. How could anyone be concerned about the appearance of the house after what had happened? He did not mourn Moh's death so much as partly die of it. His material safety had been founded on her: she was house, she was food, the comfort of everything regular. That whole ground had fallen away beneath him. And then there was what he had only purblindly perceived while she was present—the moral quality she involuntarily disguised as anger and ungivingness, but which was really her incapacity for flattery and deception, her stark perception of the necessities that sustained survival. Only now did he begin to perceive how that quality had supplied a necessity of his own survival.

Death-obsessed, ill with it, he was spiritless and paralysed. He and Dad had the house and the servant. He had his days at his own disposal and might have asked for the services of the gardener or, more to the purpose of survival, instructed the woman servant to prepare the evening meal or at least to peel some potatoes in time for Dad's return from business. But he was too listless to take thought about such things, and the cooking was left altogether to be managed by Dad, whose unpractised widower's awkwardness often roused Felix from lethargy into bitter irritation.

So after some months it became clear that they must give up the posthumous house. Dad went to a residential hotel, Felix to the less neutral retreat of Mavis's household. She, like Moh, saturated her identity into her home, ruled her house. But hers was the profoundly different style of a sophisticated generation that comfortably spent its money and conformed to its class, or at least to the standards set by a circle of friends, as well as by the fastidiousness of the husband who had complained about the neglected lawn at the house of grief.

The transplantation into this nest so redolent of other lives was an exile from which there was no hope of return, for home no longer existed.

He quarrelled with others besides Dan, and quarrelled too not so much with anyone in particular as with the temper of the times. An enthusiastic niece lent him a book about Timothy Leary's psychedelic gospel. It was too much. The world of all he believed in had suffered the shock of his own defection, his faith's collapse, so that any hope of participation, contribution, enjoyment had become elusive and uninteresting to him—and now here was a new insidious but radical assault on that world. Minds were to be turned in on themselves, submerged in their own lakes of illusion and hallucination; the fabric of outward facts, that medium by which minds defined themselves and reached each other, was to be ignored, torn down, dissolved; health and wisdom and history were all to be overturned in favour of a shapeless innocent freedom... Even a proxy survival, in the shape of a world that would still make sense to him, was no longer promised.

And when a friend pressed upon him *The Tibetan Book of the Dead* he found something like his own emptiness systematised, buried in a suffocatingly elaborate mythology and celebrated as the ultimate aspiration. The human world, like the tiers of other worlds above and beneath it, was nothing but illusion; the only reality was absolute nothingness. That the Eastern wisdom to which this vision belonged enjoyed a fashionable following was a thought that added stifling weight to his despair.

But there was another side to things. Enterprises had been set in motion before his shock and, ironically, now, during his four dead years, came to fruition. He had discovered a gifted black poet and laid plans with two young friends to find a way of publishing a collection of his work. Had his will been less sick, Felix might have given active expression to his awful negativity, offended the poet, discouraged his partners, Corinna and Basil, blocked their successful effort at fund-raising which turned the quixotic fantasy into a realistic experiment. But his lassitude allowed their determination to carry him, as though by default, into the vortex of a publishing triumph. The book was instantly, hugely successful. Because the poet was black, and black poetic voices had been rare and never so appealingly accessible, so rich in the testimony of experience, Wilson Nthuli's emergence set up a ripple that became historic.

All this was far beyond anything Felix could have planned or hoped for. Though the triumph was out of his hands, it brought him an experience of effectuality. Decisions and acts of his own were responsible for changes in the stubborn substance of the world outside himself, moreover on a scale that was quite new to him. Whenever he decided to telephone the printer to order a further impression, he had to assume the validity of his judgement; but the whole excitement the publication had generated was proof positive that somewhere he had judged validly, was capable of so doing.

And there were other scarcely lesser though less public fulfilments for him in these four alienated years. During his three therapeutic holidays at her house, Tanya insisted on his taking the opportunity of isolation and peace to cloister himself daily with a typewriter. He yielded to her pressure dubiously: this was the most unpropitious of times for creative composition. But to his surprise what poured from him was not merely introspective journal entries and notes but several entire stories that had flickered in his thoughts for years as mere possibilities. He found a refuge from the oppressive achingness of the present in the task of translating hauls of memories into the language of narratives that arrived at a final charged image and significant shape.

But before he dissolved the inner stone of his malaise, the angry impulses in his four years' depression produced several damaging contretemps, stiffened his relationship with Mavis who provided him with a home, and turned neutral circumstances to destructive results. Even the triumphant the publishing venture ended in debacle. He, Corinna and Basil had been ploughing their profits back into the business and had put three more slim volumes into print, of which the latest, just out, was a collection of Corinna's poems. This was the moment when she and Basil, recently married, announced their decision to emigrate to England. Suddenly the question had to be faced as to their shares in the venture. It had been entered on without formalities when Felix invited them to join him, and now they differed over the division. Was it, as Felix assumed, one half to himself and the other to Basil and Corinna jointly, or, as they argued, three thirds? They consulted a lawyer, and his opinion humiliated Felix, presenting him as both grasping and, in this case, unsound in judgement. He was, in any case, in no mood for carrying on the business as a minority shareholder and without Basil and Corinna's help. Moreover, Nthuli, initially genial and friendly, had lately begun to display suspicions over his royalties and imply that he was not being honestly dealt with. So Felix decided to cede the rights on the famous book to another publisher and, as to the rest, remainder the stock and simply let the business run down.

Then, having no heart for the endless trickle of tasks he was involved in through the magazine he had been editing, he decided to close that down as well.

There was another loss. He had for long cherished a plan eventually to write a biography of his mentor Johan de Waal. For many years, never urgently, yet always with fascination and a sense of destiny, he had assembled information that often deepened and complicated the paradoxes, rather than solving puzzles, and made the story seem increasingly extraordinary and important. But now, when a young stranger tentatively enquired, "Would I be poaching on your territory if I tried to write a biography of Johan de Waal?" he barely hesitated.

Knowing no more than that Gregory Hennigman professed himself a devotee of de Waal's work, he responded, "For so long I've thought of de Waal's life story as my trust. But now I'm not sure any more whether I'll ever do it. So perhaps I ought to stand aside. Perhaps you've come at the right time." Almost gratefully he yielded the whole project and all his information about sources into the keen young man's hands. Whereas he was fixed in a dispiriting grey perspective of closing days, here was someone, commended by enthusiasm, by an eagerness to be guided, and by the testimonial of appropriate timing, who could relieve him of that responsibility of witness for which, in spirit and in remaining years, he felt he had become too small.

Only when Hennigman showed him a draft of his first chapter did Felix wake up to what he had allowed to happen. The quest for a deep, difficult truth had been abandoned into the hands of an ambitious market writer who had sniffed sensationalistic possibilities in de Waal's popular legend. Indignantly, querulously, he browbeat Hennigman over the crudities of his pages, then tried to retrieve the situation with an offer to collaborate—perhaps there was a method to be found by which Hennigman's energy could be turned into the vehicle of Felix's intentions. But Hennigman had the bit between his teeth and, with reason now to feel offended and threatened, refused. Nothing could be saved. It was too late.

13

Man's Estate

With his father he went up to visit Israel—a cousin's son's wedding their pretext for making what was really a pilgrimage to a sacred site of the imagination. Emigrant relatives and friends enhanced the pilgrims' notion of inherited belonging with a dimension of intimacy and warmth. In that setting, on an impulsive determination, Felix gradually reduced his doses of Valium and, one midday, with the poison dissolving out of his system, recognised as in a ritual the return of his emotional normality. It was the very hour in which the country's normality, ever precarious, was once more overturned by an eruption of war.

The wedding was set for some days after Yom Kippur. On that holy day Dad as usual was observing the fast, so in the morning he left their hotel for a synagogue where he would do his observances until nightfall. Toward noon Felix strolled a block or two from the hotel to a nearby main road and sat down on a bench at a bus stop to gather a sense of how the Day of Atonement affected the atmosphere of Tel Aviv.

There was an almost midnight emptiness in the wide street, with few pedestrians and little traffic. On a second floor balcony opposite, a man leaned on his elbows staring idly. A spidery, bent old woman with covered head, creature of some irreducibly foreign ghetto surely, came shuffling in bedroom slippers from somewhere behind Felix and made her slow way past him and across the street at a long angle, exploiting its emptiness, and then on round the next corner. Her tortoise pace made her journey epic.

A single aircraft, strangely heavy and low, lumbered noisily across the sky. Now and again, mysteriously, a car or truck in military grey-green passed at speed with its headlamps lit though the street lay under the glare of a naked sun. Then a siren sounded in what he recognised as an air raid warning. He supposed it must mean something else: a particularly serious terrorist attack, perhaps, that had to be announced by siren because there was no local radio broadcasting on Yom Kippur.

He sat on. A group of four or five people, evidently tourists, came along. One of them carried a transistor radio. They stopped opposite the man on the balcony and began a shouted conversation with him, something to do with "the BBC...Suez Canal...Golan... Egyptians...Syrians..." After a few minutes the group moved on. Nearer Felix's bench they encountered a young couple coming toward them, whom they told almost gleefully, "There's a war. Yes, yes...The Egyptians have invaded Sinai. We've heard from the BBC. You'll have to go and fight."

The young man addressed protested, his accent suggesting a Sabra, "No, no... We don't want war..."

The others insisted, and Felix found himself intervening: "Don't spread rumours when things aren't certain." The man with the radio glared at him without replying and walked on with his group.

Then far up the street the little old woman reappeared, shuffling slowly back along the way she had gone. As she passed his bench she said to him in clear, familiar English, "Don't remain sitting here. Didn't you hear the siren? Go back to your hotel." That she should know enough about him to proffer a protective rebuke seemed a normal fact of this day's strangeness.

On his way back he passed a woman in a pink dress standing in a shop doorway. Her lounging stance, large handbag and muttered invitation identified her as a prostitute. In a remote past he had hunted such invitations, but now he shook his head and walked on. The moment was too incongruous: Israel, Yom Kippur, broad daylight, war. Yet this was a spring message to those of his passions that had been in hibernation.

In the hotel foyer a throng of guests hung on the words of one of the staff behind the reception counter who was translating the Hebrew announcements emerging from a radio—because of the crisis Kol Yisroel was now broadcasting. There had indeed been an invasion on several fronts. The forces at the borders had been taken by surprise and overrun, but the country was mobilising. All soldiers on leave, all reserves, were to report for duty immediately and were being summoned from their homes and synagogues.

Felix wondered what Dad knew of the situation and whether he was still going through the readings and rituals of the hunger hours. After a time most of the hotel guests dispersed from the foyer, but later in the afternoon sirens sounded again and everyone was herded into the basement which served as an air raid shelter. There were no sounds of an actual raid to be heard, and he supposed the exercise was only a precaution or a rehearsal. All the same the thought of Dad worried him. Was he taking refuge in some other shelter, or could he be out in the streets trudging his way back, faint with hunger and shocked by the news? When some biscuits and coffee were brought and dispensed in the cellar his anxiety increased as the plates and urns were emptied. With things in turmoil it was uncertain when or where a meal could be obtained. But finally the old man appeared while there was something left, and broke his fast in the air raid shelter.

The kibbutz wedding they had come for now lay under a cloud of uncertainties. But the only sign of abnormality to be seen in the streets was a man dabbing blue paint on car headlamps. Out of curiosity and a vague idea of loyalty, Felix was prepared to sit things out as an observer, at least for as long as they had planned to stay in Israel. But a few telephone conversations soon made it clear that any delay in leaving might result in their being trapped for the duration of the war. Schedules for flights out of the country were likely to be disrupted. Moreover, their presence here under war conditions would be a source of additional anxiety to relatives and friends. A chain of telephone calls for advice and information—a friend, the Zionist Federation, the airport—had them, almost without decision, flying out the next day, via a rushed lucky connection on a windy night at Athens airport.

Yet not even the drama of this escape brought home any sense of a desperate situation. And the first letter Felix received reported a cousin's visit to one of the fighting fronts as rather a comic escapade. But over the following weeks a series of letters presented an increasingly grim and tragic picture. The wedding took place on the planned day, but the groom, on a few hours' compassionate leave, had to return to the front almost as soon as the ceremony was over. A close friend of Felix's was assigned the duty of chauffeuring an official to soldiers' families to break the news of fatalities. By the time the invaders were repulsed, Israel was deeply wounded and seemed doomed to face a succession of wars, each more damaging and difficult to win than the last.

Felix reported his defection from Valium to the neurologist who had prescribed it. "I've been off it about ten days and I feel human again. That damned depression has lifted at last." The doctor had monitored his condition during the four years and twice had admitted him for treatment with an intravenous anti-depressant.

"Well," he said cheerfully now, "there's something else I'd like you to try. You could find this a miracle drug."

Felix had heard him use that phrase before, in recommending Valium, yet he suppressed his doubts and agreed to the experiment. After two days of the new regime his perceptions of scale, direction and time had become distorted and his face, arms and legs were tingling. Frightened, he telephoned the doctor and was permitted to stop taking the tablets and told to attend the next week's clinic.

"Well, what now?" the doctor mused when he presented himself. "Shall we try Valium again?"

"But, Doctor, you know very well..." It was as though everything Felix had reported about the gratuitous miseries caused him by that drug month after month, year upon year, had not been heard, or else not believed. "No. No more Valium." He would not come to that doctor again.

His new home under Mavis's roof lay two long blocks from the nearest bus route and during his apathy he had lacked the will to take the long walk to the bus stop for trips to town. The river of traffic he would have to cross on the main road daunted him. And then, the strength of his right hand had continued to wane during the four years. He depended on that grip for the safe mounting and dismounting of buses. So his days of travelling independently by public transport were over. He would have henceforth to depend on his family and friends for lifts, or call expensive taxis.

His new quarters had begun as a double garage, then been converted into a playroom. Now this adjunct to the family house was packed with his books, and divided by a wardrobe and bookcases into a sleeping alcove and an office. His flatlet had its separate outside door, its separate telephone, its separate shower cubicle and lavatory. The servants brought his breakfast to his flat and usually served him lunch at the kitchen table. When he joined the family for dinner and, at the week-ends, lunch, he made his way to the dining-room through the laundry and kitchen.

Another change was the proximity of the children, his accessibility to them as tenant uncle: the elder girls, one of whom had pressed the Leary book on him, the tiny boy who smelled out and raided his cache of sweets or sat on his lap and prodded the typewriter keys, the little girl who had welcomed him into the house by crocheting a shawl for his knees or shoulders as though she wanted to assuage the chill of his grief.

Every Sunday a parcel of pears, to keep his stomach regular, every month or so a packet of peppermint sparkles. Dad's solicitude still reached him almost daily by the umbilicus of the telephone, and they saw each other at least once a week.

"Do you need anything else? Batteries for your razor? Anything I can do for you?" Anything I can do for you? Anything I can bring? These words were almost his motto. This was the active side of his old fashioned mannerliness. The obverse was his reluctance to seem in any way demanding.

"Dad, do you want kitke or rye?" Mavis would ask at table.

"Anything. Give me whatever is nearest..."

One Sunday Felix reported to him, "I had a dream about you. You were telling me something, talking and talking, a long, long business, and in the middle of it came a knocking on the door. You continued talking. I knew it was my doctor at the door about something urgent, so after a while I tried to interrupt you to tell you so. But you just talked on and on."

"Ah," said Dad with sincere regret, "I'm sorry."

His work on Johan de Waal's papers was drawing to a close now that he had compiled a fifth posthumous volume, but his earlier rather lonely faith in his author had been overtaken by a durable fame which warmed him by reflection. A share of the royalties de Waal had not lived to enjoy came his way year after year, the trickle of money once swelling momentarily into a torrent when one of the volumes was prescribed as a school setwork. He reaped the harvest gratefully but with ambiguous unease. Ought he to think of this income as his mentor's posthumous gift, or was he in any sense robbing de Waal? If that was so, it would imply much more—that he had misunderstood his mentor and had helped to falsify his legend and perhaps cheapen and distort his literary reputation. That sloppiness of his which had admitted Hennigman to the role of biographer was perhaps a sign of his deficiency. If de Waal's ghost rose up, would it be to greet him with affection, or spurn him with bitterness?

Another, though less troublingly dubious, aspect of his circumstances was that while most of his income was unearned, in the form of interest and dividends and indeed, by now, those royalties, most of his work—editing, advising, reviewing and, of course, writing—was rewarded only nominally if at all. But at last this imbalance was changed. Denis Harley, an old friend who conducted a private art school, persuaded Felix to run a regular creative writing seminar as an adjunct to the school. Beginning very tentatively he was soon enjoying the classes, and in the main, it seemed, so were the students. Apart from this satisfaction, the teaching became the only department of his life that regularly afforded him the adult dignity of being paid what he earned and earning what he was paid. For not only did the fees supplement his pocket but, because his students attended voluntarily (those whom his methods, or lack of method, failed to satisfy simply withdrew), the money affirmed week by week that what he gave was wanted and taken seriously.

There often was something necessary Dad could do—clean the electric shaver, change the batteries, insert a fresh ribbon in the typewriter, attach stamps to letters for posting. But the price was irritation. The invariable sequence of set questions—the answer to "How are you?" followed automatically by "What can you tell me?" followed in turn several times by "What else can you tell me?"—the off-key comments and cautionary advice, the fussy adjustments of collars, buttons or hair in disregard of impatient protests, would finally bring Felix to the climax of an exasperated defensive bellow.

He grew to recognise a pattern in nearly every conversation with his father: Dad solicitously probing, insisting, nagging, piling irritation on irritation, until irritation exploded in a shout of protest—and only then, rebuked and silently rebuking, desisting from his teasing attentions. It was as though the anger alone had had the force to flash a real communication between them. Felix would be left full of shame at one more graceless failure to bear with the urgently clumsy caring that was symptomatic of Dad's loneliness, yet angry at having once again been manipulated into the brattish reflex. But this habit of abrasive interaction persisted, in fact, until Dad's increasing deafness and vagueness strangled conversation between them.

These ritualistically induced tantrums constituted one of the ironies pertaining to man's estate. Dad above all had promoted him to that condition by having invested money from the sale of the house in interest-bearing stocks in his name, a steady supplement to his less regular incomes. Dad and he had always employed largely different languages of reality, yet even now he remained bonded to his father's world, his father's child, with a child's pettishness and dependence.

When he had been wrought to the point of rudely yelling at his father, the old man would fall back at last, quelled, the skew lift of his upper lip betokening hurt, while his eyes hinted that he was somehow satisfied, somehow replete.

14

Soweto, Mon Amour

By the time Felix emerged from Valium's long numbing of his responsiveness and desire, Elizabeth had been the ironing woman in Mavis's house for a year or more, coming in twice a week for a few hours to ease the older maid's load of housework. He watched the yellow-skinned, tall, handsome woman arriving and leaving, with a sense of her distance from himself. He heard the warm greetings she exchanged with the the other members of the household, especially the children. But her work gave her nothing to do with him in his almost separate flatlet.

That the house (it was the house, not anyone in it) should reserve the ironing woman from him was a perfectly normal thing. There were elements in the life of the inner family that he, of course, did not share in. He was perfectly satisfied not to be expected to spend evenings with visitors who were not particularly his own friends; at first, in any case, he was blocked by depression. But simply because Elizabeth was there regularly week after week he began to feel a chill in his exclusion from her. Or was it because, as her pretty woman's proud walk suggested, it was possibly not the house but Elizabeth herself, after all, who reserved herself from him?

Then she became the second housemaid, still sleeping out, leaving work at mid-afternoon to accommodate the long journey to Soweto, but coming in almost daily and doing her share of what had to be done for him—serving some of his meals, dusting his room, making his bed. He had now to add his monthly tip to her wages and could exchange the same friendliness with her as he did with the older housemaid, Mary, and the gardener-cum-houseboy, Peter. Yet Elizabeth's prettiness in itself made her seem self-sufficient, and imposed a certain reserve on him. After all, the law of the land was such that even his recognition of her attractiveness was tainted with potential criminality.

One of the occasional services for which he turned to Mary or Peter was the trimming of his fingernails. He came into the kitchen one day with a bothersome hangnail. It was Mary's day off and Peter was at work in the garden. Felix made his request to Elizabeth with slight awkwardness, never before having asked her for so personal an attention. Without hesitating, she took his hand and half-turned her back toward him so that she could anchor his unsteadiness while she wielded the scissors. The side of his hand was pressed, in fact, into the softness of her breast and, his arm was bracketing her torso. Almost an embrace. He thought it, yet thought too that to read intimacy into the situation was to invade her privacy. She had a family in the township; she had her separate life.

But the next time he needed his nails trimmed, in vague experiment he turned to her again. She employed the same caressing incidentals to make the task convenient, and so it was the next few times, so that a warm temptation flickered, and his restraint gradually fell away. His first tentative closing of the space between their bodies as he stood half behind her could be taken as accidental or no more than an enhancement of the comfortableness she had introduced. But later there was no tentativeness in the soft pressure of his thigh and chest against her, yet she bore with it as though she felt nothing, or as though this nestling contact were natural, to be taken for granted in the circumstances. Only when at last the eloquent nudge of his tumescence against her buttock still provoked no withdrawal or rebuke did he become certain that there was a complicity between them.

But its meaning remained indecipherable. Her compliance with the liberties he was taking could mean simply that she felt the weakness of her position as a black servant. This degree of submissiveness in someone who seemed so sure of herself would be bizarre, but Felix guessed that a woman so attractive may often, to the point of weariness, have been the subject of comparable indignities offered by men against whom her social defences were futile. Then could her compliance mean that she was indifferent? This was no more likely: it presumed a coldness that did not match the warmth of her manner, the inviting tenderness with which she cradled his hand against her breast. Or might it mean that she understood and pitied his frustrated hunger and was willing to let him feed off her in this limited way, confident that he knew no way of coercing her into yielding more than she wished to? None of these alternatives convinced him, yet the thought of each was hurtful. Perhaps he ought simply to accept the attenuated sweetness he obtained from her whenever his nails needed trimming, because indeed he knew no way to take the matter forward that wasn't desperate, squalid and dangerous to both of them.

That winter became a season of pity and terror and confusion for the whole country. Beginning in Soweto, a long-dreaded black rebellion erupted in township after township. But instead of the old nightmare form of a bloodbath in the white suburbs, the conflict that developed as the shocked authorities set about suppressing the uprising took a shape more desperate, tragic and perplexing than had been dreamt of—the fighters on one side were mainly school children, exasperated by the insult of an education system designed to be inferior. This meant that most of those killed, injured and imprisoned were children and adolescents. And warring without adult direction or restraint, the pupils, exulting in the discovery of their power to defy, though seldom armed with anything better than stones and matchboxes, at times deployed their numbers, their cunning and fearlessness to bring low a police or military vehicle. But often they could not wait to identify and confront a combatant enemy armed with superior weaponry, so turned to express what they had to express on any object to hand, any part or agent of the imposed world they had been unwillingly born into. The stocks of smashed bottle stores were poured out on the ground—in token, perhaps, of the children's contempt for their fathers' paralysis by the liquor of resignation. But shops at which township people bought their necessities were also destroyed. Delivery vehicles were stoned, overturned, set on fire. Certain schools were razed. Several whites with nothing but the most benign business taking them into the townships were mobbed. A doctor was killed.

One of the scores of photographs published in newspapers fixed itself in the mind. In the foreground, a cluster of children, their faces and gestures aflame with joy and exhilaration, every detail proclaiming triumph, ecstasy of liberation. In the background, a burning bus—the township's transport. But those faces said that things were no longer what they had been. Children were warriors and leaders. Destruction was creation. The people's loss of a facility became an item of their liberation. The bus was no longer a bus but a symbol, as was the fire that consumed it, as was everything. The bus was a machine of the humiliating, no-longer-to-be-tolerated system. Or did those faces express so much? Perhaps their passion reflected only the orgasmic joy of burst-out after long restraint, the libidinous excitement of assumption into a collectivity exercising its newly-proven power to destroy.

Where Felix lived the only sign of these wild events was some unusual traffic of helicopters and other small aircraft crossing the sky, yet the conflict was happening so near at hand that Elizabeth commuted almost daily to and from the war zone. She had a son, too small to take part in the rebellion, who had been attending a school in Soweto. When the trouble erupted she had sent the child for safety to her parents in a small country town. As months passed and the unrest continued to simmer it became clear that the disrupted school system was not going to be soon and safely reinstated. Soweto schools that continued to function were in danger of wrecking or arson, and staff and children who continued to attend risked being seen as enemies, or at least defectors from the rebels' cause.

He learnt of Elizabeth's dilemma only when she said to him one day, pronouncing his name with shyness, "Felix, you can help me?"

"How?" he asked in surprise.

"I'm so frightened to send my child to school in Soweto..." The solution she had thought of was to put the little boy into a boarding school in Swaziland, but that would require money she did not have. What she needed from Felix was a few hundred rand. Her turning to him rather than to Mavis spoke somehow of her perplexity and urgency, as well as of a trust that rose above the unspoken complicity between them. Perhaps Peter had told her of his occasional "loans" from Felix—whose reluctance had never been strong enough to stiffen into a refusal. To have asked for her reasons would have been to impose a prosy complication on this gesture of hers toward himself. Her request, arising from her embroilment in Soweto's historic paroxysm, implicated him and in some remote symbolic way offered him a chance of relevance. But his urgencies thrust him beyond the point where being allowed to relieve a victim's distress would produce its own emotional reward. Explaining her need, Elizabeth stood close to him, making the transaction intimate, exposing herself in a position of susceptibility.

"Yes, sure, I'll give you the money," he said. His throat tightened with the sense of his own risk—at the least the risk of offending her—as he added in almost a whisper: "But I need you to help me too."

"What?"

"You must let me touch you."

There was faint surprise in her expression, yet her nod of assent was unhesitating and simple. He knew she understood the full sense behind his euphemism and the full force of his need. Her willingness to rescue him seemed autonomous, quite unrelated to his promise of the money.

He was often to give play to guilty doubts: had he abused the weakness of her situation? Had he pushed her into the condition not only of an adulteress but of a prostitute as well? Was he taking advantage of Soweto's agony to procure this relief? But nothing she ever said or did reflected these accusations. She gave herself to him as though she desired him equally.

Under Valium, his libido had been dully hibernating. Afterwards, lust awakening had begun to thresh around for outlets with the desperation familiar to him from the time before Tanya. But in this new phase his need seemed newly capable of summoning responses. He had become involved in several strange, brief affairs, no less teasing or perplexing than fulfilling. But now with Elizabeth occurred a more sustained and more significant chapter which, though it involved him deeply in danger, deception and moral ambiguity, was rich in tenderness and excitement. The affair that began as an agreement about money and sheer physical contact very soon deepened in passion and in sympathy so that they were, to the limits of their situation, real lovers, and also friends.

Their lovemaking was condemned always to be furtive and hurried, as cruelly constrained, in a sense, as their conversation was by barriers of language and interest. They were knowingly and repeatedly breaking the law, offending against the Immorality Act, whose very name signified a unique depth of revulsion in the law-makers and imputed a special shame to the transgressors. They gave no assent to the shame. The wrongness of the law was vivid in the lifegivingness, the human affirmation of what passed between them. But discovery threatened their caresses with the perils of criminality, penalty and some form at least of disgrace that would hurt his whole family.

There was the threat advertised in the notorious lengths the police would go to to discover and trap such lovers as they were, the thought of which was so grotesque and chilling that they usually suppressed it. Apart from that, Felix was surprised to learn that he and Elizabeth were chiefly conscious of different dangers. He more immediately dreaded discovery by any member of his family. Her first fear was of the other servants. He had vaguely imagined that they would feel a protective solidarity with her, and even interpret his loving her as an act of human identification. Her dread made him aware of her endangered aloneness in giving herself to him. The moral and political judgements she might be exposing herself to were other than he could have guessed at. And jealousy might also enter the picture: it was easy to suppose that she aroused desire in Peter who saw his wife in his distant home village only during one month of leave and half a dozen brief visits punctuating the year.

But if danger and the consciousness of contravention fed the fire between them, these were not the only elements. They liked each other with a tenderness unaffected by their relation as master and servant; Felix entertained no abstract, principled guilt on this score—servants existed in his world, and in no small measure the fruitfulness of his way of life, and perhaps even his survival itself, had always depended on their ministrations; and Elizabeth seemed to interpret his dependency as scope for intimacy and tenderness and gave no sign of resenting her position. No matter what she did for him, all sense of mastership and subservience dissolved when they were alone together. They became a man and a woman, impassioned bodies, lovers. Except for one or two extraordinary occasions, time did not allow them to undress or even lie down for their intimacies. They exchanged hungry, exploring touches whenever they were private enough and near enough to each other, and for their fullest embraces stood in the narrow strip of space that separated his bed from the screening wardrobe and book-cases.

Watching her at work while he ate his lunch in the breakfast nook in the kitchen, he would shudder with excitement at the thought of her availability to him, the recollection of the hampered and curtailed, but also wild and urgent, caresses they had exchanged an hour or so before. Something that repeatedly moved him was the expression of her face as she reached her climax. Her features contorted as if in agony. But he knew the grimace did not mean that, or if it did, it was an agony he could not understand, except that it referred to the whole complexity of her womanliness yet also somehow betokened the wholeness of her giving in that moment, and that it was an agony joined to joy.

She said to him one day: "Even if you are married, I will come to you." The affirmation was rich, but it also implied a recognition of barriers. Her fantasy held back from the possibility that they should be married to each other. Even if the prohibition of the law should miraculously fall away—a possibility about which he at times fantasised, yearning for the condition in which they could move publicly together as lovers enjoying their due of unpressed time, safety and pride—she seemed to acknowledge that the limits on the vocabulary in which they could converse with each other set limits on the fulfilment available to them in a life together. In any case, she was already married. They could never be for each other in that sense. Perhaps the same acknowledgement was implicit in the promise he was moved to make to her one day when his cup of gratitude was full: "When I die I'll leave you money. As much as I can. To help you."

He knew that without some extraordinary help she was condemned to a life of hard labour and worries. She was under-educated and burdened with the responsibilities of a house whose rent had to be found, a husband who drank too much, a child whose whole upbringing, not merely his schooling, had to be achieved against obstacles and under threats. A few times during school holidays, when she brought the child with her to play about the house while she worked, Felix witnessed how the mother's concern could exasperate her into the harshness of screams and smacks in response to some naughtiness of the little boy's. He knew there was nothing extraordinary about this as motherly conduct, though it was out of key with her usual soft humour. But it made him aware of how mothers like her were embattled against history. Her aspirations were minimal and ordinary, but they arose in circumstances where confusion and moral chaos flooded into a cultural vacuum. African culture had been ruined by the white civiliser and then had neither been restored (which, anyway, did not seem possible) nor replaced by anything adequate and durable. The whole picture was made plain in the upheaval that had begun in Soweto.

But Elizabeth's struggle, commonplace as it must be, both preceded and would outlast the dramatic dated epochs of the proclaimed political struggle. Also, she was at the mercy of that scourge of premature mortality that seemed chronically to afflict the poor. Her first husband, a security guard, had been shot dead on duty. And now, one day when their closeness had been established some months Felix heard her yell of grief at a telephone call: her young brother had been killed in an accident.

Days later, after her short leave for the funeral, Felix listened to her soft sobs as she worked on at her ironing in the kitchen. As her lover, once he had murmured his sympathy, he knew no way to comfort her except to imagine her pain and suspend his demands until she again gave him a sign that their caresses would no longer affront the roused gods of her deeper belonging. And it was that deeper belonging which his promise of a bequest acknowledged, implicitly precluding the possibility that he might so deeply enter her life that he would participate in her hardship, use up his savings for and with her, and reserve nothing that might be bequeathed.

They continued as lovers for two years. During that time some of his other friendships may have owed their expansion to his freedom from the sexual predatoriness that had so often distorted earlier relationships. On the other hand, the closest of those friendships would have seemed hollow if he had shut out from them the most urgent of his secrets. He found himself, thus, sustaining other intimacies with the story of his perilous, perplexed happiness with Elizabeth. It was perplexed and somehow coloured by sadness because, for all its life-giving goodness, that relationship was disqualified from accommodating precisely the kind of indispensable inner life he nourished by making self-defining confessions to these other friends whose understanding and absolution he needed hardly less than sex. He did not think that in making these confidences to others he was depriving Elizabeth of anything it was possible for him to give, but it sharpened his sense of the limitations her life was hedged by. They were unfair, perhaps even cruel, but they were conditions of the Africa that contained Soweto as well as this suburb where he pursued his inner life. There was nothing he could do about them.

When the ageing Mary retired, Elizabeth took on her job, though still not sleeping in the servants' rooms in the backyard but daily leaving early to be with her husband and child in Soweto. It was this fact that forced their separation in the end. Mavis decided that Elizabeth's hours were not sufficient for the work; she must make place for a servant who would be present through supper time and the washing up afterwards. Felix sometimes wondered whether this was the genuine reason for the change of arrangements. After all, Elizabeth was a particularly congenial presence in the house, earning affection from all the family, and no dissatisfaction over her hours had been expressed. In any case, Peter customarily did the work to be done in the evening. Had Mavis in some way been led to suspect the affair, which she must regard as too dangerous and embarrassing to be tolerated, and had she devised this as the most tactful strategy she could think of for ending it? If the dismissal was strategic, Felix was grateful that it was not punitive. Mavis's need to be discreet would have prevented confrontations with Elizabeth or himself, and he in particular was vulnerable since he could be regarded as having treacherously abused her hospitality.

Elizabeth worked her month's notice and, in an atmosphere of bewilderment and unreality, took her farewells. She telephoned occasionally from her new place of work, and gave Peter as well as Felix a number; but it could not be freely used since the job was demanding and her employers discouraged calls. At long intervals she visited Mavis's house keeping alive her friendships there. She and Felix sometimes found an opportunity for very restricted caresses. He usually pressed some money onto her, wanting still to be real in her life, to be of some help. She accepted, but this was not what she came for. In her slight uneasiness he read a danger that the cash gift could somehow reduce what there was between them.

But even the slender surviving connections unravelled with the drift of the years. By the time the law they had contravened was repealed they were too far from each other to use the new freedom. So far from each other's lives that by then neither of the promises they had made each other seemed real enough to be kept. Yet a certain wondering awe at the ways of passion and tenderness, a special triumph of aliveness, would always return to Felix with his memories of how they had been brought together in those terrible days of Soweto.

15

A Servant of the People

"It is time to strip away the innocent liberal mask and expose the sinister, if unconscious, tendencies behind it." Oliver Vaughn, still far from his peroration, leaned forward, his fists on either side of the lectern, as he eyed with amused remorse those of his audience who were leaving their seats and tiptoeing across to join the leakage out of the lecture theatre. They had been witnessing a rite of iconoclasm. Its target was Professor Roy Craddock, venerable prophet of rootedness and the doyen of local poets.

"Bradbrookism"—the label was Vaughn's own coinage—was "neocolonialist cultural elitism in a patriotic guise". Poem by poem, dictum by dictum, initiative by civilising initiative, he correlated Craddock's influence with "supremacist presumptions and colonial practices". He was teaching regionalism's philosopher what it meant to be truly rooted.

The parties in Vaughn's audience, whether scandalised or gratified, must surely be compelled by a sense of dramatic occasion. Had his paper not run on well into the lunch break, he would probably have held all his listeners, however heavy-going his discourse. He delivered the esoteric references and qualifying clauses with a piratical relish, flapping his flags of half-rolled dark shirt-sleeves and brow-encroaching bang, off-setting the hard subversiveness of his thesis with smiles and glances that invited collusion. It was a presentation designed to bring the theatrical potentialities of the conference to a head.

And in fact the remaining three days were full of it—Vaughn's attack on Craddock, and rumours of the professor's bewildered discomposure.

Felix managed to corner him in a lobby between sessions. "I have to tell you," he said, "I saw Roy Craddock being taken apart at a conference about twenty years ago..."

"Twenty years? Oh yes? You knew him then?"

"He'd been one of my lecturers."

"But he hadn't had time yet to spread his influence."

"True, he had just become well-known as poet, the best of the war poets. But that was enough to get him into trouble. In fact, it was the first conference I ever sat in on, and I was shocked to see how fierce academics can get about their causes."

Vaughn gave an uneasy laugh. "But why was anyone attacking him then?"

"He'd upset the Leavisites, mainly that Osbrug University crowd—I'm sure you've heard of them. His mistake was to present a paper about problems he and other poets had in trying to root their English language poetry in African soil. Those Leavisites reacted as though he had insulted them by asking them to take their minds off the Great Tradition and think about local poets' problems. They lammed into him at question time, one after another, until the chairman had to rescue him."

"What's your point?" Vaughn had bridled. "I believe Craddock wasn't present at my paper. In any case, I've never met him before this conference, and I wasn't setting out to hurt his feelings."

"O, no, I see that. You took him as your whipping-boy because he's so well-known and liked. It was incidental to your thesis. That's one difference between you and them. Some of them were colleagues of his who wanted to humiliate him. I remember Rosalie Wepener saying something like, 'Not only does Professor Craddock beg us to contemplate him rowing on the Zoo Lake, presumably instead of Wordsworth on Wentworth Water, but he appears to be asking us to tell him how to *write* his poems as well'."

Vaughn laughed, and Felix admitted, "She was funny in a way. But it's the politics I'm thinking about."

"What do you mean?"

"It was the years when English departments were fighting off anything anybody suggested for the curriculum that might take time from the classics. But why I wanted to tell you the whole story is, it strikes me that those Osbruggers' attack on Craddock was from exactly the opposite ideological direction to yours."

"Well, I don't know what you mean by ideological. But I see what you're getting at." Vaughn laughed again, a touch ruefully. "What am I supposed to make of it, though? Certain acts become necessary at certain times."

"Possibly," said Felix. "But what is poor old Craddock supposed to make of it?"

Vaughn shrugged and gave a comic grimace of sympathy, but the eyes he turned on Felix were wary.

That turned out to be the prologue. About three years later Vaughn came with his wife and child to live in Johannesburg. Now began a sort of tragicomedy to which Felix would be an agitated and agitating witness — a member of the chorus. The theme was still, after all, Craddock's theme, Vaughn's theme—rootedness, belonging, service to the place.

Constantly, there was a trickle of people leaving the country—here a family, there an individual, acquaintances, public figures, relatives, friends. Many right-minded citizens regarded themselves as simply of the world—thus heart-free, when they became dissatisfied or endangered, to transplant to wherever they chose, and there still be at home, at one. Seen from *this* home, it amounted to a constant crumbling, a negation of community. It troubled Felix. He had developed a kind of patriotism, a need to cling to his Johannesburg rooting, a belief that he always would—at least as long as he remained untested by danger. Where one found oneself, one had to discover or establish connection and meaning. To him, writing—like love, like any mode of being serviceable to one's local world—had come to imply an embracing of reality as given, an active way of belonging to the place of one's life.

It seemed still one more strand of attachment, even if an adventitious one, when he agreed to join the Guild Against Censorship that had been founded by a novelist named Henry Walters. It was a time when new kinds of censorship had been brought in. More and more classes of publications were being banned, more and more local books excised from the new little literature that was trying to grow. Verse by black poets, now that there were more of them, was receiving at least as much suspicious attention from the censors as black writers' prose had long suffered from.

Though black members would have been welcomed, the Guild had none, mainly because blacks and whites generally lived so far apart. But Henry Walters discovered a black cultural club called Pula in one of the nearer townships and invited its leader to bring poets to share the Guild's platform for readings. He did so several times, and on those occasions a larger audience gathered for what was more of a performance, with music, movement and ethnic costume being added to the verse.

Walters commented wryly on this turn: "With whistles, drums and xylophones, who needs friends?" But the Guild's purpose was still being served. Each time its members and Pula's read together they transcended one of the artificial barriers; goodwill was affirmed; discoveries were made, knowledge shared; some starving inner life was nurtured. Recognising all this, Felix subdued his almost superstitious unease about belonging to any organisation. The Guild was making a bid for a kind of connectedness that was all the more thrilling because it had always before seemed out of his reach.

It was a bid that began to be dramatically raised after Oliver Vaughn joined the Guild. He had resigned his lectureship and come, at the invitation of the directors of FrontBooks, a Johannesburg political publishing house, to replace the manager whose outspokenness had led to his being banned by the authorities. Vaughn had hardly settled in his new home and job when he sought out the Guild, joined it as a poet with a recently published collection of his own, and threw himself into its activities. Bonhomie, reputation and the torrent of his course-setting proposals soon eased him into a place alongside Walters at the helm.

He introduced Walters to the leaders of three other township culture societies like Pula. Through his black political contacts he had become familiar with a network of similar societies all over the country. Musicians, sculptors, painters and writers liked to band themselves into colourfully named groups, almost submerging their individual personalities. Performances and exhibitions seemed meant to bring credit to the collectives more than to the artists themselves. It was an African way of doing things. And it rubbed off on the Guild when the township societies sent troupes of performers to take part in readings.

A Guild member mumbled, "I don't know what these concerts have to do with writing"—yet he, they of the Guild, could only feel grateful for the new understanding Vaughn had helped them to gain, this new, nearer approach to the reality of where they lived.

"We at FrontBooks are thinking of launching a new kind of literary magazine, based on the community arts groups," Vaughn announced at a Guild committee meeting, "and we'd like to involve the Guild as well." His plan was that the groups would gather their members' literary contributions and would help to distribute the journal in the townships, where bookshops were rare. It was an ambitious, bold idea, perhaps too much so, but having noticed a few interesting voices at the readings, Felix was attracted by its possibilities. In any case, no doubts that might have been expressed by Guild members could have dampened Vaughn's enthusiasm.

So *Grassroots* was launched. The name was not promising, but the large format with many photographs as well as drawings by township artists gave the magazine a defiant panache. The network easily distributed large numbers of copies. It was linking people who were hungry for the novelty of print—their own names, voices and viewpoints in print. Even the city bookshops found some demand for it. The township contributions were wildly uneven in quality, but *en masse* they created the impression that an otherwise stifled pulse was being laid open. Vaughn had the gleeful, affectionate air of a father presenting the talents of his family to a receptive audience. The third issue was banned.

This was a sign that the authorities were already noticing *Grassroots*, but Vaughn was dismayed. In the next issue he published an open letter to the censors, arguing that there was less danger to the state in allowing a channel of expression like *Grassroots* than in blocking it. The placatory line was surprising. It implied that Vaughn set more store by the continuing existence of the magazine than by the political profit there might be in its suppression. And perhaps this had less to do with policy than with Vaughn's affection for people he knew in the network and their way of doing things.

In fact, no further issues were banned, but very soon the matter was dwarfed.

There was a new political clampdown. Some hundreds of people had been rounded up and detained, homes and offices searched, a score of organisations banned. Indirectly the Guild was affected. "Impi has been banned," Henry Walters announced. "Two of its members have been detained. And Radwell Sebetha has gone into hiding—probably left the country." Impi was one of the township cultural societies the Guild had been reading with. Radwell Sebetha, the leader of Pula, was the one poet whose talent sounded clearly above the drumming and fluting.

"We need some way of protecting the community arts groups," Vaughn declared. "We need a writers' union. If we all get together—the groups, the Guild, the Afrikaans Writers' League, some of the internationally known writers with their connections, some media people—then we'd have some muscle."

Within weeks the Guild called a conference of all who might be interested. The venue was a hall in a foreign consulate, one of the few places in the city where blacks in such numbers conferring with whites would be welcome and safe. There was a spangle of well-known writers and journalists, but the township arts associations predominated with a phalanx of mainly very young men, exuberant and challenging, full of the new power revealed by the school-children's uprising in which many of them must have taken part little more than a year earlier. Full also of a determination to bring about a Union.

In the chair, Oliver Vaughn seemed to float benignly among them, equally ready with his amused snort or a jocular phrase to welcome their expected and their unexpected gestures—as though the expected ones confirmed what he believed, while the unexpected ones taught him something new which he was perfectly happy to incorporate into his scheme of things. Both in any case illustrated the message he wanted to convey to the world. And as their ideas emerged, so did the impression deepen that Vaughn had known from the beginning what these youths and their leaders were going to demand. By contrast, when older delegates, mainly whites, expressed anxieties about correct procedure, qualifications for membership, or literary standards, he was moved either to a satirical grin or to a grimace of pain. Theirs was the sound of an old voice; his endeavour was to make a new voice audible.

The most visible face of that new voice belonged to Tshepo Msomi, a columnist on a township newspaper who had become the new leader of Pula and was evidently a particular friend of Vaughn's. He had a morose yet deceptively relaxed manner. When Stephen Malley, a poet and publisher, anxious about commitment to literary craft, urged that "membership be restricted to writers proper", Msomi struck at him: "People like you don't know about the pressures I come under every day in my job, and the same applies to all cultural workers."

The youths around him applauded. He was a popular spokesman of their own anger.

Malley was winding himself up for a comeback when Vaughn intervened: "I must point out, Stephen, the theoretical impossibility of devising a test for commitment to literary craft that is not both culture-specific and traditionalist—one that isn't unfair to writers who come from a different tradition."

Malley ballooned with disgust. "Well, if that's the line you want to take, there's not much I can say."

It was the first sign that Vaughn and Msomi were active allies, not merely friends. And from now, more and more visibly—between and behind all the other speakers—their partnership piloted the conference, which contour by contour moulded the shape of the new Authors' Union.

"If there is a membership fee, how can I pay? The same for all the workers in the cultural associations. You are excluding us from this Authors' Union."

"It can be a nominal amount. R10 or R5 a year."

"And payable by one representative of each group that wants to join."

"But are those members full members? We don't want second class citizenship." (Laughter.)

"Full members, of course. And the paying representative would be ex officio on the Union's Executive Committee."

"So this Union would be an umbrella organisation with the community arts groups as affiliates?"

"Special affiliates."

"Many townships are restricted for whites. You can't hold Union functions there."

"No, no, no, no... The Union must hold functions in the townships. The arts groups will be holding their usual readings and exhibitions in their own communities. What kind of a Union is this if its members don't go to each other's communities and read together?"

"Well, we can apply for permits. Is it safe otherwise?"

"No, look, whenever we come into the white areas we take risks. If we always think about the police and the dompas and what the regime wants we will never do anything. I challenge our white members to show solidarity by coming to our readings without permits."

At the least, the aims of the Guild were now going to be more vigorously served, and its hit-and-miss reaching across barriers regularised and hugely enhanced. This must be why Henry Walters did not seem to mind that by the time the conference was over his Guild had somehow vanished, funds, aims and most of its membership, into the maw of the Author's Union. He was, of course, elected onto the executive committee, but the significance of that was diluted, for, as he privately remarked, "If you count all the township representatives, it's at least three times as big as the national cabinet." Nominated for the chairmanship, Vaughn declined and proposed Msomi instead, agreeing himself to be honorary secretary.

Felix, who was also elected to the committee, had never before observed such conscious political activity from so close by. He shared most of the alarm of those who were troubled by the strange compromises and accommodations and biases that were being built into this Authors' Union. But this was the construction of a machine for future work—in which he might find some role for himself. This was the way in which people were to be welded into a unity that could bring about desired ends. It was a style of procedure mastered and relished by Vaughn and Msomi, and at the very least accepted as normal and familiar by Malley, Walters and any who moved effectively in the world .

Also there was sheer curiosity about Oliver Vaughn's course as a dedicated political animal. What, for instance, would he do next? Why had he elected to exercise his political skills among the tiny recalcitrant minority who practised the arts? How did he deal with such prospects as banning, detention and even murder, which faced activists like himself? One, a close friend of his, had recently been shot dead at his own front door. And how would he come out of all this eventually?

The Union presented a dubious situation, full of problems and uncongenialities. Felix might soon have despaired of its promises and withdrawn but for the softening presence of an old friend on the committee. For years, since her children had grown up and her first novel been published, Rebecca Saffer had divided her time between writing and voluntary work at an advice bureau for people disadvantaged by the law, and recently had been helping with proof-reading and correspondence at FrontBooks—which had taken on something of a public welfare dimension since the launching of *Grassroots*.

In the easy-going editorial office with its comings and goings she had come to know a number of the township contributors individually. Thus she did not even at first find the Authors' Union confronting her with a featureless mask of collective will. Her intimations and sympathies went behind the anonymity, and she helped Felix discover and befriend some of the the individual young men, helped him by her example to hold onto his curiosity—his critical interest in the life of it—and onto his hopes.

In practical terms, Rebecca's being with him on the committee meant that he was usually assured of a lift to meetings and readings. And after all, even if his own enthusiasm only occasionally flared up, all that was required of him to join this experiment was a willingness to witness.

Meetings, readings, editions of *Grassroots*, a conference, debates, a court case, foreign visitors to edify with all this evidence of a cultural rebellion—the life of the Union unfolded. It might have been too largely a matter of committee meetings and organisational business but for what went on being called the "readings". Once or twice a month a different branch played host, and most of the branches were in fact the township arts groups, so the readings involved expeditions, and each expedition was an adventure, a fresh and individual experience of urban Africa where such events as these met hungers unknown in the white suburbs.

Reading itself was only one element of a kind of variety-concert-cum-art-exhibition held in a church or communal hall. The audiences were miscellaneous, often large, usually including many children. In one township people drifted in from a dust-bowl of sun-stricken untarred streets lined for miles in every direction by almost uninterrupted rows of uniform hutches—a dormitory town laid out on a stark stretch of veld, revealing no sign of its inhabitants' haphazard choices but built under a plan according to decree. There was a broad space around each house, yet scarcely ever a tree or any cultivated vegetation, so the openness spoke not of air and light, gardens and privacy, but of desolation and isolation. Other townships they visited might be very different, with cheek-by-jowl shanties and crowded streets, or even some aspects of a modest garden suburb, but there was always the sense of displacement and unfulfilment.

No wonder the performances were met enthusiastically, no wonder the applause expressed welcome to visitors, gratitude for relief from monotony, solidarity with familiar sentiments. Appreciation of the words, the actual meaning of what was spoken, was a different matter. The words, in any case, were mostly in English, a language not taught to black children during their first few years at school. And moreover, the words in whatever tongue were often drowned by the accompaniment. Apart from a line or two of refrain in the occasional long poem, usually proclaiming one identifiable sentiment, it seemed that the words were not meant to be heard clearly, not meant to be understood.

Inevitably, there were moments of poignancy and comedy: so many young men yearning to be poets, reading their ambitious lines mostly out of identical black hard-covered foolscap notebooks; strokes of contrast brought in by figures like the Soweto Laureate, Mama-Union, King Rage, Mohamed Moosa; the circumstances differing from reading to reading, according to the venue, the audience, the pretext, the time of day, the weather, the idiosyncrasies of the hosts.

Driving away after one of them, Vaughn—who sometimes lifted Felix when Rebecca could not—was recalling an exuberantly defiant performer with chuckles of relish, when a bend in the road revealed a perspective of the huge township they had just left, a vista of bleakness spread across the veld. He checked his glee. "Oh, shit!" he said, suddenly quite sombre, "even after a revolution, this will still be here." There was an unusual nakedness to the moment which fixed it and the dusty starkness of the scene in Felix's memory.

But before long he began less to notice the unpredictabilities than the uniformity, the recurring samenesses underlying all the different shows. With exceptions—but were they recognised?—all the audible black voices at the readings seemed to become one voice. It was not simply that themes of protest and resistance were predominant. It was that—here where there had not yet been the time for European literary conformities to be imposed, conventions that might be expected to refine and tame experience for the sake of aesthetic order—the actual testimony of experience was thin and repetitious.

It was as if these poets, instead of drawing detail and intimacy from their own lives, were striving to speak for their communities, to achieve a communal voice. But to succeed at that would require rare qualities of imagination, so most of the attempts failed. What should have justified the openness of the Authors' Union and the unselectiveness of the readings—the multifarious voice of actuality, that larger portion hidden from whites by the country's habits of segregation—that voice was still mainly missing. The protest poets, those whose promise of power lay in that they could reveal, from the inside, the realities of their oppression and their anger, sounded in most cases as though they had never *been* inside, as though they possessed only second-hand knowledge of their own lives and wrote of them, coded into monumental stereotypes and hyperboles, as a matter of pious obligation rather than living urgency. Shrill tones of outrage, even when their message was known to be true, sounded of a learnt or imitated indignation, a competitive effort to shock.

And they did shock, those defiant, insulting proclamations, hungry for destruction and bloodshed. Felix was shocked, though less by the threat of possible horrors to come than by the immediate incongruities. The party of whites who made their way to the townships to participate in the readings was always warmly, even tenderly, welcomed by fellow Union members. Yet in the angry recitations that followed there might be nothing to indicate that people like these "writer friends" were exempted from the blanket of mockery, denunciation and menace flung over all whites or all "Boers".

And then, beyond spurts of gleeful applause, there were no reverberations, no apparent consequences attached to these aggressive words either by blacks or openly by whites. The few who were troubled confined themselves for the moment to frowns and murmurs. The result was that the negation of words, already effected by drums, handclaps, whistles and xylophones, was compounded. The meaning of the most terrible lines must be allowed to fall out still-born—and the deafness needed to manage this had of necessity also to close out both the most innocuous and the most magical lines. Any other response would be divisive, at the very least discourteous.

"It must be so frustrating," Rebecca commented to Felix after a particularly bloodthirsty reading, "to dare to say such hair-raising things out loud in public....and nobody seems to notice. It's like another kind of censorship."

Henry Walters and Steven Malley were not inclined to compliant loyalty, but their situations only rarely allowed them to come to readings. As for the representatives of the Afrikaans Guild, members of the very "Boer" race that was most often denounced, it was no surprise that after two or three readings they stopped attending. Their presence and, much more, their precarious standing as dissenters, had been ignored, in fact spurned.

Having Oliver Vaughn's ear—sometimes in his antique "Beetle" on the road to or from readings, sometimes in the FrontBooks office before committee meetings—Felix seized opportunities both to learn and to challenge. Once he asked, "Doesn't it surprise you that those angry orators we've just been listening to serve their own cause so inadequately?"

"What now, Felix?"

"Well, they declare their rage clearly enough, but they tell their audience so little about what causes it—I mean so little that's new, and particular There's hardly any specific, revealing detail."

"Their audience is the community. And the community knows all the details of the oppression. Hearing about the rage is new, and forward looking."

"But *we* were in the audience, and some of that rage was generalised in a way that included us."

"You will insist," Vaughn protested, wincing, "on looking at things from an individualistic point of view. The community is not looking at a few friendly whites in the audience, but the whole oppressor class. Try to see past your conditioning for once. Something very important is beginning to happen in the black communities, they are rediscovering the communal voice, their own African forms of creativity. And the Authors' Union can be a part of it."

Grassroots had become the unofficial organ of the Authors' Union. The writings in its pages—many of them the very pieces that had been performed—neither supported nor muffled by musical accompaniments, lay naked in the flatness of print, the aliveness of the few revealed, the thinness, violence or confused inarticulacy of the many exposed. But this evidence seemed to have escaped *Grassroots*' editorial collective, so innocently had poems and non-poems, stories and non-stories, art and artless gestures, been laid side by side in its pages. It was an unforgivable innocence: it withheld distinction from the better work, robbing its authors of the recognition that was their due and, even worse, of the encouragement and criticism by which they might have grown.

Eventually Felix came out with it: "Oliver, I know *Grassroots* achieves many good things, but what about standards?"

Vaughn's sidelong glance as he drove was ironical but easy. "Literary standards, you mean?"

"Exactly. There seems to to be no discrimination."

"Whose literary standards are you talking about?"

"Well, mine, yours, those you work to in your own poems everybody's..."

"There's no such thing as everybody's standards. So many of us ignore the fact that our standards come out of our history and material conditions." Vaughn spoke as though in some pain.

"I don't altogether understand that. But in any case, all we can trust and aspire after and apply as the standard is the excellence each of us has perceived, felt, been moved by. Out of that come the consensus we make judgements by. Is there any other way do justice to the talent of the few?"

"That kind of subjectivism always ends with elitism."

"But you know that not everybody is equally talented. So when there's so much being presented that is poor—stuff that's weak, or blatant and crude, the few good things by those who are potentially real writers get buried among the rest, because *Grassroots* implies that they are all equally worthy of publication."

"Have you never thought that the township writers could be in the process of making something new? They're rediscovering their communal oral tradition and they're trying to do something fresh with it under new conditions. These are early days."

"Is that what you believe is happening?" Felix took hold of the chance to retreat from a quarrel. "Okay, I'll watch for that... But in the meantime *Grassroots* is disappointing."

"Disappointing to whom?" This response was a dry little joke rather than a challenge, and all Felix answered was, "Yes, well..."

A young protégé of chairman Msomi's was charged with being in possession of a banned political publication which the security police had found when they raided his home. The Authors' Union arranged his defence, sent a number of the executive committee to observe the court proceedings, and, after the dismaying verdict, paid his fine, much as though it were the Union itself that was on trial. Rebecca fetched Felix and they sat with the contingent through the two days of fascinating though troubling ritual. The shiftiness and determination of the prosecution's police witnesses both alarmed him and teased his credulity. Were they really as obstinately fixed on securing a conviction, as indifferent to facts and justice as they seemed to be, or was his perception distorted by his connection with the Union?

The censors had invited writers and publishers to submit for their scrutiny works not yet in print, to avoid the risk of being banned. "We don't have dealings with the regime's censors," Tshepo Msomi decreed. He was putting to the executive committee a motion that would prohibit the Union's members from accepting the insulting option, even if they wished to.

He seemed to know how to use the wording of a resolution, the timing of a vote, to get the results he wanted. Again and again apparently straightforward issues turned out to have unexpected implications in terms of either democratic or communal requirements. The gift of a mini-bus had to be refused because the corporation offering it had accepted government contracts. A film-maker who wanted to make a television documentary on the Union's readings dropped the project because the committee's permission was so hedged about with conditions. Interviews for an article about the Union for the township edition of a newspaper were refused, because publishing a township edition was considered a form of racial discrimination.

Someone complained that Wilson Nthuli and Harry Fordham had been charging entrance fees at their popular one-poet readings.

"And this is discrimination against blacks because most of us can't be able to pay."

"Well, they'll have to be disciplined," Msomi declared.

Felix exploded: "You can't do that. Surely authors have the right to earn money by their work if they can."

Henry Walters put in: "My impression was that the Union was constituted to protect our rights, not take them away."

"Of course! And anyway," Felix added, "Harry Fordham is not going to let the Union tell him what he can and can't do with his own work and he's not going to accept your discipline."

"Maybe," said Msomi quietly. "But we'll deal with Wilson."

"We'll deal...who's *we*?" Felix demanded.

There was no answer from Msomi but a straight look.

Rebecca muttered, "Mafia!"

No one else commented.

"Do you go along with Tshepo's ideas of discipline in the Union?" Felix taxed Vaughn at his first opportunity.

"Yes. He's looking after the stability of the structure."

"But, come on, Oliver! What about the individual members' freedom of choice?"

"What about it?" Vaughn's tone was bantering. "The Union expresses the wishes of the community. That takes priority at this stage."

"But for God's sake! Individuality? Where else does writing begin? Look at your own style, your individuality."

Vaughn gave an irritated sigh. "I haven't been writing. In any case, it's not for us to express the people's experience. It's their struggle—their poems, their stories."

"But what about ours? All the separate stories we have to tell?"

"I think," Vaughn said with a wince of tormented acerbity, "the culture of bourgeois individualism is pernicious., sterile."

"Sterile?"

"Yes, sterile. Think of the western writer, cloistered among his bookshelves in his study, and his reader, just as isolated, playing the game of decoding the printed pages. Think of their distance from each other, their separateness from everyone. I remember once being in a taxi in New York, looking up at all those windows, all those separated lives, and suddenly feeling a desperately sad loneliness. All those individual people with their own separate concerns, knowing nothing of each other except as competitors. I felt cold, scared..."

Because this revealed as much about Vaughn's susceptibilities as his ideas, Felix's indignation was deflected. All he said was, "One doesn't have to see it that way."

"One has to if one is realistic. That atomisation is dictated by the material conditions of bourgeois society. But here in Africa we have an alternative form of social organisation for the arts. Africa's tradition of communality knows nothing of that terrible bourgeois loneliness. The artist is not an individual voice speaking with a vague hope that somebody somewhere will understand. He is the voice of the community speaking to the community."

"But why does the community need him if it already knows everything he can say?"

"He gives voice and form to the community's aspirations, its fears and its wisdom. The community needs his gifts, but he can't perform without the active presence of the audience. Think of the traditional story-tellers, the grand-mother in the family, taking her cues from the children's responses...and think of oral poets cohesively surrounded by their audiences and inspired by the feedback they get."

"That's marvellous in its way—but that's just one kind of artistry. What when the poet or story-teller uses print? He needs to work in privacy with nothing watering down his independence, because he has something new and unique to give?"

"You're thinking of art in terms of commodities, material trade, not in terms of the people's ordinary life, a healthy society."

"Am I? I don't think that's so. You're talking about a connectedness between like and like, and I'm concerned about connectedness between unlike and unlike. Without that nothing grows."

"Ah, well..." Vaughn said, with a laugh, "it's your class-conditioning speaking."

At the Union's annual general meeting, Vaughn proposed Rebecca Saffer as secretary in place of himself. She, in turn, nominated Felix back onto the committee and, to his surprise, he was re-elected. He had imagined that his comments at meetings had been regarded as obstructive. Also the onset of a pinched nerve with persistent sciatica had been tempting him to reduce his activities and drop out of the Union. But Rebecca's wish for his continuance persuaded him.

Some weeks later a newspaper commissioned him to review an anthology of black writings edited by Tshepo Msomi. The introduction contained a call to "bash and twist the old forms into new forms and spit on white elitist so-called standards that want to straitjacket the people's bold experiments and inventions." This was a warning, but Felix wrote his piece, praising what he could, criticising what he had to. He submitted it nervously, yet was unprepared for Vaughn's message some days after the review appeared: "Tshepo tells me the people say you are not their friend."

Flustered, Felix asked, "And what do you think?"

"I can see what they mean," Vaughn said.

"What they mean," Rebecca quipped when Felix told her, "is that you are not the kind of best friend who wouldn't tell them about halitosis."

"But if they don't want to know," Felix pleaded, "what's the use of my saying it?"

Rebecca shrugged.

He went back to Vaughn later and told him, "I don't seem to know what I'm doing in the Union at all. I'm going to resign."

Vaughn eyed him hard. "Oh. Is it that bad? I'm sorry. Look, don't act in haste. Things take time. Give the Union a chance."

His appeal surprised Felix, perhaps flattered his vanity. "Do you imagine there's anything useful I can do?"

"Yes, surely. Your membership is useful."

"Very well, then," Felix yielded, "I'll stay with it. But"—this was a warning as much as a promise—"I'm going to be less passive from now on. I'm going to try to make things happen. Find my own contribution."

"Of course," said Vaughn. "That's fine. That's as it should be."

His first move came at the next committee meeting. "I remember talk about creative writing workshops at our inaugural conference. Isn't it time something was done about that? How about the Union running a series of workshops? I for one would be willing to teach, for as long as I'm wanted." He knew from experience that there were things he could teach. And among the township writers he might have the chance to midwife talents in danger of strangulation by ignorance, confusion or neglect.

The idea went down well in the committee. Henry Walters indicated that he too would be available for teaching, and half-promised the absent Stephen Malley's help. Two township members were appointed to investigate practicalities such as venues, transport, demand, availability of teachers. Once his proposal had been accepted, however, Felix's urgency was lulled. More than a month passed before he felt the need to enquire what was happening. The answer, that the sub-committee was canvassing the demand, was suspiciously vague, but by then a new urgency had overtaken the first.

The surprise was how small a thing it took to sharpen the friendly running debate between himself and Vaughn into a more urgent contest. It was his second, and secondary, attempt to "make things happen". He suggested a minor addition to the Union's present programme of activities—an occasional poetry reading which, instead of being open to all comers, would present readers whose work a panel of editors or talent-scouts had found to be particularly interesting. His hope was that these selective readings would provide a way of acknowledging talent, and that aspirant poets in the audience would have a chance to discover the connection between poetic art and the listeners' pleasure.

But the response to his proposal was uneasy, almost suspicious. Question followed question until time ran out, so the decision had to be held over for the next meeting. The next day, however, Oliver Vaughn appeared on his doorstep.

"I've come to ask you," he explained, "to drop your proposal for these readings."

"But, why?" Felix demanded in bewilderment.

"It would harm the Union."

"Harm? What on earth could be more harmless than a few readings where we try to put the emphasis on the actual poetry?"

"You're seeing things from a white perspective."

"I don't know what that means. I am white—but so what? I'm trying to get our attention off race and onto poetry."

"Your readings will be seen as a white initiative. Most of the readers will be white."

"I suppose so, at first. But it depends on the talent that appears. The point is that we'll be bringing out the poetry, whoever makes it."

"That isn't the point. Your readings would carry the label of being the real thing, and the open readings would be sidelined."

This checked Felix. "Oh, I see. Yes, that could happen. That's not what I want. But surely—"

Vaughn cut in: "It could invalidate the whole Union experiment. The community writers are exploring something new and very important."

"So you've told me several times," Felix grumbled, "but I've seen no sign of it yet."

"There are signs," Vaughn urged. "Believe me."

"Well, if that really is the case..." Felix pondered. "Look, let me think about what you're asking of me."

Vaughn left it at that, but once alone Felix found his thoughts rushing in a spiral of bewilderment and indignation. It was as though Vaughn discerned, if not a sinister intention, an infection against which the health of the Authors' Union had to be guarded. But what could this disease be, so shameful that the inoculation could not be administered democratically in the openness of a committee meeting, but only in private? Or perhaps it was in the inoculation itself that the shame lay, since the disease could only be the distinctions and disciplines and liberties that made poetry possible.

For Vaughn, evidently, there was a higher cause, and Felix did not doubt its idealistic nature: there was no viciousness in that philosophical dreamer—his Authors' Union had been devised to serve a benign purpose. But that purpose was at odds with the making of poetry, and therein lay a deception. This was why the priority of the higher cause had to be hidden from its intended beneficiaries; this was why aspirant poets on the executive committee could not be invited into a debate to consider, essentially, whether or not they ought to be exposed to an exercise in quest of literary art. They would never vote to be protected against precisely what they aspired toward. Vaughn was not so crass that he would ask them to agree that the authentic pursuit was not for them.

Felix telephoned Vaughn to tell him he was writing out a defence of his proposal.

"That's excellent," Vaughn said. "I look forward to reading it. Will you post it to me?"

But his reaction to the letter was neither a capitulation nor the broadside of polemic for which Felix braced himself. Instead, there was silence, no response at all. Felix waited a week, then telephoned again.

Vaughn commented only, "Well, you haven't been quite fair to me."

Felix bridled. "Why didn't you let me know? You knew I was waiting. Anyhow, what did I say that was unfair?"

"It's a complicated matter of perception," Vaughn said. "Look, I think we should read your letter to the committee and discuss it there."

The suggestion cut from under Felix his suspicion about Vaughn's motive in visiting him. "Perfect. I'll hold back for that." But at the next committee meeting, in fact, the matter was crowded out by more pressing business. Then followed almost two months during which the Union was mysteriously dormant—no committee meetings were called, no readings took place. And at the end of that hibernation, Felix's scheme and Vaughn's objections to it were both, suddenly, equally, annulled.

Into a small theatre on a Saturday morning crowded sixty or seventy members of the Authors' Union. They were gathered for the extraordinary general meeting called to decide whether their organisation should continue in existence. There were rumours, and a mood of perplexity and anger dominated. The chairman's opening statement, however, dealt dryly with alternative ways "to address this urgent situation", as though the circumstances were already known.

Henry Walters asked, "What has happened to make this necessary?"

Msomi responded, "I think you'd better hear for yourself from the community."

Speakers from the townships then described the dilemma that they had been placed in. They had received warnings, and then, increasingly, been threatened, ostracised and harassed for being members of a multi-racial organisation. A few others brought contradictory testimony, and the debate erupted. Bewilderment, indignation, recriminations, pleas, counter-proposals, satire, insistence, despair.

"But I thought we'd formed the Union to resist racialism. We've been standing up to the censors and intimidation from the police, and fighting back all the time. Why now cave in to a splinter political group, and for the worst possible reason—someone objects to our non-racialism?"

"Some of our white members don't understand the difference between non-racialism and multi-racialism. This Authors' Union is multi-racial. Multi-racialism is racist."

Msomi had taken the chair, but made no pretence of neutrality. From early on he let it appear that he was determined on dissolving the Union, and rejected every compromise by which it might be avoided. Oliver Vaughn listened almost silently for a long time. At last he stood up and, with a resigned shrug, conceded, "Well, perhaps we have to accept that this is the wrong historical moment for a development like the Authors' Union."

He said very little else, and Felix guessed at a stoic grimness in him that precluded winces as well as smiles. There was no sign of grimness, however, during the lunch recess when they exchanged banter while he helped Felix, hampered by his sciatica, down a flight of stairs and across the street to a tea-room. And he laughed easily when Rebecca called to him, "Oliver, I'm trying to decide if it's the right historical moment for a toasted cheese sandwich or for fruit salad and ice-cream."

Deep into the afternoon session Henry Walters said, "I'd like to read out an excerpt from our constitution."

Msomi gave an impatient shake of the head, as though a fly were on his ear: "No, no, no...that document's not relevant in this situation."

"Yes, I agree with you," Walters responded, "not at all relevant—since we're spurning it." Msomi ignored the sarcasm.

Through the hours the assembly had steadily shrunk as confused and indifferent members had slipped away. When there were hardly more than twenty left Steven Malley proposed an adjournment, "...so that this important decision can be taken by a broader representation of the membership."

Msomi declared, "Yes, it is an important decision. That's why we have to have a result today. We've got a quorum. We don't need any more delays." He ignored Malley's whoof of indignation, and peremptorily put the motion to the vote. The result was twelve ayes, seven no's, two abstentions.

"For once," Rebecca muttered, "perhaps it's kosher to count by race."

Felix concurred sourly, and they tallied the ten blacks including Msomi who, with Vaughn and another white radical, had voted for dissolution, the two blacks and one Indian among the opposers, and the two black abstainers. Most of those, nearly all blacks, who had left the meeting, he guessed, were in fact bewildered abstainers, and theirs was the the true majority.

Msomi announced the result, then he appointed two committee members to assist the treasurer and secretary in the business of winding up, and declared the Authors' Union duly dissolved.

"How could Oliver vote that way?" Felix complained to Rebecca driving away afterwards. "The Union was his baby. Maybe Tshepo's instrument, but Oliver's baby. He hated the motion—did you notice how little he had to say all day?—and yet, because Tshepo demanded it..."

"Oliver's a politician," Rebecca pointed out. "He calculates what he has to do for his his cause."

"I suppose so, 'the wrong historical moment'—whatever that means. But there's something wrong, something damaged..."

A newspaper reported that on Sunday, the day after the demise of the Union, a meeting was held in Soweto at which an Association of Black Writers was founded, with Tshepo Msomi as its president. Later Rebecca told Felix that one of the first acts of the new body was to authorise its president to ask Vaughn to summon a quorum of the defunct Union's executive committee, including especially the treasurer, so that the funds of the Authors' Union could be transferred to the ABW.

"God, that's cheeky!" Felix protested. "Does Oliver agree to it?"

"Well, he says it sorts out who gets the funds."

"I'm sure that's what Tshepo says too. It's amazing how he always knows the next move."

"What he's asked for now isn't a meeting," Rebecca quipped. "It's a seance."

"And Oliver's the ghost."

Still lending a hand at FrontBooks, Rebecca brought Felix the occasional item of news. One of the township youngsters she encountered in the *Grassroots* office, Vusi, told her that the Union in its day had, in fact, organised a number of writing workshops, with Msomi, Vaughn, and some others as 'facilitators'. Vusi had found them not very useful—they had dealt mainly with relevance and solidarity, hardly at all with writing.

"So why weren't we called on—Henry, Stephen and me? Why was it kept from us?"

"Well, politics. What do *you* know about facilitating relevance and solidarity?" The final twist was Msomi's applying to the Swedish sponsors of *Grassroots* to divert their funding to the ABW's proposed new magazine, *Solid*, since it alone would be the authentic outlet for black writing. The Swedes were considering it, and the whole FrontBooks venture had been put at risk.

"I've never heard Oliver say anything against Tshepo until today, when he found out about this," Rebecca reported. "It really hurt him."

"You know, Rebecca," Felix said, "there are certain acts of selflessness that enrage me. Somehow, though Tshepo has been treacherous and I know he has hurt Oliver deeply again, it is part of what Oliver allowed from the beginning, and I can't forgive him."

"He hurt us all, in a way,"

"Yes, that is so. I never quite saw it before. And I allowed my hurt, too. Is that why I'm so angry? I should have known all along that the Union was not for me. The politics was bound to swallow up everything else."

Rebecca shrugged. "I'm sticking to my typewriter from now on." She was only half joking.

A couple of weeks later came a sequel. "Oliver told me he made an appointment with Bishop Khumalo to talk about the failure of the Union."

"But what does Khumalo know about it?"

"No," Rebecca explained. "Oliver wanted his opinion of the black writers' rejection of us whites. Do we have a place here, a part to play, or would it be better if we got out?"

"My God!" Felix shook his head. "I'm astonished! Well, what did Khumalo say?"

"He said whites of goodwill were needed, and at the least, Oliver as a writer could bear witness."

"Well, yes, of course. But the idea of Oliver, the dialectical materialist, consulting the bishop—I can't get over that. And what if Khumalo had said go?"

"I think he would have gone," said Rebecca. "He is hurt enough."

A long time after it was over, Felix had a dream about the Union. It had moved its office into new premises, a small hall in one of the shabbier, more mixed, older suburbs. There was a poetry reading. A throng of different sorts of people was miraculously accommodated on a single row of chairs lining the four walls. It included one or two rabbinical figures out of Old Jerusalem or Chagall. But the reading took the form of a church meeting. He sat with a few sheets of poetry in his hand awaiting his turn, and noticed Oliver Vaughn heartily joining in the hymn singing. An interval was announced and most of the company left the hall. Now one more rabbi, dwarfish, laden like a peddler with baskets of delicatessen, arrived. He went into the little kitchen on one side and there began unloading his packages.

Felix told him: "There's a mistake. You're making a mistake."

The little man nodded, smiled, shrugged, and went on laying out parcels of halvah, beigels, olives, snoek....

16

Faith

Felix was still full of anger over the way political motives had been allowed to destroy the Authors' Union. His account of the Union's three years, which he needed to write in order to purge his bitterness, was barely begun. At the same time, a pinched sciatic nerve was hampering his mobility and draining his energy. He was feeling a threat of narrowing possibilities in his life.

Alison was one of a handful of recruits to the seminar at the start of a new year, one of those new people who introduced a fresh excitement of expectancy. Her offerings, both creative and critical, were acute, imaginative and powerful, her stories bravely frank in their exploration of passions. His role as her teacher was to point out the occasional blurs and excesses, and to applaud. But something made it uncomfortable to pay her due tribute in the presence of the other participants in the seminar, so he wrote her a note. In response, eager to get the whole measure of his recognition, she came to visit him. Face to face they recognised a need in each that the other particularly met, so that, immediately, they were friends, and very soon after, lovers.

She was an academic lecturer, her intellectuality electrified by a powerful sense of self that was also a sense of theatre. Her bell-like voice, ready, deep-throated laugh, her lively movements, and the upright way her torso rode the broad seawave of her lower body, like a surfer, all gave her a striking attractiveness. Her eyes, wide and eloquent, and the intensity of her inner life, reminded him of Lucilla. But Alison, so frankly, unambiguously, committed to her aliveness, embodied an earthier, more humorous version of the vibrancy that had captivated him in Lucilla. Long before this meeting he had read in a magazine a story memorably celebrating a small girl's initiation by her playmates into the wild excitement of erotic games. The discovery that Alison was its author brought him not only the surprise of coincidence but also the piquancy of recognising that writer's voice, that child's hot breath and flushed face, in the woman who had come to him.

Apart from her affirmative hunger for what she saw in him and what he could give her, that which attracted him most strongly was the mystery of her fullness. She was full—signs and implications pointed to the fact—of a world of ideas and experiences, friendships and activities, a world she intelligently enjoyed, in which her astonishing appetite for him was offering him a place, even the pride of place—as he was inviting her to take pride of place in his world. He felt ready to participate in that fullness of hers, ready with her, this unforseeably complete, yea-saying mate whom he had been awaiting, to make, discover or explore a fullness of happiness.

But when they had been lovers for a while, he became aware that, beside the eloquence of her eyes and the aliveness of her thinking, there was something else that also recalled Lucilla. It was the theme of injury in her history, her way of attracting injuries. In the main they came of mere bad luck, accident, biology; but there was also a motif of compelled behaviour that counterpointed her intelligent *joie de vivre*. The first meaning of this damage, now that he was in love with her, was that he was being called on for protection. But how was he to protect her from the scars of a painful girlhood, the wounds of two failed marriages, the vulnerability of mothering a small child under the jealous surveillance of an unfriendly ex-husband, the aftershock of a malady that had almost taken her life, the inner, and sometimes outward, bruises she incurred through her intense and complicated relationship with the young man she lived with?

This last above all. If the feelings that had brought that liaison into being were now so curbed by coldness and brutality that she was able to find a space for the love that had sprung up for Felix, he soon recognised that the earlier passion was far from being burnt out. Perhaps one of the things he could do was to help her extricate herself from an entanglement which was becoming harmful to her three-year-old daughter as well as to herself. But she was profoundly ambivalent: the young man, Carl, was beautiful, strong, talented, a thrilling conquest for her to have made. The entanglement went into her innards like a tumour; to be rid of it she might have to lose so much of herself that she would not survive.

By the time Felix came to know about all this, Alison's way of being had become so precious to him that he could not think of subjecting his possession to any kind of threat. Nor could he think, bear to think, after the first apocalyptic month or two of their love, that the increased restrictions on the time she could spend in his sole company, the attenuation of the caresses she allowed him, meant anything but what she said they did. Her child, her academic work, her health, old friendships, the very appetite for living that he loved in her, all made claims on her. Meanwhile, her confusing struggle over the great change she knew she had to make inhibited her passions, required her to conserve her emotional energies, be inwardly as still as possible so that she could think through and work through her feelings and her situation. All this demanded of him only an abeyance of expectation, which became painful enough as months passed bringing no restoration. But though he went through moments of anger he could see no alternative to passively waiting.

After emerging from one of his innumerable breakdowns, Russell Hoekstra, the Beatnik poet Felix had first met in Paris and who'd bobbed up like a clownish Mephisto at intervals ever since, had come to live with his mother in her flat ten minutes' walk from Felix's place. He made a habit of dropping in. With or without warning by telephone he arrived sometimes more than once in a day, occasionally bringing a book or magazine or stick of chocolate as a gift, almost always fired by some urgent need. He had a new poem or fable to show, or wanted to use the typewriter to record an inspiration that had just struck him; he needed a cup of coffee—into which he would shovel five, six, seven, eight spoonfuls of sugar; he needed to complain about his oppressively conventional mother, or about some rival poet or some purblind editor or the whole hopelessly provincial local literary scene, or else about his headache, his anxiety neurosis or depression; he needed to lie down a while and calm himself, or to phone his psychiatrist or the fantastically perverse woman he had spent last night with.

On his way to or from Felix, he usually exchanged some chaff with Peter the gardener. Asked for his name, Russell replied, "Jesus". To Peter, not being a Christian, the joke name was as useful as any other. So in gossip thereafter between him and Felix, Russell remained "Jesus".

His visits disrupted Felix's peace and eroded his working time, but he would have been a complacent spectator of Russell's performance if he had been allowed a passive role. After all, this was a fairly amusing show, generated in a bizarre and witty imagination. But Russell loved to entangle his audiences in his farces and dramas. At times he presented Felix with an extravagant compliment or hallucinatory accusation that demanded a response, or arrived urgent with some more or less benign scheme, usually some ploy for achieving immediate fame, of which Felix was to take advantage by writing to someone in Paris, or by sending a wad of his work to Los Angeles, Athens or Calcutta. He could as easily take fire with an idea that was preposterous or vicious, one that would require Felix to forswear himself, betray friends or principles, lend or pledge sums of money, or let himself be dragged into some bizarre, inconvenient adventure.

The demand one day was, "I need to tear a book. Give me a book to tear up." As usual Felix resisted, but this time Russell insisted, pleaded, made it a matter of his health. "I have to do it. Look how my hands are shaking. I've got red sparks exploding in my brain. How can you refuse me such a little thing? Here, can I tear up this one?"

"No," Felix protested. "That one, rather." He indicated one of those unlovable slim review copies that occasionally found their way to his shelves. Emitting dog-like growls, Russell set about mangling the book and managed to inflict a ragged rip through the thickness of all the pages and the cover before losing interest. He had not broken the spine or torn pages out, so the wrecked volume remained one piece.

"Now write on the the flyleaf," Felix commanded, " 'I vandalised this book' and sign and date it. I'm going to keep it as evidence."

And, half-ashamed, half-amused, Russell complied.

More often, his manipulations left Felix as the one accused. He came out as meanly possessive when he refused to give Russell a woman friend's telephone number, coldly puritanical if he would not endorse a surrealistic slander on someone Russell wanted to punish, or as party to an unimaginative elitist conspiracy bent on suppressing all originality when he was unwilling to promote work he did not care for. Even the embarrassed quality of his amusement at some of Russell's wilder sexual boasts or fantasies was somehow to his discredit: "You're so damn prudish, so square and careful." Or else: "Your kind of bourgeois solemnity is sickening. It's pure dishonesty."

One day it was: "I don't understand how you can claim to be such an admirer of de Waal."

"Why?"

"He was a free creative spirit, he knew how to laugh and live dangerously, like Villon. He teased the bourgeoisie, like Jaroslav Hasek. He really scandalised your respectable Johannesburg."

"All that was long before I met him." The mature de Waal he had known—the warmly encouraging writing "coach" at whose feet no lesson in literary technique had been quite separable from a lesson in life—no longer went in for the defiant and satirical pranks he had been notorious for when young and otherwise unrecognised.

"That was the real de Waal," Russell insisted. "You'd have been afraid to have anything to do with him, never mind claiming him as your mentor."

It was one of those moments when, under siege, Felix wondered if there could be some truth mixed with the paranoia and sheer fanciful mischief of these charges. Now the doubt touched his relation to de Waal's complicated spirit: how dare he confidently assume that he had understood it sufficiently and faithfully expressed it in speaking and writing about his mentor and in editing his posthumous volumes?

He took refuge in mock admiration: "Russell, sometimes you display a truly Satanic power of insight." Russell's indignant scowl gave way to a grin and a triumphant guffaw.

Week by week in the afternoon sessions of the writing seminar a young school teacher, Tony, had been charting the course of a ruinous love affair in a series of tortured poems. He arrived one day not, as once or twice before, in the company of his heart-breaker, but with a woman dressed in a white caftan whom he introduced as Velma. Felix's first guess was that the destructive romance had been broken off at last in favour of this stranger whose black hair fell in a screen, helping to conceal the eyes she seemed unwilling to show except in sidelong glances, just as she hid the lines of her body in the tent-like caftan. The way she clung to Tony, exchanging whispered remarks with him during the readings and discussion, turning her gaze mainly onto him when it was not bent to the table in front of her, suggested intimacy and an immature nervous excitement. Felix was mildly irritated at this visit to the seminar by someone who seemed not quite interested in the proceedings, but he mentally congratulated Tony on acquiring a warmer, prettier partner to replace the elusive girl who'd been tormenting him.

He proved mistaken on several scores. Velma was present again at the next week's session. This time her attention was less concentrated on Tony and it seemed she was interested in the work. She made her critical comments with laconic brevity indicating not shy reluctance but a sulky self-assurance. Her own presentation was a long prose poem abundantly decked with symbols in a pre-Raphaelite manner. Matching the exotic style, the content at first seemed fantastical. But as Felix followed its surreal flourishes he began to recognise allusions to things of his own that had been published—the story of a Jewish child who imagined himself the incarnation of Christ's second coming, others about certain amours, disappointments and betrayals—as well as references to characteristics of his face and movements and to the very table they were sitting at. Could this be a disguised letter to himself? The signs were many, cunningly chosen for his particular recognition. But if he was the person addressed, it was a romantic, canonised version of him, and the coding was dense enough for doubt. So he hesitated to make any response to her obscure message—her possible confession of compulsion, her plea to be recognised in some special way—and offered nothing beyond the objective aesthetic assessment that was proper to the seminar.

And might indeed have left it at that, except privately to savour a vain man's bemused gratification at this curious baroque item of flattery, might even have interpreted as a warning all the uncongenial signs in Velma's manner and her writing style. Might have, but for the perplexing turn in his love relationship. If he had been enjoying Alison's closeness, even merely been certain that he would again enjoy it, he would have noted Velma's eccentric overture with the detachment of immunity to its temptation.

As it was, since the affirmations he derived from Alison's love were more and more being eroded by delay and doubt, he suppressed the suspicion that he was beginning to re-enact a sterile pattern he had lived through several times before: he allowed Velma's prose poem to fill him with bewildered excitement and an irresistible curiosity. Before the next afternoon seminar he wrote her a letter intimating his interpretation of the poem and the feelings it had stirred. He handed it to her as though it were one of the notes of critical advice he occasionally gave to students whose problems needed more than an impromptu comment.

Startlement, circumspection, curiosity and excitement smouldered in her answering letter. Whatever she'd known of him had driven her to try to know him better. Now that he had acknowledged her signal she was half afraid of the mood he had expressed. Her life was embedded in her role as wife, housewife and mother of grown children (it pleased Felix, somehow, to discover that she was not what her appearance suggested, a girl in her twenties, but a woman past forty). "But you have become necessary to my inner vision," she wrote. "And, Felix, I know you will soon learn that I, too, am necessary to you." She gave him her address and telephone number, so their communication was no longer confined to the seminar.

And so the strange game between them began, at first a romantic exploration of a mystery, then the testing of limits, finally on his side a grasping for the consolation of erotic intimacy, on hers compliance, for the sake of something else hinted at but not defined. Two or three times she drove over to visit him, but her domestic situation, her Christian principles, precluded any bodily expression of their excitement. Their exchange was a matter of words, thoughts, letters. This hunger for a louche, papery surrogate for sex seemed to be his particular vice which took hold whenever the game appeared attainable. And he recognised that though it had germinated from his limitations, it was rooted within the heart of the talent that empowered and freed him—his relative skill with the written word, his native manumition in the province of language. Aspiration and depravity involved the same gift. The game did not concern love.

In any case, he was in love with Alison and clung to the distracting possibility that she would come back as his lover.

When finally Alison summoned the strength to dismiss Carl from her house, Felix had played only the negative role of wishing and waiting for this resolution. But instead of releasing her for him, the break plunged her into a state of grief. Now less than ever, while she mourned and waited to mend, was it possible to demand anything of her. He had to hold himself from impinging on her, even with sympathy, even with understanding. All he must do was endure her waiting, wait for her healing.

For him too this phase was a dark passage, full of deep pain, disappointment, bewilderment. On top of everything else, his sciatica was worsening, robbing him of sleep, redoubling all his ordinary disability, making it impossible for him to remain on his feet for more than a few minutes, virtually imprisoning him in his flatlet except when there were strong arms to help him through to the house or out to a car. The shadowiness of the room to which he was more and more confined began to seem a larger sort of twilight. Well into spring that year Johannesburg received one of its rare snowfalls, and Gail, understanding how he needed to be lifted out of himself, took him for a drive to see how the suburbs were transformed. Felix recognised the loveliness of the quilted roofs, trees and gardens, but he looked through it to three days of intermittent snow a decade or so earlier, when the sifting whiteness had seemed to bring the city a magical renewal that caught everyone up in its huge euphoria: this time he felt no joy, but a remote melancholy.

As his hopes of an easy cure receded, dismay filled him: it seemed that his life was beginning to close down. In recent years he had found and nursed the proposition that to be reconciled to the inevitability of death was to be made unafraid and therefore liberated to explore and enjoy the fullness of life. But now that he was sensing his mortality, his power to explore and enjoy was reduced by the new feebleness of his body. Another idea of his had been that the point of experience was the pursuit of meaning—meaning that would off-set the nullity of death and also would accumulate through human history until a great, complete Meaning was understood, or rather, brought into being (he could find no more satisfying sense to attach to "God"). But now that so many things he had hoped or even intended to experience were drifting beyond possibility, he sometimes avenged their frustration with fantasies of abandoning all restraints in a hunt for sensual and sensational gratification—moods in which any quest for meaning was stripped of meaning.

He was reluctant to betray his own secrets, as much as any friend's, to the scandal-monger—who, anyway, was quite capable of inventing scandals to his own Rabelaisian taste—but inevitably Russell sniffed out the fact of his sexual frustration. Inevitably, too, he played on it, raising his art of embarrassment to new heights by a long drawn out campaign of homosexual overtures. He interpreted Felix's uncomfortable resistance to the wooing sometimes as mere humourlessness, sometimes as the pusillanimous reflexes of an unfeeling spirit. Felix took these accusations no more seriously than any of the others concocted by Russell, but his feelings were affected by something stronger than the cunning mischief of the game.

The suggestive teasing was kept up for week after week, deep into the time when Alison's inaccessibility became a perplexity and torment. Her withdrawal renewed the sentence Felix had for such long spells and so often before lived under, the sentence of exclusion from any erotic intimacy. The deprivation magnified and distorted the idea of erotic contact so that it came to seem the only source of real aliveness, the only language of real meaning. Its proper context was the sort of love he had expected to share with Alison. But following such expectation, the fall again of that sentence of exclusion turned his lust rebellious, negated order and defied restraints that were necessary for the sake of meaning. Russell's love of sensation for its own sake made no pretence of meaningfulness. It offered an erotic contact and a dive into the madness of total licence. And suddenly, in this damned mood, Felix desired just that. After wrestling with the fatefulness of this attraction for a few days he met his visitor's expected lewd suggestion one morning with an awkward nod of assent.

Russell gave a look of startlement. "Go *on*!" he exclaimed, and burst into a laugh that was half surprise and half mockery. Felix's surrender had either called his bluff or, if he had not been bluffing, by its intensity had somehow quelled his desire: perhaps after all what he needed in Felix was sanity. Or had the moment of defection presented him with an opportunity for a new and irresistibly piquant form of embarrassment? Whatever the case, this particular farce was now at last over, but its ending left Felix with a bitter, unclean taste of humiliation. As also with a certain dread, since Russell would surely one day incorporate this episode into one of his sensational boasts or slanders.

He did not, though, just yet give up haunting Felix's flatlet. Attempts to discourage him were either ignored or overwhelmed with contemptuous indignation: "How can a supposed man of letters be such a locked-in petit bourgeois? How can a poet be such a cross-thighed virgin?" And while he continued to visit, he continued to provoke and tease, and above all to probe for confidential information about acquaintances, about anyone he happened to see in the vicinity, and especially about Felix himself.

Some weeks after the seduction fiasco, Russell offered, if Felix agreed, to arrange a visit by a woman he had encountered in some hotel lounge. Her name was Tossie and he was sure that for a negotiable sum she would be glad to come to Felix's room and give herself for an hour once in a while. The squalor written into the proposition dismayed Felix, who had imagined long since that he had done with the lovelessness that resorts to prostitutes. Besides, there was always a risk of prankish treachery at Russell's hands. So he held back for a while. But Alison's elusiveness eventually drove him into a mood in which he wanted to forswear her and settle for Velma in his head and Tossie in his bed. He gave Russell the word. But, either because Tossie had moved on, or because Russell's caprice had changed, or the proposal had never been serious, nothing came of it.

In spite of disappointment after disappointment, Felix was kept from despair over Alison by the strength of the friendship they had established. By now she no longer attended his seminar, but they saw each other most often in a circle of writing friends who met regularly to read to each other. He knew what satisfaction she derived from these meetings, and the affection she felt for several in the group. Even during her convalescent retreat after her loss of Carl she attended several times, her manner only slightly subdued. This connection was not one she would willingly break, and she could hardly avoid doing so if she cut herself off from Felix. In any case she had made so many affirmations of many-sided love for him and gratitude for the kinds of recognition he had given her that he could not doubt the bond that had grown between them was real and durable.

Meanwhile, with Velma the game of hot intimacy by letter and telephone went on, though some of the secrets she confided to him seemed to invite sympathy rather than erotic excitement. And there were times when he could not tell what was game and what was troubled history—whether she was advertising her lasciviousness, or hoping by confession to exorcise a frightening compulsion.

Sometimes, though, her narrative spoke clearly of peril and of pain: "I had a kind of breakdown two years ago. All the discipline I need for running my fitness classes just collapsed. I couldn't get up, cried or slept all day. And I hallucinated and I was violent, suicidal, and I don't know what else all I did. I was really in hell."

Yet something in the terms of her survival put a restraint on his sympathy. "Actually it was a blessing in the end. In hospital I started to sculpt and write poetry, and I made friends with two of the other patients who told me things that opened my eyes and changed the direction of my spiritual life."

He had no impulse to enquire what those illuminations had been. So, for all she revealed to him, she remained swathed in a certain secretiveness. Also, despite the special wildness they shared, the language of her thoughts and feelings was foreign to him. She fetched him one Saturday afternoon to take tea at her house and meet some of her family. He was received with bewildered politeness as Velma's invalid writing teacher, the talk punctuated by dutiful enquiries about him flowed more comfortably as it veered away.

Beyond awkwardness and guilt, something else discomposed Felix. The things Velma surrounded herself with, many of them paintings and sculptures from her own hand, were alien to him. Her work was in a ripe flowery style that insisted on a dimension of piety. Did taste matter so much? Or was something other than taste at issue? He had the impression that her decorations were tolerated but scarcely noticed by her family. This was one of several dislocations—the husband seemed precariously uneasy, and so did the daughter, while in her boyfriend's bonhomie there appeared a kind of smugness, expressed also in the flirtatiousness between him and Velma. Felix wished himself away from there.

Many weeks after the breach with her young lover Alison remained inaccessible behind the barrier of her grief. The delay was bringing Felix to a point of embittered bafflement. But when a friend in the reading circle gave a party, he went to it nursing the hope that tonight might mark the completion of his love's recovery. He sat ensconced in the easiest chair trying to ignore his aching back and leg, waiting to see her. She had promised the hostess she would come. It was past ten o' clock when she arrived, and she was escorted by a new handsome young man. Her manner in introducing him to Felix was slightly embarrassed and so all the more eloquent. Later, when the newcomer was engaged in conversation with someone else, she came to stand by Felix again.

"I've been naughty, I know," she said, looking enquiringly into his face.

He nodded glumly. She'd never outgrown the hot-faced child of her story. "Felix, you do understand." Anger surged in him at her words. He understood that he was not young, strong and beautiful. But before he could produce a syllable, she was squeezing his arm and saying, "Whatever else happens, I will always love you, Felix. With the same love." He knew what love she spoke of, and he knew that what she promised was true. Just this was his part of her.

He pressed his anger down.

An outsized window in Mavis's house had been broken. At his typewriter, between sentences of his article on the Authors' Union, Felix watched the glazier at work through his own window, and became aware that that the man was repeatedly glancing in his direction. Peter came by and the glazier engaged him in conversation. The play of their eyes told Felix that he was its subject. When the job was done the glazier knocked tentatively at Felix's French window. "Can I talk with the boss?" he said, and entered the room to stand closer.

"Yes, of course." Felix was mystified. An artisan driving a van would not need to beg for bus fare.

"When I saw the boss, Almighty God told me to come to the boss. God told me to pray with the boss, for Jesus to come into the boss's heart. Can I pray with you, my boss?"

This was an invasion, but so well-meaning was its gentle agent that Felix could not find it in himself to refuse. He nodded, and the glazier placed his hat on the floor, went down on one knee beside Felix's chair, clasped his hands and raised his face and voice in fervent supplication.

Shortly after this incident Velma phoned and, still bemused and amused, Felix told her the story. She met it with a few moments of silence, then said, "I have to come and see you." Half an hour later she was with him. "That was one more sign," she told him. "Another one was that my husband and I decided to separate last week—he's gone to live in a hotel. That man praying with you makes me realise I have to stop procrastinating and give my mission priority. I've been appointed to help you to take our blessed Lord Jesus Christ into your heart."

"No," Felix protested. "I'm not available for that sort of thing. For one thing, I'm Jewish."

"Exactly." She nodded and took hold of his arm. "Listen, you feel not available now because you're still blind. But I have to use my body to bring you to the truth."

"Your body?"

"My sex, and your lust. God can use any instrument."

He had his own—not truth, not yet achieved truth—but his own struggle toward truth, his own frail yet hopeful devices of survival amid tides of irrationality, his own evolved fragments of faith. And his very selfhood, whatever it might be, was bound up with those. Velma, with her designs on a self she perceived but which he could not imagine, was requiring him to default on all these allegiances. But the extraordinarily youthful, splendidly moulded, cunningly instructed body she was now presenting to his eyes and his touch was indeed a powerful instrument. On the barren ground of his desert a kind of manna had snowed down, and he bent to gather and devour.

17

The Lower Parts

At a narrow gap in one of the city's east-west ridges the steep flanking koppies almost nudge each other like friends standing shoulder-to-shoulder. Over the poort, like a shared cloak, is spread the public garden of indigenous flora called The Wilds. A busy road lined with jacaranda trees twists between the shoulders, bisecting the garden and displaying it to the traffic. For some years now the old horizon formed by the shoulder on the west—that primal, rounded skyline rough with rock and bush—has been overtopped by the hulk of the new hospital. A score or so of mansions and their gardens in one of the oldest suburbs were demolished and cleared to make way for it. As seen from points on the road, the structure usurps the koppie's skyline—an enormous shoebox or coffin of naked concrete, almost windowless, with a single iron chimney. The square black pipe climbs like a narrow pilaster up the near end wall, then protrudes high above the block. With its rust-coloured mock-decorative band near the top, it jabs the sky like a rhetorical finger, proclaiming for the hospital, for the city and the age, the rights of functional ugliness. The fumes it emits are usually invisible.

For weeks the hospital became a focus of yearning.

Felix's sciatica had grown intolerable, draining him, pinning him down. Eventually, lumbar spinal surgery had been prescribed. The power of drastic cutting held out the only promise of relief, of restoration. But it was delayed and delayed. Velma, his lover and would-be converter, shared the yearning, helping him storm the hospital's blockhouse fortress. And at the same time, she again and again assailed his agnosticism with the full power of her sensuality and complicity in his fantasies. He swirled in a vortex of bodily distress, mental affront and sexual gratification perplexingly mixed.

She chauffeured him to and from the hospital and dealt for him with enquiries and forms and entanglements of red tape, as his admission for surgery was repeatedly obstructed. First when the in-house neuro-surgeon who was taking charge of the case ordered a preliminary experiment in "conservative treatment" at home; then when additional X-rays were ordered; then when a "long weekend" was found to be imminent; finally when, just as he was about to be wheeled to the operating theatre, Felix confessed to a sore throat and was sent home to recover. And at home, spending hours with him daily throughout the extended waiting time—her attentions most needed when the anti-inflammatory and aspirin prescribed for the conservative experiment doubled his distress and helplessness by drenching his stomach with acidity—Velma, his paramour and his soul's pursuer, was virtually his nurse as well.

Arachnoiditis. The tortured cobwebby membrane enclosed in the bonewalls of his vertebrae had not shown up on the X-ray plates, so the condition had not been given its precise, malignly poetic name before the surgery disclosed it. Now he had imagery for his malady. Inflamed spideriness. Inside the tower of his spine, the little bone dungeon at the hinged pivot of his symmetry, spiders had been at it, scarlet-black and hot, writhing with agonies of their own which they tirelessly avenged on his most inaccessible tissues. Their insidious penetration of that protected chamber of his machinery, that station of the brain cable, had had to be compounded by the neuro-surgeons' metallic assault. Their invasion was in the cause of routing the invisible spiders, relieving the destructive pressure on trapped nerves that produced intractable pain and threatened to paralyse his legs, bowels, bladder and loins. They came as his rescuers, his protectors. But he was a territory broken into, further reduced and full of new damage.

He woke to find himself packed among pillows, naked but for dressings, surrounded by machines and claimed by them as a component, connected via terminals, wires, needles and tubes. He lay inert on one side through dim confused hours between routines of being rolled over, his weight crushing his opened back, to lie the other way. The nurses' timed ministrations displaced all his volition. At their set hours they came, some of them young delicate girls, efficient and nonchalant intimates of mortality and its filths, to wash him and remove blood, pus and urine. The leakings of his wound were constantly sucked out into a teacup-sized plastic vessel like a Chinese lantern or concertina, a little box of sticky blood that had to be manipulated through the bars of the cot-side each time he was turned, obstructing the smoothness of the manoeuvre, extending the seconds of agony. His bladder was invaded by a catheter inserted through his urethra. This narrow plastic tube was anchored to his thigh by a patch of strapping plaster; it discharged into a longer, thicker tube that ran on to empty its trickle into a polythene bag suspended on a frame at the foot of the bed, which slowly bulged with urine and had to be emptied through its outlet tap every day.

He had anticipated the lumbar wound, though not its ferocity. But why was his leg still being wrung by the old pain of sciatica? As he recognised it he became aware also that there were regions of numbness on his lower body, and that his right foot constantly tingled, as though buried in electrified mud. Doctors questioned and tested him. His foot flopped disobedient to his will. His right buttock was unresponsive to pinpricks. The emancipated nerves had been damaged during the surgery, how badly, how permanently, only time would show. His body, like many of the routines it was subjected to, had become a system of obscurities. He kept asking for explanations of what he was feeling, what was being done, but every fact he elicited seemed partial or ambiguous, or refused to be translated for his imagination out of the code of the medicos' terminology.

Soon after his promotion from the intensive care unit to the ward, a brace of physiotherapists lowered him from his high bed and tried to stand him on his feet. His numbed right leg seemed empty air from hip to floor, and the left, in an immediate violent spasm of sharp pain, shot up doubled against his chest. The women's strong hands prevented him from falling and they bundled him back onto the bed. "Too soon," they pronounced.

Over the days, the leads, drains and terminals, one by one, were detached from his body. But when the indwelling urinary catheter was removed, his bladder swelled for hours without emission and eventually protested with rhythmical spasms of pain. Untrained in the elaborate ritual of re-catheterisation, the night nurse had to send out a call for a doctor. So the unmanning contraption was re-inserted in the guise of rescue, the visible bag a noisome insignium of his uncertain, waiting condition.

In the hope of reactivating his bladder a drug to induce contractions of striped muscle tissue was prescribed. The effect was dramatic, but not what was wanted. His solar plexus, oesophagus, lungs and throat were gripped by an unrelenting tension. Breathing and digesting became laboured, and his voice was strangled to a whisper. The drug was withdrawn after two days, but it had triggered a syndrome that persisted. He often lay and writhed, searching for a position in which he could breathe, could find some relief from the sensation of being congested to the point of bursting. Only for a brief spell when he awoke in the mornings would he feel released, relaxed, but no sooner did he swallow anything than his oesophagus began to burn and twist and pull taut—so he became reluctant to eat and drink.

And none of this helped the trench along his spine to heal. His writhing disturbed the dressings and the wound repeatedly became infected. Twice more he was taken to the operating theatre to have the incision re-opened and cleaned. Soon after the second of these treatments Alison visited him. At the sight of her he wept helplessly in protest against the pain of the new cutting and scraping.

"I'm frightened," he told her. "I don't want more of this. I'm afraid to suffer, and I'm afraid to die."

To anyone less loving and permissive than Alison he could not have spoken so nakedly. And once the words were out they affected him like a message from an inner voice—they informed him of his fear, which now began to haunt him. He lost the balanced view of death that he had worked out for himself, the comfortable assurance that to accept death's inevitability was to earn a liberation from dread and from futile crippling cautions, a freeing into the fullness of living. That brave equanimity now became inaccessible. He was assailed by the knowledge that he had nearly died and that he remained in peril and with prospects of bodily miseries for a long time to come. A raw fear settled in him.

The lonely selfishness of his dread soon, paradoxically, took on a new, supra-personal dimension. His imagination, sick but in its sickness newly vivified and enlarged, mysteriously opened itself, and he found himself horribly participating in all the pain and death in the world. All human sentience was suddenly his own. Thus the news that trickled into the ward by radio disturbed him in quite a new way. A war over the Falklands, invasions in Lebanon and Angola became personal calamities. He was obsessed by thoughts of the casualties. The agony and horror of the wounded involved him personally; he was with them in the same pit of awful mortality, his own shock and damage compounded by theirs. And every fatality added its volume and darkness to the annihilating flood that saturated the world, diluted every reality, and gathered for him.

News of a particular death cut still deeper. It was the murder of a handsome brilliant political journalist whom he had known well, had for long admired and liked, and who was still dear to Gail and Dan and other friends of his. Her political commitment had years ago taken her out of the country and then into a bewildering allegiance with enemies of Israel whose aims, he thought, were scarcely her affair and whose violent methods repelled him. Now she had been killed by some other terrorists' parcel bomb. The explosion became his own, blew all politics (except the politics of identification and non-killing and non-hurting) into insignificance. The possibility that she had not died instantly haunted and tormented him, his new sensitivity seeming to force him, too, to suffer the content of her violated dying consciousness.

Other deaths, injuries, illnesses, even the most anonymous routine accidents he happened to hear of, took on a power to afflict him: in impinging on his awareness they immediately threatened him. It was a vision of all human life as an appallingly thin skin stretched over the blank immensity of unlivingness. Only in terror could it be apprehended. What began as the most egotistical kind of anxiety transmuted itself into an identification with all who suffered and moved deathward. This was a vision that involved him in something like compassion, and it was real because distressingly felt, personal—but too painful to tolerate for long, too intense to live with.

The damage to his nerves under surgery had distorted and deadened sensation in his loins. But the negation went deeper. Even to imagine desire, excitement, passion, had become impossible. With Velma's first visit to him in the intensive care unit, he found that the whole force of the sexual explosion there had been between them was now translated into revulsion. Lust being cut off he was emptied, and the void was filled partly with dull remorse over what was now out of reach, but much more with a new flaming antagonism.

It was in part a feeling of punitive bitterness against her for having involved his passions where his tastes and interests had had no scope.

There was, for instance, her rite of requesting his judgements on piles of her writings and then angrily rejecting his criticisms as "intellectual", "cold" or "petty". There were her displays of suspicious resentment on meeting women friends of his, and even on hearing him speak about them. Some of these were his long-cherished confidants without whose sympathy his inner life would have withered. But the signs were that though, in the passionate sense, Velma loved him and was urgent to possess him body and soul, she neither knew nor, had she known, could have liked, the person he really was.

And in part his new antagonism was an eruption of angry disgust over the romantic religiosity she had tried to convert him to. During their lovership, it had generated its own series of bitter, exhausting quarrels as he resisted each assault, and she raged at his pride, blind obstinacy, perversity, spite. But now, stripped of the deliciousness that had complicated it, her campaign to claim him for her Christ stood exposed as an attack on his inwardness and his truth. The attack on truth was what especially enraged him now that he felt so close to extremity: he needed to know absolutely what was happening to him, what was the nature of things. He could afford no lying comforts, no false sentimental hopes. And the decoratively bleeding Jesus image which incarnated Velma's truth and on whose behalf she was so greedy to annex him was to him the epitome of offensive falsity.

Her compassionate participation in his bodily predicament, everything she had done for him in the weeks preceding the operation, all her trouble and concern, amounting to the attentions and anxiety of a loving wife, gave food now to his resentment. In his weakness and indebtedness he had been half-allowing her to claim him. Now in his greater weakness he found the claim intolerable. He nursed these feelings without word or sign to Velma, waiting for an occasion when it would be easier to declare them. Yet when his release from being her lover was suddenly spelled out, the form it took left him not simply relieved but, instead, almost superstitiously discomposed.

Russell Hoekstra had encountered Velma several times at Felix's and, in the same self-mockingly intense, teasing manner he used in bidding for any attractive woman who came into his vicinity, had been wooing her for months. Though Velma had responded to his brokenness with Christian pity, his playful demonism had affronted and disgusted her, and with a double motive she had repulsed all his advances. Thus when about a week after the operation Felix was visited by a dream that she had finally yielded, it affected him as simply bizarre. Yet the day after he'd dreamed it they came together to visit him. Velma was subdued, but Russell glowed with the brilliance of a new happiness and, as innocently as though he knew nothing of her other attachment, confided that he and Velma had become lovers. The preposterous dream was being promptly and accurately bodied forth.

This in itself was disconcerting. But beyond that, even though the reality neither threatened Felix nor took from him anything he wanted, the thought of the new partnership appalled him. After all, it represented the joining of two streams of wild sickly romanticism—Velma's predatory born-again idea of Christian spirituality, and Russell's neo-Beatnik readiness to flirt with any perversity for the sake of excitement. What would they do to each other? What would they do together?

Yet, thinking sanely, he had no good cause to be troubled by a partnership between those two that might relieve him of their attentions. After all, they were appropriate to each other, and their very air was inimical to the critical realism and rationality that was now desperately necessary to him.

By now, instead of monitors, pumps and receivers, the vaster apparatus of the whole hospital machine was beginning to take hold of him. The building itself was a machine in its newness and functionality, but a machine that was body-like in the complexity of its hugeness—tunnelled with corridors and shafts through which a throbbing corpuscular traffic of the sick and their attendants flowed, threaded by fragile systems of pipes and cables, apportioned into specialised departments devoted each like an organ to its own arcane process. The playschool decor ineffectually disguised the machine: a uniform thick colour on skirting, doors, frames and curtains always indicated which of the five otherwise anonymous, huge segments of the kilometre long hospital one was in—orange block, green block, red block, yellow block...

Navy blue was the block-colour of Felix's ward, and in this sombre medium the patterning on the curtains read like rows of tombstones. Neon lighting, windows (unbreathing, subservient to the air conditioning) which peered out onto grey walls that were relieved but unrelieved by the grey opacity of other similar windows, polished linoleum floors extending their hygienic gleam into anonymous corridors that stretched hundreds of metres toward the convergence of perspective and branched off into lobbies that served banks of grey metal lifts with soft implacable electronic tones to announce their arrival—all of this cohered into an aesthetic system that involved and denied him at the same time.

In a wheelchair drawn backwards through the tunnels of those corridors—by a porter who chose to trundle two chairs at once, back toward back, pushing one before, trailing the other behind—he would undergo a sort of dream-nausea, feeling that not he but the endless corridor was moving, its glassy floors, near featureless walls and ceilings, the traffic it contained, sliding away from him, as though it were time, life, the world that was slipping away. In the ward, patients and staff withstood the impersonality of the place by exchanging the shibboleths of cheery bonhomie, and tuned portable radios to filter in an interminable mutter of pop-chart music and frenzied advertisements. But such jollity only increased his sense of being at at odds with, remote from, his surroundings.

The efficient building was powerful enough to sustain his survival, to contain the chaos of hundreds of the sick with all their various maladies and injuries, but as it grew more familiar, though no less alien to him, it became itself an element of another kind of illness. This was a depression that, even months after his return home, would still discolour his days, an obsessive, dismaying notion that the falsely cheerful, factory-vast hospital, enemy of everything inward and individual, continued to own and claim him.

The hospital, however, by virtue of its power, permitted him allies and weaponry for his struggle against its own grey influence. There were a few nurses who had that patience for conversation—even only a minute or two at a time—by which they rescued both themselves and him from being mere instruments of function. Nothing of consequence might be said, but they provided relief from the strain of trying in his strangled voice to communicate urgent needs to staff who were distracted by their own urgencies, and sometimes, perhaps, too lazy of limb or wit to attend.

A particular ally was the occupational therapist who took him in charge for a long session on most mornings. The serious Irene made time for conversations that were better than perfunctory, and patiently bandaged his feet to the pedals of the dummy bicycle, so that he could kick them round for a few minutes and gain a little strength, exercise a little balance. But her particular boon was to give him an hour to himself each day at an electric typewriter. When he did not need to write his monitoring doctor a message more complicated than the hurry of speech allowed for, he used the time to tap out observations and reflections. They were mostly fragmentary, mere notes of his days' oddities—yet necessary as he struggled to attain some tolerable control over his feelings and groped toward some remembrance of his selfhood. He would fold and pocket these scraps of paper then give them to Mavis to take home to his desk.

And there was Sister Pool, a moon-mother presence. She was one of the two most senior sisters on the ward, alternately in charge. Her ample build and tender manner had supplied the moon simile to Felix's ideas when she floated comfortingly amid the confusion of his first days after surgery. Like the full moon she was present, it seemed, only seldom, but then produced a tide of kindness. Unlike other staff, she did not take the patients' discomfort as a matter of course, but listened with care and deployed her intelligent sympathy to seek the quickest possible easement.

Nor did she stop at giving merely what was asked for. When Felix's strength began to return he was provided with a chest-high dressing trolley on castors to cling to while inching himself along the ward and corridor for exercise. Sister Pool perceived that he needed something more and one day guided him further along the corridor to a room that served as a lounge for walking patients and their visitors. She called it "the sunroom".

It was at the end of the building and had large, clear-glass windows which not only admitted sunlight but gave on a view of The Wilds below and the tree-rich, flowery suburbs beyond. His mood at first attached significance to the visible part of the name painted on the roof of a nearby building, RUIN. Only later, after several visits, did he realise what medicine there was for his spirit in even so little sensory variety as the sunroom offered.

The other senior sister was a martinet he thought of as the Gunboat.

She habitually browbeat not only junior staff and patients but technicians, paramedics and even the occasional doctor, all in the cause of hierarchical order and the rigorous efficiency of the ward. It was as though she had been elected to represent in a single voice the ethos behind that overwhelming hospital building.

Felix drew her fire a number of times, as when he tried to make a suggestion concerning one of his medicines. "*Mister* Greenspan," she trumpeted, "the Professor has spent eleven years studying his subject, and if he prescribes a particular medication for you I don't think it's for you to question whether he knows what he is doing."

Any response to such a tirade except mumbling submission simply fuelled her indignation. Yet, like the hospital itself, she was so assured in her power to control and dismay that she could afford to be conspicuously kind at moments of crisis. One day he was being conveyed from the ward to the lavatory seated on a commode that consisted of nothing but the open seat in a frame on castors. All his pyjamas were away for laundering and he was covered in only a "surgery gown" of the kind that gaped open down the back. An exclamation from the nurse who was trundling the commode made him look back. On the floor of the corridor lay a large turd. The sight wrung from him a desperate wail.

At his cry the Gunboat strode into the corridor from the ward, calling, "*Mister* Greenspan!" She came to his side and, still almost hectoringly, told him, "You must remember that you are still in the early days after your surgery. This kind of accident is not unusual among post-operative patients. All sorts of things are likely to settle down as your back heals and you recover your strength." She spoke as though she were giving professional advice or instructions rather than offering comfort. But this met his need better than any gesture of consolation could have done. In fact he *was* comforted, and his gratitude was mixed with admiration for the insight displayed by her timing and choice of information. But why did such a person choose usually to terrorise the ward, conceal her potent compassion, go to such lengths to seem hard?

Alternating spells of incontinence and constipation cycled through the weeks and threw him again and again into crises of anxiety. The Gunboat had performed her act of mercy at one of those times. Possibly worse than the dramas, were the dreary trivia of squalor caused by his loss of control in this and all directions. He had to resign himself to having his bedside locker do extra service as a laundry bin for the filthied pyjamas bundled in with his other belongings by busy nurses. He had to see Mavis burdened with the recurring chore of taking his soiled pyjamas home to be laundered. He had to let Becky help him clear his nostrils with a cotton bud because he was too weak to blow his nose. He had to make a duty of eating heavy-smelling microwave-heated food when he had no appetite, and drinking when he dreaded the acid protest of his stomach and its weakness in holding down its contents: if he ate inadequately he would remain weak, his wound would not heal, his bowels would clog; if he drank too little his bladder would fester with infection.

He underwent hope and disappointment again and again through strangely regular weekly successions of improvement and backsliding—what was the curse on Thursdays? His body, in rebellion against itself yet desperate for its chance of survival, seemed to have overrun and commandeered the realms of his tastes and choices, of his selfhood.

Reaching beyond to express himself in thought, he blundered. Another of Sister Pool's favours came one Saturday morning when there would be no expedition to the occupational therapy department, but instead some blank, uncomfortable hours in the ward. She took him to the ward secretary's office, not in use over the week-end, and made him free of the typewriter there. The demands of the unfamiliar machine distracted his attention from the tyrannies of oesophageal spasm and dread.

Moved by both gratitude and vanity, the next day he showed her the fragments he had typed—a gesture that let in the perverse imp of complication. One of his notes ran: "A strong man of well-rounded character and rich experience tells his Afrikaans fellow patients, `Ek haat 'n kaffer...' as though he were showing them his badge of membership."

" 'Badge of membership' ?" Sister Pool queried. "Does that mean all Afrikaners hate blacks? People say that sort of thing, but I'm Afrikaans and I know it's not so."

"Oh...but no, I'm not generalising," Felix protested. "I don't mean that... I wouldn't..." But he saw that he had generalised. Why had he noted that the patients were Afrikaans? That *she* was was concealed by her unaccented English and her married name. Had he known, would he so innocently have shown her his note? In any case, she must now suspect he was one of those whose cheaply-bought badge of enlightenment was a show of contempt for Afrikaners.

Dad was now close to eighty, more deaf, more forgetful and more nervously solicitous than ever. His residential hotel was near enough to the hospital for him to walk across and he took to coming to sit with Felix for an hour or two nearly every day—the staff was easy-going about visiting times. He spoke in subdued tones, a grimace of profound gravity rarely leaving his face: he was watching by a deathbed. Felix hunted for points of conversation and tasks he could ask to be done for him—pour a glass of water, moisten the face-cloth, shave him, clean the electric shaver—but essentially these visits were blanks during which he could neither read nor listen to his radio, neither rest nor reflect nor try in some way to find distraction from the imaginable peril of his condition. Finally, feeling ungrateful and sad, neither brave nor diplomatic enough to do it himself, he asked Mavis to find some way of discouraging the old man's visits.

By contrast, visitors to whom he could confide his feelings and reflections, or could recount the anecdotes of his days, allowed him to re-approach the selfhood from which he seemed to have been exiled. There was even more to it one day when the visitors were Henry Walters and Professor Roy Craddock. The latter came to Johannesburg infrequently on academic or literary business. That Walters should have thought to bring the doyen to see Felix, and that he should have agreed to come, amounted—since neither was a particularly close personal friend—to an assertion that he was seen to participate in their shared world of inward aliveness. He was moved, grateful for the affirmation, for the implied call to him to resume his creative life. A call that came when, in the main, what he felt was his distance from his fullest being—when, in a double sense, his voice was lost, and he had no assurance that it would return.

Behind the hospital's rearing chimney, protected by its nine-storeyed wall, subjected to all its benign, righteous power, he had been invaded by terror. The most primitive dread—that of his own cessation as an isolate animal—had overwhelmed him, and when he tried to think his way out of that intolerable loneliness, the sense of the remotest stranger's defenceless mortality had become equally terrifying to him. The vulnerability of all creatures was suddenly now symbolic, symptomatic, of his own.

This vision had bloomed out of terror. Only in terror would he have embraced this limitless identification—so close and intense that it was as though his own senses extended into every person whose particular peril or distress he was made aware of. But because it sprang from terror, it was too close and intense to amount to altruism. Altruism required a more endurable and lasting, more living and rational form of fellow-feeling than merely a horror of mankind's mortality. And in return for this broader, warmer sympathy, altruism offered participation in the relative immortality of the race—immersion in the river of what was inherited from and bequeathed to others, generation by generation: aspirations, ideas, stories. One could understand and cultivate this philosophy, this virtue—it was wise, healthy, self-rewarding, a ground of civilisation.

This vision of shared aliveness, this consolation, could never be as deeply rooted, as profoundly felt as that visceral dismay, that selfish dread, which descended like an affliction at moments of susceptibility. In contrast to that, without that malady as its concomitant, wasn't altruism nearly always bound to be a mere matter of conscientious intention, a pretension? The vision of common mortality and suffering had come as a thing of sickness, a thing involuntarily incurred, but the shock of it, surely, would leave, once it was passed, an enduring remnant of illumination, a buried knowledge of connectedness that from time to time might find its expression in altruistic forms.

In a similar way, he had experienced, long ago, exacerbations of lust that were volcanic. Their magnificence or malignancy, defying all order, refusing reality to all but the self and the desired, was endurable for only an explosive moment. Then the fires subsided under the liveable patterns of sanity. But the eruptions would have left a fertile lava, a subliminal knowledge of transforming possibilities. His capacity for desire seemed, where he found himself now, quenched by the asphyxiating breath of the hospital. As for the always hidden access to those huge rich potencies underneath, the whole stratum seemed to have been impenetrably sealed under the grey weight of damage and discomfort which sickness and the hospital had poured onto him. He could not help believing that henceforth he would never again be striving for joy and excitement but but only for endurance and survival.

His despair of ever being other than a foully incontinent invalid, dependent, vulnerable and useless, his terror of suffering and meaninglessness, at times overwhelmed his terror of extinction. He had heard that a polythene bag pulled over the head would cling suffocatingly to the mouth and nostrils. More than once, during short stays at home, he lay gazing at the plastic packet left close at hand in case he needed to vomit, and contemplated using it to make a quietus. Once for a few moments it became a temptation, an impulse of mad automatism, that he had to fight down.

When Gail arranged for a psychiatrist who was a friend of hers to come and see him, he unburdened himself of the secret idea that had been with him for some weeks: "If it becomes clear that I can't realistically expect to get much better, and get back to my old life, my real life, and if I find I can't bear to go on with endless helplessness and sickness and pain and incontinence and meaninglessness—then, I wouldn't want to continue just for the sake of continuing. Could I be helped to some way of ending things?"

The psychiatrist pondered for a bare moment before replying: "Yes... I think something could be arranged."

His detached assurance chilled rather than comforted Felix. "Oh," he said, "that's good to know. Thank you" and, suddenly, needed the conversation to end as soon as possible.

He realised that what he had really wanted was an appalled, somehow loving response (such as would have come from Gail herself, or Alison, or even Velma) that would jolt him into a more resolute commitment to life. But perhaps the result was the same. After this close approach to the convenient accessibility of cessation—not just as a solipsistic fantasy but as euthanasia, an administered mercy at the hands of a responsible doctor—he pushed the idea aside with a surreptitious revulsion. He was not ready to face leaving even the most diminished version of aliveness.

18

Recovery: A Journal

NO ONE SEEMS AFRAID, I ONLY...
Fallen among surgeons
I turn to blood, pus, faeces and snot...

The nurses' training aims at the cure of all idiosyncrasies, yet achieves the licensing of all manner of idiosyncrasy. The patient longs for consistency, or the kind of individuality that expresses intelligence and sensitivity. Instead "training" often intrudes as the "reason" for mechanised unthinking procedure. On the other hand, amazingly, this is how the world's work gets done.

They face daily into the pit
and accept that the only way
requires some cruelty, some waste
and some blindness.

Doctors make no distinction of feeling between good news and bad. Equally cheerful whatever the message, they are like traffic guides, pointing one's particular route to the inevitable destination while trying to ensure that we don't exceed the speed limit.

My urine is my treasure which I keep like a purse.

The hospital as archetype of civilised institutions (yet it represents hell to many of the patients in its custody);
as symbol of the human body;
as an instance of human collaboration.
What would become of mankind if all institutions were dismantled?

Patient (joking after taking a revolting medicine): Brr! You are cruel.
Nurse: I'm not cruel.

P: You give me this terrible stuff to take.

N: I wouldn't choose to give you horrible stuff to take.

P: But you've just done it.

N: The nursing staff have to give you the medicines but the doctors order them.

P: You'd do anything they tell you to.

N: No, not anything.

P: Oh, yes. I'm sure you'd all stand on your heads if they told you to.

EPISODE FROM THE FIRST DAYS

One of the four patients in the intensive care cubicle was an old man with a head injury and pneumonia, in a coma or semi-conscious. His only sign of life was the gargle of phlegm in his throat: sometimes it rose to a loud groan. Day and night, perhaps every half hour, a nurse came to "suction out" his throat, a process that took five or ten minutes during which she cajoled him to cough and he seemed to respond. A real case of fighting to keep him alive. I particularly noticed old Sister M's ministrations. As though she was trying to call him back, or somehow to sweeten the time for him, she lavished endearments on him: "Come on, Mr Desmond, cough, my darling...cough..."

It went on throughout my time there, in the dark, imperilled place of half-sleep, pain, tubes, monitors, restrained voices, gentle hands. Sister M put her heart into the fight for Mr Desmond. As the days passed I picked up some bits of his story. He had not undergone surgery. He'd been living alone, terribly neglected, sent here from another hospital.

I feared for him when Sister M went off duty for the weekend. On the Saturday afternoon came his first visitors, a son and daughter or daughter-in-law. After a few minutes the son seized the old man by the wrist, bent over him and prayed with fierce intensity: "In the name of JESUS sickness leave this body—in the name of JESUS germs leave this body—in the name of JESUS pain leave this body—in the name of JESUS disease leave this body—in the name of JESUS Satan leave this body!" And then, bending close, with even more passion: "Dad, can you hear me? Dad, listen, we are praying for you. You must fight back Dad, we are all praying for you, we care for you. And, listen Dad, Jesus loves you, that is why you will pull through, that is why YOU ARE NOT SICK."

Mr D's steady desperate gargle had run on as an under-note to all this, registering no recognition or response. But no sooner had the young couple left than his voice came through in a sort of bubbly croak that amounted to a shout. A nurse was there instantly. The curtains were drawn round his bed. Shortly after, I and the other two patients were moved out to another cubicle. Over the next couple of days I gathered from odd remarks here and there that Mr Desmond had died.

CB comes to see me. I tell him I've been very frightened and he remarks, "So have a lot of your friends." This makes me more afraid.

THE BLACK WIDOW

With the heavy haunch and short stature of Bushman ancestry, she is no spider. But she is genuinely a widow of two months standing. Grief could well explain her sour face and the grim rage she puts into her work. She seems to hate it and the economic necessity that binds her to it. I quail when she is one of the pair who come to bed-bath me and make my bed: when I must roll to the side so that the sheet can be spread, she will pull me to the very edge where I go rigid with fear of falling—these beds are mercilessly high. She scorns my terror: "You can't fall. I'm here."

The sisters have absolute authority over her. One morning while she is bed-bathing me, this time solo, Sister A looks round the curtain and orders her to bring a bowl of water for my dentures. Sister B (the sister-in-charge, the Gunboat) catches her half-way down the ward and gives her a contrary order. When she flounders and tries to explain what she is about she gets a broadside: "Betty, you do not keep the professor waiting." Betty puts the bowl of water down on the nearest dressing trolley and turns to do Sister B's bidding. At this moment Sister A reappears at the door and demands the completion of her order. Betty whirls and blurts in her helplessness. I half expect her to throw herself on the floor and howl. The prof suddenly tires of the delay and says he will do the examination at some other time. Let out of her dilemma, Betty returns to her first task but can't immediately find the bowl.

It has been a minute charged with authoritarian mindlessness on the part of the two sisters—which as a patient I witness with alarm. A day or two later Betty is again bed-bathing me, and has prepared a basin of hot water with Savlon for my feet (in accord with an instruction from Sister A who has decided that I have Athlete's foot). Curious about Betty's response to unreasonableness in her superiors I remind her of that incident—and "remind" is the right word: she has pushed the episode so far to the back of her mind that it is halfway to being forgotten. But she recalls it after a while with little more comment than a dismissive chuckle. In fact, however, her equanimity seems to have been disturbed: she forgets entirely to wash my legs and soak my feet. My attempt to remind her brings forth an indignant, "But I did. You forget. I did!" I let the matter drop.

The Gunboat, The Thinktank, The Fairy Fay, Mickey Mouse (my nicknames for some of the nursing staff).

> Super-matron Thatcher pays
> a few hundred lives
> and expensive machines
> for the Falklands.
> But the rules she plays by
> strictly and of course humanely
> forbid euthanasia.

In a way that is new to me I identify with everyone in whom agony and fragility are manifested. Even the thought of the illustrious long-dead chills me: I experience their extinction as a sort of eternal suffocation. So after all, my disturbed emotions have brought me round to a kind of immortality—but a hellish kind. Yet it is also the absence of the dead, their expulsion from everything that had concerned them (and might—such as their world's reception of their death) that troubles me.

The body must exert itself or the mind grows poisonous. (When my mind had slipped into the cold grip of the terror of death and was freed for a while by some mild exertion.)

Nurse Gloria, speaking of her training, told how everything was demonstrated before the trainee was expected to try her hand—with the exception of last offices. Here she was required to perform not after example but under instruction.

Honesty manifests itself more in how people work than in what they say.

Inaccuracy is a weapon in any hierarchical power struggle.

Evasion ditto.

A dishonest person forced me to lie.

Evidently uninterested, someone asks me what it is I teach. Trying to rebuke her coldness I respond, "Humanity". Once I have said it it loses its arrogance and becomes the truth.

WRITE TO SAVE YOUR LIFE, NOTHING LESS

(Saturday. Sister P has allowed me to sit in the ward secretary's office and use the typewriter.)

I trace that dangerous border where mind struggles to overcome matter. In any difficult physical achievement there comes a point where cause-and-effect breaks down: there is a quantum gap that can only be overleapt by something like faith. Self-hypnosis? Yoga? Something of that sort. We've all seen it, found it in ourselves. But what is it?

Along with the yoga, or whatever we call the power that bridges will and deed, there has to be an instrument, e.g. this typewriter, without which I would have sat through this morning putting my energy into writhings in the grip of spasm. The machine dictates, and I am grateful.

I, even I, am walking a tightrope. I have to make the rope as ordinary, as flat, as the floor.

Last night a patient in pain said, "Ek wil doodgaan". Half an hour later, when the pain was relieved, he said "Ek voel soos 'n koning". (I don't know whether "Ek wil doodgaan" means "I want to die" or merely, rhetorically, "I'm dying".)

Even if one can't believe it one knows that one's body is subject to one's ideas. I can walk if I sufficiently want to. I can walk if I know I can: I have proved it—by doing it—yet I permit doubt to remain.

I aspire to a sort of rational yoga, free of mysticism. It must reside in reason and the consistency of reality, yet it can never depend on logic pure and simple. It must move from received fact to logic to new fact: e.g. with my body in its present condition I have walked under circumstances that bolster my confidence—those circumstances (the parallel bars hedging me, the nearness of the physiotherapist) affect me mainly as ideas, producing confidence and hence relaxation, since there is no physical contact: logic says it is thus within my physical capacity to walk relaxed with no support—I must absorb this idea, and then, easily, rhythmically, confidently, walk.

The air-conditioned hospital hums in my ears. When I leave the building my ears buzz in the unusual silence.

There seems to be a sort of wholeness to all these fragments...
Cunning wholeness, innocent fragments.

The ward's sealed windows look out upon
sealed windows, blank as one-way glass.
Week after week we are locked
in the hospital's solipsistic block,
oppressed (in the corridors)
with the smell of metal,
the taste of sickness (even in the water)...

THEATRE
On the crate-sized box
white stencilled letters declare:
CRISIS STERILE STOCK.
This is where the world ends,
where someone explains to me,
"Everything green is sterile."

NURSE M

Her beautiful African-mask face is dead. She knows only that she must hold her job (despite her head-cold, despite her injured neck in its brace —"I'm also a patient") and not miss days of work and pay. She clings to some rule about not removing the thermometer from the patient's mouth too soon and some general notion that patients are untrustworthy; she sees them not as people but as things she works with (so I say despite her habit of chirruping "Hullo Mr G.... Hullo my love..." when she comes on duty).

One day, while waiting out the regulation two or three interminable minutes until she may take the thermometer from under my tongue and read it, she notices an imperfectly closed window in the two-bed room I'm in and demands, "Why do you open your window? Don't you know it's cold, Mr G? Hey, Mr G? Why you open your window?" The weirdness of it is that she actually expects me to answer, she actually does not know that I couldn't stand up to open the window if I wanted to, nor that the thermometer makes it impossible for me to speak.

A film director has been half paralysed by stroke. In OT he struggles to master childish skills. He rarely attempts to speak. When he does what comes out is, "I dee dee did dee dee dee OH diddy diddy dee..." accompanied by agitated gestures. Into that OH, it seems to me, is gathered all his desperation.

Mankind has institutionalised death, pain and all the horrors of existence. At one and the same time this gives us a sense of control over our fate, masks the terror of our individual fate as animals, and licenses the things institutions do to individuals—in the name, say, of healing, law, education and order. There is a dilemma. The institutions represent our humanity, our civilisation, our power of thought, our historicity, our capacity for fear and compassion. We might have chosen another way, the way of the fish, say, the way of the uncommunicating, unremembering animal. Is there a third way? Life as play, as savage simplicity, without technology and without record beyond stories and songs? Pain, illness and death would be swathed in mystery. This looks like an answer, but even if it could work (by means of instituting a universal anti-institution), there is something deeply dissatisfying about any arrangement that reduces man's capacity to comprehend. I find myself thrust toward a notion I hate: Man is potentially God only because he suffers. Somewhere, somehow, the state of the innocent unthinking animal contains more truth.

Every hour seems to bring something significant

I was sitting up in my usual chair after breakfast yesterday. They'd given me a capsule to dissolve under my tongue, something new for my stomach discomfort. Suddenly my whole insides began to seize up. My voice has been very weak lately, and now all I could get out was a choked whisper: "Call Sister!" Yet the nurse on the far side of the ward responded immediately. And all I had to say when the sister came was, "I can't breathe." Within minutes she'd given me an injection of Valium and had me bundled back into bed to sleep it off.

By what power did I manage to summon help so promptly? Perhaps my face spoke louder than my voice.

SM tells me she works by choice with the dying—terminal cancer patients at the Hillbrow Hospital. Many don't know they are dying, and opinions differ as to whether to tell them. She mentions the cultural barrier between black and white. I reflect on the vaster barrier between those who know death is imminent and the rest, including the institution people who minister to them. (I cast no general reflection on the latter: even the most sensitive and well-meaning of them would be paralysed, I think, if they shared that knowledge.)

In the gym suddenly there looms up in front of me a boy strapped to a narrow padded board which is being raised vertical, as though for a crucifixion.

"Ek gril my stukkend, maar ek moet myself hou..." (I shudder to pieces, but I must contain myself...)—patient, referring to the black nurses whose ministrations he must endure. He happens to be a Bible reader.

A girl in a corridor pauses to tell me: "Jesus loves you", and minutes later by a slip of the tongue a physiotherapist comes out with "the water" when she means to refer to "the floor" I'm walking on. (Most floors in the hospital gleam like water.)

The Jesus Alternative keeps popping out at me. But I can't take the smug irrationality nor the implied institutionalisation—the latter symbolised by the neat ubiquitous package of the Gideon Bible. (What presumption, what insensitivity, what disregard of individuality there is in its distribution in hospitals, jails and hotels!) I have seen it being read by two patients in my ward, but in a brief ritual "reading", very different from the way they read other things. Yet when I read a page or two of Gospel there is a literate cleanliness to the prose, writing that gets on with its story-business and has nothing to do with religious promotionism.

At home for a week-end I dream four times that I am walking without support. Back at hospital I tell someone, and in the innocence of her professional interest she remarks that paraplegics have similar dreams. My heart sinks, but later at physio I do walk a few steps unaided.

Alison tells me that when she came to see me weeks ago "I couldn't see you in your eyes."

Already my memory loses so much. Even the details of my "rough time" in the first few weeks fade and become inaccessible.

Deaths in this time: Moke, RF (I needed to know from Gail that the bomb had killed her outright—I can't bear the thought of someone desperately injured suffering for hours before death comes), Battiss (Doreen tells me she has not wept for him because he had lived so fully: this perspective was natural to me but is so no more—not to deny that now I am becoming less appalled than I was some weeks ago).

MARK

He is a young engineer visiting SA from England who was seriously injured in a car accident while hitch-hiking. His childlikeness, his innocence—memory expunged—his will to be whole and free of the hospital. The hospital staff, relishing the drama of his troublesomeness, seem to feel a special affection for him, as though in putting his pieces together they had somehow created him—with his youth, physical beauty and spirited rebelliousness. At first he makes repeated attempts to run away, then he resorts to affirming "There is nothing wrong with me" etc., and begins to rebuild his memory bit by bit—intently reading newspapers for their references to places, people, things he knew before (finding that a name can evoke an image or other kinds of association—for example, he asks me "Is Kotze k.o.t.z.e.?", wanting to connect a remembered sound to the printed word, and "Is it Dr Hendrik Verwoerd?" i.e. the Dr H.Verwoerd referred to in a newspaper article). When in conversation there is a reference that calls up nothing in his memory, he says "I don't know that." His "reality" ("There is nothing wrong with me except..." "I'm going to get out of here.") and the hospital's reality begin far apart but gradually come together as he heals. His youth and sheer will make him a symbol of the powers of recuperation.

After one of his escapes, he is dragged, resisting, into the ward by the professor who shouts an order for a sedative hypodermic. This sounds like a melodramatic threat meant to quell Mark into docility, but it turns out to be in earnest. Staff rush up to help, Mark is bundled into his bed which, with its cot-sides and grid-lid, is virtually a cage, held down for the needle, padlocked in, and left to sleep off his frenzy.

Image of him standing naked in the bathroom doorway asking the empty corridor "What must I do now?"

His interactions with other patients in the ward. There is the fatherly Afrikaner with his own notions about the physio-therapeutic discipline Mark needs. A tug of wills. Mark yields where he must, then the other seems to lose interest. He demands an exaggerated military-style march (to counteract M's shuffling). For M this is anathema. He marches, but only when he is in view of the other, so the swagger-strut becomes a kind of send-up (subtly English).

As he walks in his ill-fitting hospital pyjamas he innocently exposes himself. The others call, "Hey, your front door is open." It is as though he has to be resocialised.

FOR I.N.

(who asked me, "What is the truth to you"?)

Truth is never had, always being sought. It is built out of facts, but the changing facts of experience. The cement of the structure is reason. But, experience and reason being the fallible things they are, it is always having to be rebuilt. So truth is almost a matter of faith. It becomes, not a system or a religion but, a way of living—an open, brave, rational way of life. Truth, or the desire for it, is what holds you together, your integrity. The desire for truth presupposes somewhere a system, but the subtlety and mystery of the system keep it always beyond the reach of the intellect. Religions provide symbols of the system, philosophies provide approximations.

CT described the funeral of MW, the historian, as if it were a wonderful party, full of delight and pleasure and fun.

I want to probe what enables one to carry on in the face of one's appalled apprehension of this mortal human condition: work, absorption in the present moment, its effort, its humour, its loveliness or whatever.

TWO PATIENTS

Nortje: (to the effect of) I can do nothing. I might as well be dead.

Barbaross: A man doesn't have to do anything. As long as he can watch the sun going down and coming up, life is beautiful.

What right have I to dub Nortje "The Hillbrow Cockroach" and wonder, even momentarily, why the doctors are as solicitous of him as of me?

Is every bit of (human) life precious? To whom? Society? Posterity? God? Whoever happens individually to know of its existence? What then of life saturated with pain or irremediable misery? We see that often it does not choose to hold on to itself.

If we particularise (e.g. about the value of specific moments) we can find an answer, by witnessing or experiencing palpable results. If we try to generalise about some absolute value of life, the best we can come up with is a theory.

RZ is looking at the problem of survival in different contexts: 1. the holocaust, the Judenrat, the sheeplike victims; 2. Israel's invasion of Lebanon.

One may choose for oneself to place some other value above survival, but no one has the right to dictate that choice to another. Violence or indoctrination or conditioning may induce that choice.

My emotion of dread is so strange, so raw. It draws its power from the stark realism of my vision of mortality and suffering. To carry on one must be absorbed in (you could say distracted or deluded by) work or play, or one must be drunk. But after all, life as it has been lived through the duration of human history is as much of a reality as death. So it comes back to the emotions: they are not determined by "the facts"—they determine the Reality one lives with. One must begin with doing.

Art faces both ways. It confronts, names, forms Reality. It is a doing.

A girl in the typing room. I stop her when she begins to talk to me about Jesus. Then we talk about her depression. I tell her work helps. She agrees and goes back to her typing.

I don't know what work is doing for me. Spasm is receding but depression remains. I suspect that if I were forming something—if this work were creative, if it were art—the depression would give way to the creative excitement.

How one is reduced! Yesterday was spoiled by spasm, vomiting, incontinence, yet I walked a good fifty metres and back and, with catheter removed, passed a tot of urine—but that's not good enough so the horrid tube and bag have to be replaced. Now Dr M says, realistically, that I can't go to live at home before I'm rid of the catheter.

Today begins with depression, after a night of leg pain, yet while waiting for my bed-bath I set about stripping myself, but I rip the waist-button off my pyjama pants. I negotiate breakfast without starting a spasm, and afterwards for the first time I manage the toilet independently from first to last.

Yesterday the Black Widow surprised me with her genuine pleasure when she saw me crossing the ward, aided only by the walking frame.

ON A WILDLIFE PHOTOGRAPH

The black baby hippo trots behind its mother
while the white gambols in front...
They have moved, will move like this
for ever and ever.
The patterns of the wild are more implacable
than the patterns of institutions.
Outside that cage of patterns
which we find beautiful
are we inside the other?
There is no outside except in the
broken-off moment.
There is no outside
except within.

Purposed custom? Random inheritance of habit?
In any case, institution of the wild.
But the wild is the opposite of institution.

A porter who is afflicted with a gross tic makes werewolf sounds as he proceeds along the corridors, and explains to anyone who looks at him askance (as, inevitably, some do, with broad grins), "Dis nie ek wat so doen. Dis die anner man wat werk in teater." ("It's not me that does this. It's that other man who works in theatre.") He needs both to do it and to deny it. I wonder how many of us display the same pattern in less gross forms.

THE PORTERS

On wheel-chairs and wheel-beds
the porters transport us for hospital purposes,
deposit us, patient load on the disabling vehicle,
to wait for hospital purposes.

One makes were-wolf noises
down the corridors;
one rebukes a couple of blacks,

"Moenie wild speel in die passages"
then promptly plays at running down
a cleaning maid.

One, taking me to the operating theatre,
flirts with the escorting nurse,
asks if she speaks Sotho or Zulu.

One stops a nurse-aid pushing the wagon
from which a ward lunch has just been served:
"Hey, ausi..." and begs her
for a couple of boxes of meat.

Before the surgery, before my admission, I asked a porter to take me to a toilet cubicle.

New, not yet their property, "Yes, you can leave me now," I said. "Yes, I can manage now"—though the door was too narrow to let the wheelchair in and I had to negotiate its awkward footplate to stand at the bowl, the vehicle waiting behind me in the open doorway while I urinated. When done I had to lunge—avoiding the footplate one couldn't stand on—into the unstable chair, witnessed by a radiographer.

"Which porter," she demanded to know, "was responsible for leaving this patient to nearly break his back?"

The indignant word of blame flew round and stuck, no matter how I tried to absolve. One porter with a closed idiot face pointed me out to anyone who'd listen, accused me of accusing him: unreachable, he embodied a power I could only dread.

IN THE WORLD

First is the resolute way of a fleet
climbing the seas to a rendezvous with right
whose devices will end a few hundred lives.

Another is the way of sitting in the sun,
the way of the fish.

Others peel off the mortal skin
and place it in God's hands.

I hug myself in my shivering skin,
no worshiper, no fish,
counting off armies and hospitals.

There is no point in making a story about facing death unless it involves a significant discovery about life. For example, that the courage to continue and the light by which meaning may be discovered are of the body. The body has to move, to extend itself, to act, if joy, peace of mind, sanity are to be possible—it must be body, not mere unfunctioning flesh.

Is this true? How does it hold for the paralysed? If pleasure is of the body, why should pain be of the flesh?

Monday. Just returned from a weekend at home. Amanda is intensely active in her art, doing so much, planning so much, burning bright, but so exposed to Jhb's violence and other threats. She tells of witnessing a troop of whites assaulting, possibly murdering, a black in a Yeoville street. As a young girl alone in her car late at night she mistrusts the police, and is helpless to help.

While our writing circle is sitting round waiting for Giles who has gone astray, she sleeps a somehow desperate sleep in a chair. Do I infuse my sense of peril into her, and much else? It haunts me all day at Becky's, though otherwise this is my first successful day there—no spasm, I have my voice, though keeping the walker in front of me I walk without touching it.

Alison read us a tremendous new section of her novella and I responded at places with stirrings of my flesh. So...

THE HOUSE ON THE HILL
It commands sweeping views
of tower blocks and suburbs,
yet many windows within are blind
to all but blank blocks of the house itself,
as if, there, we can see only inward—

hospital, war office, abattoir, laboratory,
prison, ministry, funeral chapel—
places where, faceless, we face
into horror, or are numbed.
This is the human thing,
vulnerable, exposed, fragile,
channel of pain.
This knowledge would atrophy me,
yet those it empowers
do the world's work,
while we labour to recollect
faces, words, selves.

I long for when I will no longer belong to the hospital. Watching the drift of a variety of people with a variety of ills or duties along the corridors—especially along "Hospital Street" with its strange pretence of being outside—I have felt that the institution claims everybody.

Pain, discomfort, loss of function, humiliation and fear of death raise the question, how is the soul to be preserved? That is to say, how is the self to recover itself as a being that continues to be what it was, responds to what is (what is not itself), continually discovers itself, and grows? How, in the face of the circumstances that the wrecked body presents, is life to be fulfilled?

For me, it cannot be a matter of religious faith but of experience. I can't settle for a belief that my being is imbued with some transcendent value, in virtue of which it will survive in some sense outside of my time. I have to undergo my livingness with my nerves, my energies, my appetites, my expectations. The body's horror of mortality must be displaced by, or at least placed in a context of, liveable emotions; the paralysis of terror must give way to action; metaphorically, pain must yield to painting or poetry.

I can take nothing for granted—not even the salutary effects of peace or work or nature's loveliness or art, or the lovingness of friends. The virtue of each has to be proven every time by the raising or comforting of my spirit, just as the goodness of food has to be tested meal by meal on the tongue and in the stomach. I dare not subside into a condition of faith:

that would lead to symbolism, passivity and transcendentalism, as well as to a kind of falsity. Acting in faith, friends brought me pots of flowers, but my gratitude was faint: I could not share their faith in the healing goodness of growing things—it was their faith, a public faith, and I had not the strength to be gracious enough to pretend to share it. Had not the strength —stronger, more alive, I might have been capable of the mutuality of giving (the flowers to me and me to the flowers)—that brings the goodness of flowers into being not as a matter of faith but as an experience.

So this is about the struggle to be; in a meaningful (oh, what an unmeaningful word!) sense, about soul-making. So I must investigate the soul of the city and the soul of the century. And I must ponder the way surroundings bear upon the soul. Why am I so affronted, so hurt, by the way the smokestack of the hospital towers over the Wilds? Is it merely the prominent ugliness of the structure? Is it the way it contradicts the purpose of the public garden by destroying its effectiveness as a place of charm, a retreat from the city? Is it because it so arrogantly advertises the hospital and its claims—its claim to each of us the moment we grow weak enough, its claim to a beneficence that demands our uncritical piety, its claim to the authority of efficiency which licenses such ugliness and precludes the wastefulness of soul-making? Or all three? It signals a threat by those who are good and useful in society—a threat to disallow the self.

19

Halva

Like a huger, more implacable Sphinx pedestalled on the ridge above The Wilds, the hospital seemed to lay claim to the whole suburban plain it overlooked, seemed to be waiting to summon in the course of time each moving human body in all those streets and houses. Any glimpse of its blank bulk Felix happened to catch, or be caught by, as he was driven about, would stir his dismay. He had to go back routinely to have his wound dressed and, at longer intervals, to have the catheter into his bladder changed for the sake of hygiene. He still belonged. And his voice, still breathless and weak as though strangled by after-shock, constantly reasserted the fact. He still belonged.

Home again. But the place he returned to was not exactly the same, and nor was it the very same self that returned. The arrangement of his furniture to lend him handholds for moving between bed, desk, armchair, basin and door was now not enough to give him independence in the flatlet. And his biggest bookcase had been unpacked so that it could be moved along the wall to unblock a formerly hidden door to the room his nurse-aid would use, and the books had been put back without regard to the order they had stood in—the order that had been lodged in his memory, enabling him to locate any volume. Moreover, the bookcase now stood behind a settee, lower shelves hidden, upper shelves largely unreachable. The part of himself that was the conscious presence and accessibility of his books—even though so many of them after so many years remained unread—that part and potentiality was now cut off.

Another sort of amputation threatened when Mavis, fired by one of her peremptory enthusiasms, took up the cause of arranging a state disability pension for him. When her enquiries discovered that his invested savings made him ineligible under the means test, she suggested, to get round this obstacle, that he transfer his investment to the name of some other member of the family. She fell in love with this neat ploy that accorded so well with her sense of filial responsibility. But it made Felix deeply uneasy. He was being expected to show responsibility toward the family, whose burden he would be if he became destitute or his needs became exorbitant. Instead he worried about deceiving the pension authorities and about his access to his funds if he transferred them. Half-ashamed of such reasons, he put up an awkward, inarticulate objection that left Mavis indignant over his evasion of resposibilty, infuriated by his prissy childishness, the obstinacy with which he frustrated her plan for his welfare.

There were often job-seekers going from door to door in the suburb. Felix was walking in the garden, supported by the agency nurse, when a woman presented herself at the gate. She exchanged a few words with the nurse, then asked, "You got a job for me, boss?"

"Yes," Felix said, "I want someone to help me, dress me, wash me, bring my food, clean my room."

Whenever he'd been let out of the hospital for weekends, Mavis had hired a nurse from an agency to see to him, and one had been in attendance during the five or six days since he'd been discharged. But he had to have more permanent and less expensive help. He required to be bed-bathed, dressed and undressed, supported to and from the dining-room when he joined the family, to and from the lavatory, serviced in the emptying of his urine bag, cleaned—body, clothes and floor—when tubes, bag or bowels betrayed him. After a few more questions and answers the dwarfish, solidly built woman at the gate, with her odd doll's squeak of a voice, gave a solemn nod to the wage he could offer, and he found that he had hired her.

Inexperienced as he was—having never before contracted a servant—he had omitted the ritual of asking for her references, but he was lucky: Nomsa proved in some respects especially suited to the job. She had worked as a nurse-maid for infants and her temperament fitted her to carry out the intimate tasks he needed. She performed them well enough, reliably enough. He was irritated by her exuberantly treating him lik
more of her infant charges, to be cooed at, teasingly or sooth
dictated, his protests to be laughed off as childish pe
the more because in many respects he had been cast b
But he endured her innocent lack of tact as the price o
ingness with which she gave her service—at least at first

persisted in all its virulence, and his voice remained a tense whisper, only seldom, when he was particularly relaxed, recovering something of its normal resonance.

Velma and Russell had after all not yet done with him. They, or Russell alone, had visited him several more times in hospital and occasionally still did so now that he was home. Their unannounced arrivals always jolted him into tension and strangled his voice. They brought him none of the peace he needed for his convalescence.

The first time that Velma came alone, conversation went stiffly between them at first. He resisted asking her why she had come. The caring she had given him months ago had earned her the right to enquire after his health. At length he said to her, "Please, take back your sculpture." The piece on his chest of drawers was prominent in his small space and stood like a monument of the passion at the height of which she had given it to him. He imagined that she would share his embarrassment at its presence here after the collapse of their affair.

But she demanded, "Why?"

"It belongs to something that's over," he answered awkwardly.

But her reaction was so bitter that he might as well have voiced what was the unspoken part of his reason for wanting to be rid of the statuette—his distaste for her style of work: "You know, Felix, I've never met anyone who is better than you at hurting my feelings. Do you realise how insulting that is?"

He had wanted a cleansing. By banishing its symbol he had hoped to close off that falsified chapter of the past, release her as well as himself from its imaginable claims. But his gesture had turned into one more instance of his clumsy aptitude to deal unintended hurts. Moreover, by once again igniting the anger that had soured their relationship his request had thrown them back into some kind of entanglement.

She took her statuette and left in a rage, but within weeks came to him again, this time in a state of shock and anger over a quarrel with Russell in which he had punched and kicked her. It surprised him that Russell's demonism should take this witless violent form, and more that Velma should come to him in her distress. Did she—because she had met Russell through him—regard him somehow as Russell's keeper, his controller?

Surely not. Her own power of control was proven, perhaps, in the fact that, game as always, Russell had readily yielded to her persuasion to embrace her faith and join her church. And even if the proof of it was dubious, her control was far greater than any Felix would claim—which she must know.

Her coming must have to do with what remained between herself and himself rather than what she thought there was between him and Russell. At this moment it seemed to be the comfort of his sympathy that she was seeking. In the form of a sharp judgement on Russell's lapse into brutality, Felix gave it with enthusiasm. But anything else she might want of him remained unspoken for the time being because a contrite Russell arrived by taxi (he had never learnt to drive and hadn't the patience for municipal transport) to confess his remorse and claim her and his place beside her in her car.

Nor, for the time being, did Felix have any but a vacuously idle, cold curiosity as to what further she might want of him. She had exhausted him by her missionary assault, her aggressive pride in tastes he could not share, and above all her almost automatic antagonism toward every aspect of his reflective self. Moreover, his faculty of lust, which had made her delicious to him despite the absence of sympathy, had been numbed since his surgery. For all he knew, the neural damage he had sustained might have left him impotent, and it might be this fact, rather than shock and depression, that accounted for his loss of desire.

It was through Velma, however, and the very next time she visited him, that he received the first clear indication that this was not the case. He was reading on his bed when she arrived. He sat up on the side of the bed and she seated herself beside him. While they spoke an impulse—was it some ghost of year-old passions that had flared in this very place, or mere curiosity?—prompted him to move a little and press his thigh against hers. She neither enhanced the contact nor withdrew, but that was enough. Despite the patches of numbness and distorted sensation, he could feel the engorgement of his flesh.

The discovery was surrounded, for the moment, by too many uncertainties for any action. But over the next weeks it stirred up his ponderings on his own condition, and on Velma. If sexual excitement was available to him, it meant, perhaps, that much else was recoverable as well. So much that had been placed at a distance could be called back, restored to him. He could return to what he had been. No, it was larger than that. His stripping, his near effacement, meant that he was free to make new choices. People he met, books he read were constantly plying him with alternative visions of reality—from Marxism through astrology and Buddhist quietism to Velma's Christianity. Shed of his virginal shames, he could (like Russell?) yield his assent to any philosophy he pleased to adopt, or pretend to. It was as if he had no past, no history to be loyal to.

And it went even deeper. Since the force entailed in libido was still vouchsafed him, he could use it, use it in new ways, ways that were perhaps perverse, demonic, but which would have the virtue of displacing that humiliating, sick obsession of his, that relentlessly self-renewing horror of mortality. With Velma as his instrument, he could employ lust as an enemy of depression. He neither loved her nor felt he owed her love, but, as he had now discovered, her body retained for him the power of arousal. And whatever she wanted of him, her pursuit of it was a betrayal of Russell to whom she was now sworn. That very perfidy held the promise that she could be seduced into the complicity he needed.

His attempts to do that were confused and constrained in the first instance by his own reversals of mood when the unconscionable conduct his fantasy was projecting became distasteful to him. Hovering between moods, turning toward and away from Velma without either quelling or unleashing his desire to take inconsiderate advantage of the fact that she chose still to be a presence in his life—he discovered, involuntarily and piecemeal, what, in fact, she wanted with him.

It was, of course, as from the first, to proselytise him, to "save his soul". She broached the subject now only tentatively, either being contrite over her defection from him to Russell, or sensing Felix's new fierceness. But her hints were enough to re-complicate whatever plans of seduction he might have formed. They implied that she still set herself a pious course of action: she would not be ready at his mere word to throw herself again into deviant wildness. On the other hand, the survival of her designs on him testified to a commitment, even a passion, that he could exploit. She needed to keep alive her hope of his conversion and, no less important, her ambition to be its agent, and he could put his price on that hope and that ambition—a renewal of some of the flagrant intimacy they had attained and then discarded, but without the assumptions of bondage to each other that had accompanied it before.

But there was contradiction—ambivalence? hypocrisy?—in his side of the contract: only deceptively could he help her keep alive her hope of conquering him for her Jesus. And when he pictured to himself the gestures which that hope would require of him, and beyond those the acts of huge submission her ambition would demand, he knew that they were impossible. The tablet of his old self, after all, had not been wiped to such a blankness that nothing remained to blur or check his will. He might have chosen, by signs and attitudes, to flatter her wish to believe he would eventually surrender. But a superstitious aversion kept him from even hollowly promising such things.

In the meantime, while he felt no immediate call actively to disabuse her, each of them hesitated plainly to speak the name of what was wished, and they teetered on a see-saw of sickly ambivalence.

The emotional malaise of his convalescence still lingered, but if he was to restore himself to himself he saw that he had to renew his attention to things outside himself. One of his regular visitors was Rebecca Saffer who occasionally still brought him news of Oliver Vaughn, Tshepo Msomi and others who had been in the Authors' Union. Her bulletins rekindled his indignation over that fiasco, and her urgings encouraged him to take up and finish the account he had begun writing before his surgery. Rebecca now worked for a journal covering social issues, and mentioned Felix's article to her editor, who, when she had seen a draft, became eager to publish it. Publication was nothing new to Felix, but now, after the breaking off and breaking down of the past year or so, there were healing implications for him in the editor's message. His piece was "very necessary, a cautionary chronicle about the way things might go". His thoughts, his contribution, were still found valid.

A few weeks later came another message, more unusual but of similar import. Professor Roy Craddock was turning sixty-five that year, the official age for retirement from academic posts, and his colleagues and fellow writers were compiling a *festschrift* to be presented to him during a conference at mid-year. From Professor Tom Warden, a convenor of the ceremony, came a letter inviting Felix to make the formal presentation of the volume. At any other time, though hugely surprised and flattered by such a request—one could not be chosen to convey honour to someone like Craddock without being honoured oneself—he would yet have qualified the compliment by the reflection that this was a gesture in a system of ceremonious gestures, a tradition in which meaning and need were wholly conventional, perilously artificial.

But now, such subtractions had no scope. A primitive urgency gave the invitation a different meaning. It was a call to him to rejoin the stream of the reflective life, the continuum of hearing-and-saying-and-being-heard that implied a fellowship of writers and readers. There was more to it than that. Ceremonious ritual, by enacting and asserting continuities across the divides of time, implied something much more. For the moment, however, the sense of fellowship was enough.

He could scarcely imagine actually accomplishing the journey to Fort Gifford, Craddock's distant town, and delivering the speech. He wrote explaining that his ill-health prevented him from making a commitment. In that case, Tom Warden asked, would he write a message that could be read on his behalf. This reinforced the import of the invitation. Thoughts and words were the substance, the life of the fellowship; their being wanted was the unifying gravitational force that drew the individual voices into one stream—and his thoughts and words were required.

He became confident enough to invite students to his flatlet, where it was possible to squeeze in some borrowed chairs and seat seven or eight, and resume running his weekly writing seminars.

For him to stand at his wash-basin while he attended to his denture, brushed his teeth and washed his face was not, when he achieved it now, though only once in a while, merely the restoration of a routine ritual. Because loss, recovery and tentativeness stripped each act of its former ordinariness, it became also the accomplishment of something new, an earnest of a different power. The same was true when he made his way, propping his balance with a walking stick, down the step at his threshold and out on the brick-paved patio to warm himself in the winter sun. And again when, disregarding the susceptibilities of his digestion, he indulged desire with spoonful after spoonful from a punnet of halvah his father had brought him.

These were forays against his still prevailing dismay. It was only his being remote from independence, strength and enjoyment that gave such moments their force. Discomfort, frustration and anxiety continued to be what was ordinary. One Tuesday afternoon, Nomsa's half-day off, he could only wait, scarcely daring to move from where he sat, through the four hours until she returned and could clean and change him.

The occasional visit, with or without Russell, the occasional telephone conversation or letter, the indications that she was aware of his erotic susceptibility, and nursed her own compulsive purpose, maintained Velma in his thoughts, an active idea. It kept alive his intention: he would exploit her potency for his arousal as a weapon against depression. Yet there were times when her actual presence—the voice, the face, the curve of the shoulder intimating vulnerability and aspiration—was what made his project seem preposterous, even monstrous.

Russell's comings and goings, though less frequent now since he no longer lived within strolling distance, were as always for his own reasons and on his own terms. He came to show his work, to complain, to flatter, to tease, to rebuke, to cadge, or to recruit Felix's alliance in one wild cause or another. Inevitably there were assertions and appeals Felix resisted, and inevitably times when he incurred Russell's displeasure. He never knew which particular offence of his it was that finally inspired Russell's malign valediction. He telephoned one day and, with no more prelude than a dry "Hullo, Felix Greenspan", pronounced: "May you die a painful, lingering death in the Jewish Aged Home," and cut off.

Felix had sent a typescript copy of his chronicle of the Authors' Union to Oliver Vaughn. No response at all had come after three months, and then Rebecca Saffer's editor, having subbed the article and scheduled it for her next issue, sent a photographer to take a picture of Vaughn. Only now—the photographer having idly enquired what he thought of the piece and suggested that he would be well-advised to examine it—did Vaughn read what Felix had written. Immediately, he telephoned: "I can't tell you how much I hate this thing of yours about the Union. I don't want it published."

"What's wrong with it?" Felix's voice was close to strangulation.

"Well, everything. It's so destructive. You put everything the wrong way round."

"Isn't that a matter of perceptions?"

"It's a matter of wrong interpretations, and bias, and guesswork. So much of your information is inaccurate. There are things you don't know or understand, and your memory for facts is terrible."

"Facts..." Felix protested. "I sent the article to you months ago. Why didn't you say this before? It's already been set for printing now."

"I didn't imagine you'd come up with anything so bad. You can't publish it."

"Even if I wanted to stop it, it's too late now. They've had costs, and they have a deadline to meet. I'm sure they'll publish any reply you want to make."

"Not good enough. It won't prevent the damage," Vaughn snapped. "I think I have to come and see you."

When he came the next day his features had swollen and taken a purplish tinge. Distress no less than rage was evident in his attack, and distress, in turn, did more to set Felix at a disadvantage: it had been no part of his purpose to cause such deep hurt. Imagining himself as something like a cowering mouse cornered by an indignant rotweiler he put up what squeaking defences he could. Each comment he offered was brushed aside with irritation. Finally he struck back: "Oliver, your anger and the way you avoided reading my piece during all the time since I sent it to you make me suspect that you'd prefer the whole story of the Union to be forgotten."

Vaughn flared: "That's not it. But a distorted history is worse than none at all."

"You haven't convinced me that it is distorted."

"Because your perceptions are distorted." With this stab he rose to leave.

"As I say, if I could I'd change what's incorrect and unfair," Felix insisted. "But it's too late."

"Well—if this stuff gets published there'll be some kind of trouble."

"He is in a rage," Felix told the editor by telephone soon after. "I know there's nothing to be done about it, but thought you'd want to know. I've never seen him like this—he looks apoplectic. Won't hear of any kind of compromise. I made it clear that it's too late to stop or postpone publication, but he's not interested in corrections or a reply in your next issue. Simply hates the article, wants it not to be published and threatens trouble if it is."

"I wouldn't worry about that from our point of view," the editor replied. "But what do you feel?"

"Well, I want my article published, of course. But he did point out some mistakes of fact and some unfair interpretations. And I'm very sorry to have hurt him so badly."

"Why the hell didn't he read the thing when you sent it to him? We could have got his reply and printed it alongside. But what do you want to do about it?"

"Well, it's too late to do *anything*—as I told him."

"But what would you like to do?"

"Ideally, I'd like to withhold publication until I've made some corrections and he has written his reply. But I can't expect..."

"All right, we'll withhold publication."

"Could you *do* that?" For a few seconds dismay overshadowed his incredulity: "No, I couldn't bear to cause you all that trouble. For goodness' sake, your issue is set up,. your expenses, your time..." But the permitted relief was irresistible. "How am I ever to make this good? You are a saint."

"It's not you who hurt him, it's Tshepo," Rebecca Saffer reminded Felix when he reported the two conversations to her. "And, as you once said, he helped to hurt himself by doing the correct thing. That's why he'd prefer to forget that the whole Union story ever happened."

"In any case, my article opened up his wounds."

"But I think you're over anxious about making corrections. I didn't notice any particular mistakes."

"You'd be equally anxious if you saw how upset he was. I'm so relieved that Shirley is letting me withdraw. I think she's noble."

As he spoke he became aware of something else. "Good god! Rebecca, do you know what has happened? This whole thing—this row with Oliver, the shock of his anger, all the rest—seems to have shaken me out of that bloody depression of mine at last. Suddenly the weighed-down feeling has gone, and that horrible fear..."

When Felix phoned to tell him of the reprieve Vaughn mentioned, "I've shown your piece to Tshepo and he's none too pleased."

"I didn't expect him to be. If he has any mis-statements of fact to point out, I'll correct them."

"The facts aside," Vaughn said, "there's an important matter of perceptions..."

"But isn't that ground we've already covered? That's how things are. Different people, different viewpoints."

"We haven't had nearly the time to talk those through," Vaughn persisted, then, with a flicker of his old bonhomie, announced, "I'd like to take the discussion further. Can we talk some time?"

Felix was surprised. "Well...okay."

"Don't let him talk you into suppressing your article altogether," Rebecca warned him.

"No, certainly not."

And the article duly appeared in print, titled "Muzzling the Muse—the story of the Authors' Union", along with a short theoretical riposte from Vaughn. But by that time his visit for further discussion had taken place and been followed by several more. In fact, though nothing he said was to alter Felix's understanding of the Union affair, they soon jettisoned that quarrel leaving its loose ends dangling, and settled into a custom of weekly visits for a friendly hour of sparring about ideology and literature.

"One never knows how things will turn out," Rebecca commented. "Perhaps, since the Union collapsed Oliver's become lonely."

His dispelled depression had been his pretext for taking advantage of Velma's designs on his "immortal soul". But the impulse to play dark games with her still lurked in him. The deliberate stoking of excitement fed by excess and contravention was after all not therapy for a malady, but the waking of a dormant appetite. It produced vengeful moods when he knew without caring that his lust would have dissolved and negated Velma's or any sexual partner's separate otherness, the person consumed as fuel or absorbed as a mere function into his aloneness. In other moods this possibility disgusted him, shamed him, or went forgotten. But now that he was stripped of the medicinal excuse, he had to acknowledge that his urge to abuse any latitude Velma gave him came of something in his nature. At best, claimed no more innocence than an acquired addiction.

A form of the latitude she displayed was the impulsiveness of her visits and telephone calls to him, as though, often, her only purpose was to let him know that she was awaiting a message. One such call ignited an opportunistic impulse to press one of his fantasies into her consciousness: "There's an image of you that keeps returning to my mind. You came from the bathroom naked and stood at the foot of my bed, and—I don't know what it was you did, something with your eyes and mouth? Something about the way you laid your hand on your hip? The way you bent one knee and thrust your hips forward? You were displaying your erotic power to me. And somehow it throbbed out of you, like heat, or radioactivity."

"Yes," she said. "I know what I was telling you."

"So you remember that exact moment?"

"Of course. Or others like it. It's the meaning that matters—not the precise day or time."

"I want to write to you again in that mood." He spoke in a fever of excitement that made him clench his jaws. "Will you let me, will you go along with me, like you did in those letters at the beginning?"

"Of course," she said again, and the very simplicity of her assent implied enigma.

But her enigma was not what he had in mind when he said, "I want to explore. I want to go even further than we went before." Her intentions were mysteries that did not interest him.

He was working on his tribute to Roy Craddock when Alison visited him. "This invitation has done me so much good," he told her.

"How so?"

"It came at a time when I was so wrapped up in being ill and just surviving that I felt cut off from the world of writing. So it was like a message from writers, telling me that they think of me as belonging among them. Also a challenge to turn my thoughts away from myself. And Craddock's life somehow says that once you've done something real, you continue in your work—you don't get cut off by physical things like distance, or race, or illness, or dying."

"It would be so nice if you could be at the presentation, to say those things," said Alison. "Why aren't you going?"

"It's just not practical. I can't manage on my own, and it wouldn't work with Nomsa."

"I'll go with you."

"You? But it isn't so much a matter of going with me as taking me," he pointed out. "I don't mean paying—I mean physically."

"If I can get away, I'd love to take you."

"Oh, but you've no idea of what's involved, what could go wrong, the squalid things you'd have to do."

"Tell me," she said with a laugh.

And Felix, anxious to forefend embarrassments and disappointments—also, not feeling quite brave enough, perhaps half-hoping to persuade her that the adventure was impossible—told her.

She would be able to get away. He telephoned Tom Warden to announce the change of plan and explain Alison's role. They would put up at his house, Tom said. The flight tickets would be arranged. The conference would pay Felix's fare. Old friends of Felix's had been hoping he would be there. Parties and readings were planned. It would be worth staying several days. Felix realised that Alison was ideal for all this. She would not be merely his nurse. She would meet his friends and add a vibrancy to his own encounters. She would bring her bright avidity to parties and poetry readings and even to sessions of the conference.

Two days before they were to fly to Fort Gifford, he wrote without restraint to Velma.

The adventure was triumphant. Alison was splendid, just as he had anticipated. Yet the single adverse moment was shaped by her. On the morning after their first night in the room that had been assigned to the two of them, she said, "Felix, I hope you don't mind, but I have to find another room to sleep in. You're such a noisy sleeper I kept being disturbed. Is that all right?"

"Of course, of course. I had no idea. I'm only sorry I..." Unreasonably, he felt chilled, demoted, set at a distance. And the feeling endured faintly during the whole time, though he remained conscious that these three brilliant days were her dispensation, an enactment of her affection for him.

She was standing close at hand when it came to the moment for his speech. He had warned Tom Warden that stress might strangle his breathing, in which case he would give Alison the signal to read on his behalf. She would enjoy the task and do it with panache. But while he listened to the introductions a trance-like state set in. Roy Craddock, standing nearby, was accessible to him. So too the two or three hundred assembled who stood waiting now for him to speak in Craddock's praise. He must at least try, at least begin his address. As the first words emerged he knew that they were reaching across from where he sat to everyone in the hall. He would not need to break off and let Alison take over. His message was in control. His voice was back in his possession. He had never before used it with such a sense of its power.

On the flight home Alison's warmth, her pleasure in the whole adventure they had made possible for each other, eclipsed the reality of that shadowed moment of the first morning.

Velma had delivered the letter by hand while he was away. It was several pages long. "For a while I thought I could go along with you on your twisted path for the sake of winning you over eventually. But now I feel too much disgust. I see how hard you are, how my humiliation means nothing to you as long as you can play your twisted game ... I realise I have to wait. For now you are still obstinate and blind blind blind ... Go to your other women for the time being. A day will come when you will realise Who I Am—and then you will seek me out. I can wait."

She claimed him, but her revulsion at his letter had in fact set him free. And there was another letter on his desk waiting to be read.

20

The River Gift

She comes through his door at the appointed time, on the evening before he is to fly across the land to Fort Gifford. They have never previously met. His niece Amanda, now an art student with a pad near the university has been drawn to an amusing, protective older woman in her building. This friend, Dorothy, practises one of the alternative healing disciplines, and Amanda, concerned about her uncle's slow and complicated recovery after surgery, has asked her to visit him. The visit has resulted, not in a prescription for pills or powders, but in good conversation and more visits.

One day Dorothy announces, "My best friend has read your stories and wants to meet you—if you're agreeable."

Mere politeness dictates his assent. "What's her name?"

"Edith."

"Tell me about her."

"No. You'll see."

Now he sees, or hardly does. He is self-absorbed, savouring the challenge and glamour of his imminent adventure to Fort Gifford. He doesn't really know why, with her tentative air, she has come to visit him. But Amanda's friend, now his friend, has sent her. He gives polite attention to some poems of her own that she reads to him. He makes polite enquiries about her occupation, her family, the nearly grown-up children, the disappointing ex-husband. Something in the way she speaks of him, though, makes Felix ask, 'Is he lovable?'

She may be surprised at the question, but her reply is not tentative. "Yes."

Her certainty is interesting, but tonight this stranger is someone to whom he can tell the story of his mission of praise.

When he returns from Fort Gifford one of the two envelopes awaiting him is from Edith. It contains twelve lines of playful witty verse, astonishingly celebrating their meeting. He awakes to her.

Edith comes through his door at the appointed time, on the evening that opens their new life. Her certainty is unlike anything he has encountered. It presupposes love, and brings it into being. Before their first embrace, he hesitates: "I don't even know if....what I'm capable of."

"I don't care."

And now he discovers what there is to be discovered, and his capability—damaged, flawed, but sufficient—is the least of it. Their bodies' sweetness is huge: the height of it brings her to a kind of wildly joyful sobbing, at which he—in surprised recognition of what he is being entrusted with—also both laughs and sobs. Yet she has said, "I don't care," meaning that this benison is additional, incidental to what she has brought and wants.

And every time thereafter, the same intensity reasserts the same paradox—love-making matters so deeply because of the context of tenderness and rejoicing it occurs in, and therefore the act is allowed to be expendable. She wants him, knowledge of him, time and experience with him, laughter with him. Much of the laughter they generate together arises in love-making and has to remain their secret. Compromises, devices, contrivances give rise to laughter, find places in their comedy.

She is with him several times a week, alcoved behind book-case and wardrobe, one door of which stands open against a net-curtained french window to enhance their privacy, on his narrow bed, making joy. They have to subdue their noises because Nomsa is there in the next room behind one flimsy door. Late in the night Edith drags herself from the bed, groaning with reluctance, dresses, lets herself out, locks the door and drops the key inside through a window, before driving away in her "Beetle" to her house on the city's outskirts. He tells her how he pictures her chilled exposure to the stretch of sleeping suburbs, but she answers, "Oh, no... I feel I'm flying through the night."

"How have I deserved to find someone so centred on loving?"

"How have I had the luck to find you?"

"That is what I mean."

Edith's presence lights the months. They bring better health, benign excitements, a flourishing of friendships, the revival of the seminars at Denis Harley's art school. She imagines explorations and adventures.

"Let's one day go up in a balloon. Let's go to Greece. I want to see you on muleback climbing Parnassus."

Because she is there for him Felix can accept an invitation to a literary banquet—a "black tie" occasion. They dress—she in an evening gown, he in a borrowed dinner jacket and bow-tie—then, since she by now is a familiar of the house, go through to show off their finery to the family. In the kitchen she calls, "How do you like us, Nomsa?"

Nomsa turns from her task to examine them. Gasps. Claps. "Oh, wonderful! You look like...queens!"

It is a time of drought. The veld, grey and hot, stretches beneath a sky that is empty except for the sun. Certain curves in the road make it possible for the rear-view mirror to catch, beyond folds of countryside, the increasingly hazy, crinkled silhouette near the horizon where the city's towers and tower blocks mass. Half an hour's drive from home they turn off the main road and rumble over a rough farm track where the rolling of the veld begins to steepen and tilt them more consistently downwards, toward a piled complication of low hills, down into which, up into which, they are drawn.

"There's the river," says Edith. "And there's the castle..."

The river, wide as a big road, winds in its fold between the hills, shining and running as though there were no drought. When Edith stops the car near a gateway, the sound of the river becomes audible, the birdsong and the inexhaustible song of the water.

"And up there...there's the cottage."

Up there is atop a mound of boulders and bushes over the bank where the river bends. Gregory, a friend of hers, is the tenant of the cottage, and has told her she is welcome to make use of it while he is on a trip abroad. "I want to go away with you," she has told Felix. "Somewhere lovely, where we can have days and days alone together..."

Jonty, the owner of the castle, expects their arrival and meets them with two strong black men to carry Felix and their luggage up the rocky steepness to where the cottage is perched on its bushy spur of the promontory. Thick-walled and rough-lined, it sits low and easy amid the rockiness. The fancifulness that built the castle shows also in the mouldings and balustrades that decorate the cottage, and there are Gregory's lighthearted posters, pictures, carvings and mobiles. And the deck verandah and the picture window in the bedroom are designed to receive, from without, the presence of the river, whose bend just here seems to enfold the spur, the cottage itself. By day cycles of river light suffuse the cottage, alternating with evening's lamplight and hearthlight, while the unquenchable soft sound of the running water is always there.

They, too, are unquenchable.

They are fitting this week at the river between two of Felix's evening seminars, but there is also the midweek afternoon seminar for Denis Harley's painting students which Felix has not been willing to cancel. So, on their third day they climb down with some help from Jonty, and drive back to town to meet the students. On their return to the river they walk through the gate and skirt the castle's moat. Edith remarks, "There's no flag on the turret. Jonty must be out."

"What are we going to do about getting up?" Felix asks.

"I'm sure we can manage."

"Oh, God! I hope you're right."

After the lawny curves that skirt the castle the rough veld reasserts itself, and there is the rugged path that soon begins to twist its way, alternately by slopes and uneven steps, up to the cottage. The first steps are shallow and even enough. They begin to climb. It is nervous work and Felix keeps his eyes on the ground and his feet. At the steeper places Edith stands facing him, grips his hands and climbs backwards, drawing him up after her. They have mounted some way when they pause to rest and he looks up. The vantage they have gained above screens of bush and rock shows more of the river's breadth and reach, so their ascent seems, mysteriously, to have raised the surface of the water, brought the river closer.

Climbing on, they they come to an outsize step. It is made of a boulder nearly knee-high, with no flatness on its surfaces, and perched where the path closely skirts a steep drop. It daunts him.

"Impossible. I could never get up that."

"We've managed so far. Come along."

"But this one's different. You're not strong enough to haul me so high. We could fall, and it's so near the edge. Please, let me sit here, and you go and find someone to help us up."

"No," Edith says. "We can manage, beloved, I'm sure you can. Put your right foot up here."

She indicates the spot with her own foot. It will mean he will have to bend his knee, lift his foot high and plant it on the lumpy boulder, sway his suspended weight forward, then lift himself as his leading leg straightens, lift the weight of himself all those inches, and balance, balance, until both feet are up there near hers. It seems impossible, beyond his strength, too perilous. But Edith is certain. She is there to share the weight, safeguard his balance.

He lifts his foot, plants it on the rock, leans, thrusts, thrusts.

He rises. They rise. The river, seeming closer yet, embraces them, sings and laughs.

Finis